10641608

BONES OF THE REDEEMED

KARI BOVÉE

BOSQUE
PUBLISHING

Copyright © 2020 by Kari Bovée

Published by Bosque Publishing

ISBN-13: 978-1-947905-09-2 9 (e-bk)

ISBN-13: 978-1-947905-10-8 9 (p-bk)

All rights reserved.

No part of this book may be reproduced in any form or by any electronic or mechanical means, including information storage and retrieval systems, without written permission from the author, except for the use of brief quotations in a book review.

This is a work of fiction. Names, characters, places, and incidents either are the product of the author's imagination or are used fictitiously. Any resemblance to actual persons, living or dead, is entirely coincidental.

KariBovee.com

CHAPTER 1

LAS MONTANAS, NEW MEXICO, 1952

She never wanted fame. All she wanted was redemption.

Ruby Delgado sighed with relief as she walked from the brush-laden desert onto the archaeological dig site situated at the base of the southern foothills of the Las Montanas mountain range. She set her duffle bag down for a moment to relieve the ache in her fingers, and to catch her breath. She then picked it up again and walked past the common work area. A dusty tarp hung over neatly aligned tables, and glittering, emerald cottonwood trees, twisted with knotty bark, protected the work area from the harshness of the desert sun.

Several men sat at the tables, their heads bent over bones, shards, reports, and cups of coffee. They were oblivious to her presence.

Swallowing the dryness strangling her throat, Ruby tried to still the hammering of her heart. She approached the lead archeologist, Dr. John Yates, and dropped her duffle bag. She held out her shaking hand to meet the man she'd idolized for years.

"Dr. Yates? Sir, it's such a pleasure to meet you. I'm—"

The man's Gregory Peck-classically-handsome face twisted

into an unpleasant sneer. "I know who you are, Miss Delgado. You're the pot hunter who discovered the treasure of the Noche Triste."

Ruby flinched. *Pot hunter?* Had he really just called her a pot hunter? An amateur hobbyist? She was in the PhD program for chrissake. She bit down on her lip, hard, afraid she'd say something she'd regret. Hostility was the last thing she'd expected from the world-renowned anthropology professor.

"Dr. Yates, that find was the result of hard work," she told him.

"Sheer luck," he said, not meeting her eyes.

"Not to mention that in finding it I almost got killed." She wished he would look at her.

Recovering the long-sought-after treasure associated with the Noche Triste two years ago had profoundly altered the course of her life, yet Yates called the discovery and her hard work simple *luck*? Luck may have had a small part to do with it, but the find— the long tail feathers of the Quetzal bird, thought to be part of Montezuma's lost treasure—was proof that Aztec riches had been smuggled north during Hernan Cortés' siege of Tenochtitlán, and had ended up in the American Southwest. The achievement also had served as the catalyst to turning her messed up life around.

Yates glanced at her, just for a second, and then his gaze wandered over her head to the Las Montanas mountain range.

The hope in Ruby's heart wilted, making her knees feel like they would buckle. The opportunity to work under his tutelage had held such promise, a desperately needed new beginning for her. She'd read every academic journal he'd ever been featured in, every book, every paper. She wanted to be the female version of Dr. John Yates—with even more renown and respect.

"How'd you get here?" He tilted his head to look behind her.

"I drove, but my car broke down about three miles back. I walked the rest of the way."

He sniffed, took a cigar out of his shirt pocket and lit it, sucking until the tip glowed an angry red. "Peter!" Yates called out.

A young man emerged from the shaded area, his attention completely absorbed in the notebook he was holding. He flipped it shut and strode over. His slim, muscular build and dark hair made Ruby think of a panther. His mussed T-shirt hung loose over dusty brown slacks and gave the impression of someone who cared little about his appearance. But somehow, it was refreshing. With a jerk of his head, he tossed back his perfect curls before his eyes settled on Ruby.

"This is the *famous* Ruby Delgado." Yates puffed on his cigar, eyeing her through the smoke. As deflated as she felt, his obvious disdain made her wanted to take that cigar, break it in two, and throw it in his face.

Peter held out his hand. "Hey, Ruby. Pete Marshall. So you're the woman who discovered the treasure of the Noche Triste. I've heard a lot about you."

"I'm sure." She resisted the urge to roll her eyes. Lord only knew what Yates had said.

"Give her the tour." Yates took a long, sharp look at Ruby before walking past her and heading toward the dig site.

Pete shoved his hands in his pockets and rocked back and forth on the balls of his feet, his discomfort as evident as a whore in church. Goodness Lord, he was good-looking . . . and she was a mess. Her dungarees were wrinkled and dirty; her blouse, though knotted and airy at the waist, stuck to her back with sweat; and her hair had escaped its neat bun. She raised a hand and tried to smooth the loose tendrils into place.

Pete picked up her duffel bag. "The living quarters are over there." He pointed east of the work area to a smattering of tents pitched below sagging telephone wires. "You'll be the only woman here other than Cynthia. It's taken her a while, but she's gotten used to coexisting with us cavemen."

"It won't bother me." Ruby hoped her uncertainty wouldn't come across in her voice. Living with a bunch of men would be the least of her problems considering Yates' startling opinion of her.

Pete's gaze roamed over her disheveled hair, her face, then down her body and right back up to her eyes, as if he could see right through her confident façade. Shaking off the intimacy of his gaze, she hurried toward the tents. Pete caught up to her.

He pointed to an area behind the tents where there were ramshackle plywood huts. "The toilets and showers are there. Cold water only, of course. If you want a hot shower, you can go to the church rectory in town. They always welcome Dr. Yates' students." He stopped at one of the tents and frowned. "Don't you have a car?"

"It broke down a few miles back. I'm pretty sure it's the radiator."

Pete opened the tent flap and threw her duffel bag onto the tent floor. "I can give you a tow. There's a garage in town, but the mechanic is drunk most of the time. I doubt he'll be able to help you."

Ruby shrugged. "I just need the parts. I can fix it myself."

"You can fix a car?" A dubious grin crept across his dimpled cheeks.

"It's 1952, Mr. Marshall, not the Dark Ages." She straightened to her full five-feet-seven-inches. "There are a lot of things I can do that would surprise you. I promise."

"I can't wait to see that." Condescension rolled off his words. "Make yourself at home."

He left her standing in front of her tent while he gracefully glided back to the work area. The rear view of his taut physique held her attention, but his arrogant swagger made her want to spit on his shoes.

How dare he? And how dare Dr. Yates with his rude behavior? It was not at all in keeping with a man of his reputation, and definitely the last thing she needed. It *was* unusual for a woman to work in the field of archaeology, but not that unusual. She hoped to follow in the footsteps of Hetty Goldman and Alice Fletcher, and planned on exceeding them both.

She plopped onto the canvas cot with a thud and stared at the blank tent wall. The air in the tent was musty, and infused with the faint odor of mildew. She fingered the rolled red bandana at her neck, scanning her new living quarters. A small desk and chair sat opposite the cot, a trunk for her belongings occupied the other end of the tent, and a gas lantern hung from the ceiling beam in front of her like a hypnotist's crystal.

What the hell did I get myself into?

Loud clanging woke her. She'd slept in her clothes, slept right through dinner, slept through the entire night.

She crawled out of her sleeping bag, stood and stretched, kicked her duffel out of the way, and stepped from the tent into the gray, early-morning light. The bright coral of the surrounding mesas cast a mellow glow as the sun tried to warm the chill of daybreak. The crisp air nipped at her skin, making her shiver. She went back in the tent to put on a sweater. Warmer, she emerged again, and this time the smell of food reminded her she hadn't eaten since breakfast the previous day.

Scanning the site, she guessed the tent with the smoke pouring from the roof was the mess tent. The silver Airstream trailer next to it, gleaming in its metallic glory, was no doubt Dr. Yates'.

She entered the mess to see other students and crew sitting at picnic tables. All heads turned as she walked toward the warming trays, which steamed with the aroma of chilies. She caught Yates' gaze and forced a smile, but he turned away. Pete, who was sitting next to him, lifted his chin in greeting. Out of place and on display, Ruby felt her face grow hot. She wanted to ask Pete about that tow of her car he'd promised her, but she supposed it could wait. Seemed she was late to breakfast, and she didn't want to make matters worse for herself.

"Line starts here!" A large man with a sunburned face and bristly blond crew cut stood behind the buffet table, gesturing for her to come over. Grateful he'd broken the silence, she made a beeline for him and picked up a plate.

"Name's Spike." He offered his hand.

She grasped his rough, callused fingers and tried not to stare at the deep scar on his face. "I'm Ruby."

"I know." He grinned broadly, revealing a few missing teeth.

"Right." She forgot everyone here seemed to have heard about her.

"Sweetheart, you're a superstar," he said. "Enjoy it."

She resisted the urge to roll her eyes, both amused and embarrassed at the reminder that her name actually meant something in the world of archaeology now. She glanced toward Yates and caught him staring.

"Well, thanks." She leaned in toward the cook and lowered her voice. "I just want to dig—do the work. That's what makes me happy." Ruby loaded her plate.

A short, boy-faced man who looked like a barrel keg on legs lumbered up to the buffet table for a second helping. He adjusted his canvas jacket. "Miss Delgado, I'm Carl Bishop. It's a pleasure to have you here."

She gave a small smile. "Call me Ruby. And I'm glad to be here."

"I'm Cynthia." A slender woman with long brown braids came up behind Carl and put her arms around his waist. Her eyes shone with warmth and reminded Ruby of rich, strong coffee. "It's nice to finally meet you, Ruby."

"Thank you. It's a relief to meet some friendlies." The tension drained from Ruby's shoulders.

"Don't let Yates bother you. He's getting cantankerous in his old age," said Carl.

Ruby raised a brow. "He doesn't seem that old."

"He's not. Just cantankerous," Carl said. He and Cynthia shared a laugh. "Don't let us keep you from your breakfast. We've got to get to work. See you in the trenches."

Ruby sat down, the food tasting better with each bite. *Cantankerous* was a massive understatement. More like ill-mannered and offensive. Regardless, she'd still have to find a way to break into Yates' good graces. But if she couldn't, she vowed not to let the man's disrespect stop her from getting back to her work, her doctorate, her career. The last three years had blanketed her in black clouds, and it was time for clear skies.

Somehow, he'd teach her. She'd *make* him.

After breakfast, Ruby consulted the bulletin board posted in the mess tent for the daily assignments. She took a pencil from her pocket and jotted down the grid number assigned to her.

After grabbing tools and a notebook from her tent, Ruby again stepped into the sunshine to search out her assignment. The spring air had warmed, and she breathed in the earthy scent of sage. The newly bloomed desert verbena spread out like long, skinny fingers, its delicate pink blossoms a soft contrast to the rocky ground. She walked past Carl diligently working his shovel along a smooth ridge he'd carved from a red layer of soil.

"Found something already?" she asked him.

"Maybe." He grinned. "Stick around a minute and we'll see."

"I should probably get busy in my own section." Ruby scanned the site, looking for Dr. Yates. She didn't want to make a bad impression on the first day of actual work, although his words and actions told her it wouldn't matter. His impression of her had been made already.

Carl lay on his belly, supporting himself with one elbow while the other hand worked the soil below with a brush. He looked like an enthusiastic child in a sandbox.

"How long have you been digging?" he asked, not looking up from his work.

"Ever since I can remember," she replied. "I used to go out with my grandfather."

"Where are you from?"

"Los Caballos. It's about one hundred fifty miles from here."

Carl raised his head. "The tumbleweed capital of New Mexico?"

"The very place."

"Was your grandfather an archaeologist?"

"No. Just insatiably curious about the past."

He smiled, and his eyes met hers. "I guess the fruit doesn't fall far from the tree. Dr. Yates says you were born to dig."

"He does? I was under the distinct impression the man hated me."

"I didn't say he liked you. I said he thinks you were born to dig. Hey, this is a beaut." Carl blew sand away from the half-unearthed pot. A lovely white pattern adorned its middle. "Dr. Yates guessed the burial ground is somewhere around here . . . Looks like we may be on to it, after all. Where are you working?"

"G-125."

"Right over there." He pointed. "Make sure your sketches are clean. Yates is pretty particular. He wants everything put back just the way it was found, too. Got a camera?"

She patted her satchel. "Right here."

"Even better."

Ruby approached the assigned ten-by-ten-foot grid. To her left, just outside her grid line, the ground sloped at an unnatural angle into a six-foot hole, indicating the possibility of a burial place. Why hadn't that been included in her grid? She sighed, then squatted and studied the depression. Above it, on the right side, weeds and small rocks jutted out from below an earthen lip. The dank odor of damp soil made Ruby shiver, a sudden chill washing over her shoulders.

Falling rocks from above. Heart thumping. Earth trembling. Ground shifting beneath her. Dirt and debris rushing down on her head like an angry waterfall. The wrath of Mother Earth. Throat tightening. Nostrils clogging. Chest collapsing. Whimpering cries filling her ears . . .

She wrapped her arms around her middle, clutching herself to stop the adrenaline burning through her veins. *Breathe.*

She thought she'd slain that demon.

Ruby peeled off her sweater—and the memory of Matthew's death—like an unwanted layer of skin and threw it next to her satchel. She studied the area again, forcing herself to see it with a clinical eye. The weeds along the depression lay in an unnatural, scattered pattern, as if someone had yanked them out and then tried to put them back in a hurry. Had someone dug there already?

How much trouble would she be in if she dug outside the grid? She knew if she did, she'd have to defend her rationale for choosing intuition over protocol. She let out a lungful of air, weighing the possibilities. If she worked outside the grid line and found nothing, she'd definitely get grief from Yates. He'd look for any opportunity to get rid of her. But if she did find something—and every instinct told her she would—then his feeble respect for her might grow.

She scanned the site again. Carl was still working at extracting his pot. Several men sat at tables under the tarp, their heads bent over artifacts and notebooks. No sign of Yates.

She swallowed. Her instincts had never let her down before. With that thought, she pulled her Pentax camera from her satchel and snapped photos of the soil depression in the area outside of her grid. Afterward, she stowed the camera, flung her satchel over her shoulder, and inched her way down the recess. When she reached the bottom, she fingered the jutting weeds and looked for signs of excavation. She ran her hand along the earthen lip above her, noting the uncharacteristic way in which the earth had been removed from the wall, like someone had clawed at the dirt with untrained fingers. Or perhaps it had been an animal?

She set her bag on the ground, took out her tools, and dug. After several minutes, her small spade hit something hard. Hard, but not rock-hard—more like hard with a mellow finish. She dug around the protrusion, loosening the earth and prying away at the dirt's grasp on the object. She dug faster, and a slight oval began to take shape. She pulled out her small brush and swept over the bulge, removing the thick, silty layer of dirt.

The object beneath looked familiar. Ruby stopped short, holding her breath.

A section of what looked like a human skull.

Could this be the Anasazi burial site Yates had sought for the last two decades?

Her hands trembling, she dug faster, sinking the spade into the earth, pulling the dirt toward her, trying with every movement not to damage the skull. When she'd completely exposed it she sat back and collected herself. She grabbed her satchel and camera and took a few quick snapshots. After setting her satchel some feet away from her, she then used careful fingers to extract the skull from the earth.

She turned the bony, partial skull in her hands and frowned. It didn't look ancient. In fact the bone wasn't entirely bleached. Traces of sinew were still attached around the eye sockets. She recoiled, her stomach lurching. She set it back down and stumbled backward, wiping her hands on her dungarees.

"Hey, Carl!" She hoped he could hear her. He needed to see this. Who the hell cared if she dug outside the grid lines?

Suddenly, the earth seemed to move beneath her feet. Dirt spilled into the recess behind her and the ground wavered, beginning to pull her downward. It slid in around her ankles, calves, and then her knees.

"Carl!" she screamed, flinging out her hands and clutching at the dirt.

⚜

Ruby threw her upper body against the slope and clawed toward the top, but her movements made the dirt rush toward her even faster.

"Carl! Somebody! Help! Please . . ." Her voice cracked, and time slowed as Mother Earth pulled her under. It oozed in around her waist, then her chest, holding her like a vise.

She popped free and fell through nothingness, like Alice down the rabbit hole. She hit the ground with a hard thud, the air rushing out of her lungs. Pain spread through her body, and she gasped for breath. Dirt and sand fell in on top of her, pelting her hair and shoulders. She spat grit out of her mouth.

When she could breathe again she looked up into the shaft of sunlight streaming down from the hole she'd fallen through, dust particles floating like birds in formation above her.

"Hey! Anyone! Help!" She looked up at the daylight and strained to listen.

No one.

She took stock of her injuries, blinking against the contrast of light and dark. It felt as if hot knives were stabbing at her hand and her hip. Something poked her leg. She shifted to ease the pain.

And what was that *smell?* She blinked again, struggling to focus in the dark, and looked down toward her hip. Darkened, leathery eye sockets stared up at her.

Ruby screamed, scrambling to get up, her legs tangled in a heap of limbs. She shot up then slipped, falling onto more skeletonized bodies. She flung herself toward a clearing on the floor and landed hard against the earthen wall. Her stomach heaved at the sour stench in the cavern.

The walls closed in on her, the hole above her darkening. Her breath came short and fast and shallow.

Don't pass out. Stay in control, or they'll never find you.

She closed her eyes, pulled air into her abdomen, and then forced it back out. She did it again and again. Soon her breath lengthened and slowed, the panic subsiding. After a few minutes, she opened her eyes to face the bodies in various stages of decomposition once more. She took another deep breath, her rational mind finally taking over.

She counted ten bodies in the pile, but those on the bottom were completely decomposed. The body with the leathery eye sockets hung limp, partially detached from the rest of them. Streaks of black streamed from the rotting hairline, into the eyes, and down the waxy cheeks. Ruby shuddered at the realization.

Blood.

The cavern spun as she went into shock. It was all too familiar: his muffled cries, her helplessness, him slipping away from her faster than she could control.

⚜

Ruby's lids fluttered open. Pete's face loomed above her. Had she passed out?

"Come on." Pete nudged her arm with his foot. "Come on, we have to get you out of here."

Ruby shook her head, trying to clear it. The stench assaulted her again and she gagged, her belly threatening to vomit.

"Oh, no, you don't. Look at me, Ruby. Look only at me."

She lifted her chin, still gagging, and tried to focus on Pete's face.

"Get a hold of yourself, Ruby. Concentrate."

She swallowed hard and refused to turn away from his penetrating, dark gaze.

"Deep breaths," he whispered.

She followed his orders, still concentrating on his face. That beautiful face.

"Okay," he said, pulling a rope from around his waist. "The others are going to pull you up. We're getting you out of here, all right?"

She nodded and let him tie the rope around her. "But what about them?" She pointed to the blackened, blood-stained skull. "That one—it looks like it was bleeding, Pete . . . Bleeding!"

"Don't worry about that right now. We just need to get you out of here."

She shook her head, the movement making her dizzy. "We have to tell the authorities."

Pete pulled her to her feet, easy as a rag doll. "Listen." He leaned in so close to her that she could smell his wintergreen-scented aftershave. A welcome treat compared to the stench of death. "I think it would be best if we didn't tell the others about this."

She blinked, his words breaking through the cloud of pleasant mint. "What? Why not?"

"You don't understand what this is. You shouldn't tell anyone," he said darkly, as if in warning.

"What do you mean not tell anyone? Why? What are you saying?" Confusion fogged her brain.

He let go of her and she swayed without his support, struggling for balance. He put his hands on her hips, steadying her again.

"Right," he said. "Let me tell them. I'll explain why later. You need to see a doctor."

"What do you know about this?"

His eyes shifted from hers to something behind her, and his brow furrowed.

"What is it?" She turned to see what he was looking at, and a heavy blow slammed into the back of her neck.

The cavern spun and whirled and flipped upside down, until darkness enveloped her again.

CHAPTER 2

He watched her drop to the ground, unconscious. He'd panicked. How would he keep her from telling the others? He turned to the corpses, his heart racing.

When he'd climbed down into the hole he'd stopped short, unable to believe what he saw. The bodies had been dumped into this cavernous hell with less care than one would throw away the trash.

When he saw the body with the black blood stains streaming into its eye sockets, he fell to his knees. So this is where they'd put them. These people had deserved an honorable, decent, even privileged burial. But this? This is where God's chosen were laid to rest? Could one of these poor souls be his brother, Ricardo?

It had been two years, two years of a painstaking investigation, of unanswered questions, of sorrow and anger. The authorities claimed there were no bodies, no evidence, and yet here they lay. The state investigation had been a sham, a cover-up, conveniently inconclusive.

But here was the evidence. The most important evidence of all. But who could he go to? Who could he trust? He needed more time. He needed a way to prove his suspicions.

He crouched next to Ruby, still unconscious. He had her to

thank for this incredible miracle. Why had she dug here, outside the grid? No wonder she'd been nicknamed *the ferret*. People claimed Ruby Delgado had a gift, an uncanny way of knowing where ancient objects, ancient worlds, and now evil secrets, lay buried beneath the earth. Now he understood Yates' contempt toward her. Yates had spent years honing his senses, refining his intuition, and now he had to work with an amateur *woman* with the instincts of a veteran.

Pete sympathized with Yates, but with this find Ruby had unwittingly become a part of Pete's quest—his enduring and secret quest.

Could he trust her? Would she understand? She'd ask questions, want to know everything, maybe even follow her own plans rather than his lead.

Anything she learned could be dangerous.

His gaze roamed over the lines of her face. In sleep her features were soft, angelic. The tough set of her mouth and the hardness around her eyes had vanished. Her face was innocent, like a child's. What kind of burden did she carry that made her look so harsh when conscious?

Perhaps they could have been friends, but now he'd have to keep her at a distance. She couldn't know his secret, no matter what.

◈

Ruby opened her eyes to see a throng of faces above her. Carl and Cynthia hovered like worried parents, and she tilted her head up to see Spike standing at a distance. Yates stood next to him, arms folded, his expression etched with suspicion. Pete, winded and sweaty, stood over her, removing the rope from around her waist and beneath her legs. His closeness and his hands on her limbs sent heat to her face.

"What's going on?" she asked.

"You fell," Cynthia said. "Does anything hurt?"

"You were digging outside the perimeter," Yates said.

"I'm sor—"

"Dr. Yates, please." Pete held up a hand. "We can deal with that later."

"Does anything hurt?" Cynthia repeated.

"My head." Ruby rubbed the back of her neck. She looked up at Pete but he avoided her eyes, finished coiling the ropes, and stepped away from her.

"You must have fallen headfirst," he said, still avoiding eye contact.

She rolled her neck, trying to ease the tension. She vaguely remembered standing in the cavern—could see it in her mind—but everything was jumbled and hazy.

"What happened?" Carl asked.

"I noticed the ground just outside the grid line looked odd. I had a hunch and decided to dig there. I remember going to the bottom of the recess. I'd found something . . . and then the ground sort of . . . swallowed me. I don't think I went in headfirst."

"Must be a sinkhole," Carl said. "Lots of 'em around here."

Ruby wrinkled her brow, trying to remember—her mind fuzzy, her body tired. An image of Matthew passed through her mind, his sweet face contorted in agony and fear. She shook her head to rid herself of the vision and regretted it when a wave of pain left her lightheaded.

"Anything down there?" Carl asked, directing the question at Pete.

"Just a cavern." Pete's voice sounded overly casual, almost cavalier. She couldn't remember what it was, but knew it was *not* just a cavern. And Pete seemed to know it, too. Pain seared the back of her eyes and she pressed her fingers to her temples.

"Damn sinkhole," said Carl.

She tried to open her mouth to say there was something more down there, but Pete spoke before she could get anything out. "We should block off this area," he said. "It's dangerous."

"That's why we didn't include it in the excavation." Yates glared at Ruby. He rattled off an order in Spanish to several of the workers nearby.

Carl and Cynthia helped Ruby to her feet. "C'mon, girl. We need to get you to the clinic," Cynthia said.

"No, no. I'm all right, just a little woozy." Her knees buckled, and they caught her.

"You need to be seen by a doctor." Cynthia squeezed her arm.

"I'll take her," Pete volunteered.

Yates took his hat off, pointed it at Pete. "I need *you* to catalog yesterday's findings."

"I've done the cataloging. Besides, I need to go into town anyway."

Yates plopped his fedora back onto his head, turned, and stomped toward his trailer.

Cynthia and Carl led Ruby toward Pete's Ford pickup. Carl gently lifted her into the vehicle. Still, the movement hurt her hip and her head. She tried to find a comfortable position, but settled for leaning in a way that took pressure off her hip. Pete jumped into the driver's seat, jostling her and sending pain shooting up her lower back. She gritted her teeth.

"What year is this thing? Thirty-nine?" she asked, trying to distract herself from the knives in her back.

"Yep. Got it from one of the scientists who worked in Los Alamos."

"No kidding?"

"German guy. Sold it to me cheap." Pete turned the key, and the engine roared to life.

"What were you doing in Los Alamos? I thought that area was full of top-secret government stuff."

"The guy brought it to Santa Fe. I was there for some supplies."

A sharp pain in her hip and lower back diverted her attention once again.

Over the next fifteen minutes she shifted her position half a dozen times, the rutted dirt road giving her aching body no mercy. She sensed Pete's eyes on her from time to time, adding to her agitation.

"What?" she finally asked, voice clipped.

"How's your head?"

"Like someone took a baseball bat to it, but it doesn't hurt as much as my hip." She winced as she shifted again.

He shrugged. "You're probably fine."

Fine?

"I think I fell more than ten feet. But it wasn't headfirst." Ruby distinctly remembered standing.

Or was it sitting?

"But you were unconscious," he pointed out.

"Not when I fell in. That, I know."

An odor came from her clothes—the pungent smell of decay. Wrinkling her nose she put her hand up against the window and leaned her head on it, struggling to remember. Incomplete images tumbled through her thoughts: Matthew, rushing earth, a skeleton, a hospital bed, strong arms holding her, her body sinking to the floor, a blood-streaked forehead, and cavernous eye sockets.

She gasped, sitting up straight.

"What's wrong?" Pete asked.

"Bodies. There were bodies down there. Well, skeletons— with leathery flesh on them."

His face tightened.

"I'm not imagining it, if that's what you're thinking. There were dead bodies down there. All piled up. I fell on them." She quivered. "I fell on still decomposing corpses."

"Ruby, I was down there with you. I didn't see anything."

Something niggled at her. He was being too casual again. "How could you *not* have seen them?" she asked. A wave of pain seared her temples again, and she grabbed her head.

"Hey, take it easy," Pete said. "You don't look very well."

She didn't feel very well, either. She leaned her head against the window again. She saw the bodies. She knew it. Why was he lying?

"Don't tell me I didn't see those corpses," she said at the glass, "because I did. They were there, and I fell on top of them. And you saw them, too."

He stared straight ahead, his face as stony as a marble statue.

"Pete, you're not getting off the hook here. I know what I saw, and so do you." It was slowly coming back to her. Something had slammed into her neck. "I also have an idea of how I ended up with this concussion."

With a quick glance in the rearview mirror, Pete veered off the road and stopped the truck. "No one else can know about what was down there," he said, putting the truck into park.

"Did you give me this concussion?"

"I'm sorry. I didn't mean—"

"Didn't mean it? You knocked me out cold, you bastard!"

"I'm sorry. I want—"

"Apology *not* accepted. At least not until you tell me what's going on. Why the secrets?" Did you have something to do with those poor souls in that pit?"

She realized the gravity of her words. She could be in the car with a murderer. Yet somehow, she knew she wasn't. Pete was hiding something for sure, but he wasn't a killer.

Anger narrowed his eyes. "I had nothing to do with those —bodies."

"Then why don't you report them? What are you hiding?"

"*I'm* not hiding anything."

Ruby crossed her arms. "I'm waiting."

Pete slammed his hand against the steering wheel, making her jump. "My brother was killed two years ago. I think he was murdered. Do you feel better now?"

She turned away, letting his words sink in. He was grieving, just like she was. "I'm sorry. But what does that have to do with the corpses?"

His voice was soft. "I think he's in there."

"Well then you of all people should want to report what I found." She wrapped her arms around herself and tried to rub away the sudden goose bumps.

"When my brother died, everyone—my family, my friends, the whole village—just accepted it. Nobody questioned anything. A perfectly healthy young man just up and dies out of the blue, and no one finds it strange? It didn't make sense." Pete drummed his index finger on the steering wheel.

"What did they think caused his death?"

"Heart failure."

She nodded slowly, carefully. "People can die of heart failure at any age. It's not unusual."

"No. He was murdered." He swiveled his head to look her in the eye.

"You have proof?"

"Not yet, but I will."

"Does your family think he was murdered?"

He shook his head and laughed, the sound tinged with sarcasm. "No. 'God took him,' my father said. 'He wanted him by his side.'" He sighed. "They won't accept that he was killed."

"And what about the others? What do you think happened to them? Why were they just thrown in there? Is that normal burial practice for this village?"

"Not since the eleventh century."

"So how did they get there? And why?" Ruby pressed.

Pete took a deep breath, probably wrestling with whether or not to divulge more. She forced herself to wait, enduring the silence when all she wanted to do was pelt him with questions.

He kept silent.

"What aren't you telling me?" she asked.

"Nothing," he said, his palm in the air.

"Then what's your plan?"

"I don't have one yet. The bodies were a surprise to me, too." The timbre of his voice dropped off, almost to a whisper.

Ruby felt for him, but she still didn't understand. And she

definitely couldn't just let it go. "What about the victims' families? Those people had no proper burial."

Pete turned his gaze back to the windshield. "We've had a series of deaths here over the past few years. They told the families the victims died of the plague."

"The plague? Honestly?" She'd heard of a few reported cases throughout the years, but that many? "Why didn't anyone hear about a loss of life that big? And why weren't the bodies disposed of? And who is *they*?" she asked.

"State officials. People in authority." Pete looked out the window into the desert. "That may be why the bodies were thrown down there. They should have been burned, but the church forbids it..."

It wasn't adding up. "But you said your brother died of a heart attack."

"Brought on by disease," Pete said. "Or so they claim."

"*They* again."

"Dr. Mendenhall. That's what he told my family. He even quarantined us and some of the other families. There were memorial services, but no funerals."

"And the families accepted this?" She knew Las Montanas was a Catholic community. A community that held fast to tradition.

"What could the families do? These people aren't educated. Mendenhall's a doctor. The people trusted his word, and the word of the authorities. They were scared. They had novenas, prayer circles, and days of fasting. Then no one else died. The spell had passed."

Ruby stared out the window, mulling over Pete's words. He said his brother died two years ago. The bodies she'd found were in various stages of decomposition—mostly void of flesh and muscle. An arid climate would be responsible for slower decay, so it would only make sense that the one was so . . . intact. But, still, not ancient. She shuddered at the thought.

"I know it was hard for you to tell me this," she said.

"I don't want anyone to know about the bodies. At least, not for a while. I don't know who to trust with this information. Can I trust *you* to keep quiet?"

"I don't agree that we should keep quiet." In fact, it went against every fiber of her being.

"We don't know enough yet."

"But we can't just leave them there. We have to tell someone." She rubbed the sore spot on her head, then sighed. "I guess the real question is, can *I* trust *you?*"

"I am sorry about hurting you."

She raised a brow at him. "Why should I keep quiet? What good will it do?"

"It will give me time. There are so many people at the site, they'll probably find the bodies anyway. I just want a little time to figure out what's going on before they're discovered. It will create a maelstrom."

Ruby bit her bottom lip. "I don't know . . ."

"Do you really want to stir things up? You're already on Yates' shit list."

Oh, right. But was not being the focus of Yates' wrath truly worth it?

"He'll hate you even more if you do anything to call attention to yourself. I promise we'll report the bodies. Just give me some time. Please." Pete looked directly into her eyes, and Ruby was struck by the sincerity she saw there. Or at least she hoped it was sincerity and not the charm of a practiced killer.

"All right, but not for long. I don't like keeping this secret."

"Thank you," he said, still meeting her eyes. "I *am* going to get to the bottom this." He put the truck into drive again and Ruby lay her head against the window, her thoughts reeling and her body aching.

⚜

Twenty minutes later, Pete swung the truck into the empty parking lot of the medical clinic. The building, made of rose-brown stucco over adobe, blended with the landscape. Enormous, proud pine trees served as a backdrop, reaching high into the luminous blue of the sky, while fat, gray-green chamisa bushes hugged the walls of the clinic.

Pete stopped with a jerk. Ruby sucked air in through her teeth, her head pounding even harder with the sudden stop.

"Sorry," he said. He hopped out and circled to the passenger's side to open the door for her. He reached in to help her out, but she pulled away.

"I can manage." She climbed out of the vehicle and tried not to grimace as her feet touched down. A wave of dizziness overwhelmed her, and she grabbed on to the door for support. Pete stood by, his arms crossed, a look of helplessness on his face. Still, she didn't want his help.

He led the way into the clinic, and she hobbled along behind. She let him open the door for her. Inside, metal folding chairs lined the plain, unadorned walls. No plants, cushy chairs, or artwork to offset the austere coldness of the place.

"Isn't there a doctor in town? We are still in the middle of nowhere. This place is a little—" She noted the brightness of the linoleum floors and the buzz of florescent lighting as it rang in her ears.

"The nearest hospital is about ninety miles away. Dr. Mendenhall is the only one we have out here." Pete indicated for her to sit in a chair. She ignored him.

Just then a gray-haired man with intelligent blue eyes behind thick, dark-rimmed glasses appeared at the reception window. "May I help you?" he asked, his voice thick with a German accent. "Oh, Mr. Medina, how are you?"

Ruby looked over at Pete. Medina? His name wasn't Medina. It was something else . . . *Marshall.*

Pete raised his chin in greeting. She couldn't help but wonder why he didn't correct the doctor.

"Who's your friend?" Dr. Mendenhall asked.

"This is Ruby Delgado. She's new at the site."

He smiled at her. "It's a pleasure to meet you, Miss Delgado. I'm Bill Mendenhall. How may I help you?"

"She fell into a sinkhole," Pete said before she could answer. *Again.*

Ruby bit her lip in annoyance. She could speak for herself! She shot him a quick glare, then turned back to the doctor. "My head is pounding, and there's something wrong with my hip."

"Why don't you come in the back and I'll look at you, eh?" Dr. Mendenhall waved his hand toward the hall door as the front door opened, sending a shaft of sunlight into the gray room.

A Mexican man wracked with a fit of coughing stumbled in. He wore far too many layers of tattered and dirty clothing for the summer heat. He clung to the doorknob until the fit ceased, then waved a greeting to the doctor and made his way to one of the metal folding chairs. Another surge of coughing overtook him. When the coughing stopped, he hugged his coat closer to him.

"I'll be outside," Pete said as the doctor led Ruby through the door into the examining room.

Dr. Mendenhall helped her to the cushioned table situated adjacent to his desk. "So, what happened?"

"I'm not really sure. I was digging for something when the ground gave way. I fell into a sinkhole."

And landed on a pile of rotting corpses.

She wished she'd never promised Pete she wouldn't say anything yet.

"Do you have a headache?" the doctor asked.

"Yes."

"Blurred vision? Dizziness?"

"A little dizziness."

"All normal for a bump on the noggin," Dr. Mendenhall said, the corners of his eyes creasing with a reassuring smile. "Let's see." Gently, his fingers probed through her hair as he examined her scalp. She jerked away in pain when he found the sore spot on the back of her head.

"Ah yes, a little contusion there. Did you lose consciousness?"

"Yes." *But not from the fall,* she wanted to add.

"How far did you fall? Do you remember?"

She thought for a moment. "I'd say ten, twelve feet."

"I see." He pulled out a small light and shined it in her eyes.

"You probably have a mild concussion. Now, let's look at this hip." He gave her a gown, told her to undress, and left the room.

She put on the gown and then sat patiently, tapping her fingers on her thighs, feeling silly for all the fuss. She wanted to get out of this office, to go lie down somewhere cool and quiet. She longed for the little cot in her tent, although the thought of going back to the site and Yates didn't appeal to her, either. She knew he was going to give her hell for digging out of her assigned excavation grid.

Her eyes scanned the desk, the bookshelves. Several of the books were about radiation, and she wondered if he'd studied radiation because of the war. She'd been fascinated with and appalled by the effects of Little Boy and Fat Man, the bombs used to decimate Hiroshima and Nagasaki.

Dr. Mendenhall knocked, then opened the door and entered the office. "Okay, Miss Delgado. Let's see what's going on." He palpated her hip, moving the edge of her panties to reveal the bloom of a purple bruise right below her hipbone.

"That looks painful," he said.

"Yes, it definitely hurts."

"I don't think anything is broken, though." He covered her with the gown again. "You'll feel sore for a week or so, and this ugly bruise will be around for a while. You also have a minor concussion. Aspirin and rest for a few days."

"A few? Like two? Three?"

"Let's say two and see how you feel." He smiled. "Is there anything else I can do for you, Miss Delgado?"

Ruby couldn't resist. "I see you have a number of books on radiation . . ."

"I do, yes. It is an interest of mine—how radiation affects the body."

The old man's raspy cough resonated through the wall again.

"Well, Miss Delgado, I have a patient waiting."

"He sounds horribly ill," Ruby said.

Dr. Mendenhall frowned. "I'm sure he is. The people of this village prefer the ancient remedies. When those don't work, they come to me. Often, they wait so long that they are very sick by the time I see them . . . I'll let you get dressed, and I'll get you something for your hip pain. I'll meet you at reception."

Once the doctor left Ruby stood, her muscles stiff from sitting. Still intrigued about the books, she walked over to the bookshelf to look at them. A spike of pain jabbed her hip, and she faltered. Instinctively, she caught herself by placing her hand on the doctor's desk, but it landed on a book, and the book slipped out from under her palm and fell to the floor.

"Crap." She hobbled around to the other side of the desk to pick it up. A piece of paper had fallen out of it. She picked it up to place it back in the book, turned it over, and stopped short.

It was a photo of Dr. Mendenhall shaking hands with a man in a black uniform with a swastika on his left sleeve.

What was Dr. Mendenhall doing with a Nazi?

CHAPTER 3

R uby left cash on the counter of the reception window, not wanting to encounter Dr. Mendenhall again after what she'd just seen in the photo. She would make do without pain medication.

Jumbled thoughts and nerves on edge made her long for the privacy of her tent. Walking through the parking lot she noted the sky had turned a searing, bloody shade of orangey-red. The entire day had passed her by.

Pete startled when she opened the door of the truck. He'd clearly been snoozing.

"Well?" he asked, rubbing his face and yawning.

"I have a mild concussion," she said.

"Oh."

"Yeah. The doctor says I need to rest for a couple of days. I don't want to, but I guess I'd better listen. I'm a little worried about my car, though."

"Yeah. I'll get it first thing tomorrow," Pete said.

"Thank you." Ruby leaned her arm across the back of the seat and lay her pounding head on her arm and closed her eyes. Her mind swirled with images of the dead bodies. She felt herself nod off and forced her eyes open. Why couldn't she stay awake? Probably the concussion. The pain in her head was shutting out her thoughts. Her mind drifted away from the pain, away from the jolting of the truck, and away from the light.

⊙⊱⊰⊙

Someone tugged on Ruby's shoulder.

"Ruby, wake up. We're here." Pete stood at the open door of the truck and helped her out as she groggily awoke.

Gas lamps burned near one of the excavated ruins. A night dig was highly unusual, but several people huddled around one of the grids.

"What's going on?" Ruby asked.

"Pete, Ruby! I'm so glad you're back." Cynthia raced toward them, her face lit with excitement. "We found it! We found the burial site. Come on, you have to see this. Yates is ecstatic." She waved them forward.

Ruby and Pete exchanged glances.

"Would you hurry up?" Cynthia pulled on Pete's arm, dragging him behind her. But she wasn't headed toward the sinkhole; she was headed in the opposite direction, toward the grid to the north of the site.

When they reached it, all heads turned toward them.

Yates beamed. "Pete, Ruby. We found it. There are only a few bones at the surface, but from the look of it they're ancient."

Ruby stood dumbfounded.

"Think they're Anasazi?" Pete asked.

Anasazi. A lost civilization. Her find of the treasure of the Noche Triste proved that commerce existed between peoples of Mexico and into the territory of New Mexico, but no actual trace of the Anasazi had ever been found. The world had been looking for years.

"Can't be sure right now," said Yates. "But, you never know."

"That's incredible, Dr. Yates. Congratulations," Annie said.

He acknowledged her with a nod. "Get your tools. We're working until we've unearthed every last skeleton."

Ruby saw Pete visibly sigh with relief. Probably because the crew's attention would be focused on this find rather than the other fleshy skeletons two hundred feet away.

Going against every instinct and ignoring every ache, Ruby kept her mouth shut and headed toward her tent to get her tools. Despite her pain and fatigue, the idea of working on a find like this made her giddy. It would only further the reputation she had already established with the Noche Triste treasure. She could get her career back on track, create a new life for herself—perhaps even leave the debilitating sorrow that had hovered over her for years behind her once and for all. The work would make everything better.

But she felt a responsibility to those bodies in the pit. Her ambition had been the reason she'd lost so much before. Lost him. Matthew. She couldn't let it get away from her again. Never again.

Yes, she would allow Yates to have his moment in the sun, and Pete could have his deep, dark secret.

But not for long.

⚜

Yates had kept them so busy digging for the next few days that Ruby's body was unable to fully recuperate from her fall. She still ached, and her head felt like it was caught in a vise. Finally, at week's end, Yates gave her some time off.

After sleeping in 'til nearly noon, Ruby sought out Pete to help retrieve her car.

There hadn't been time after finding the burial site.

By the time they came back to the site, her car towed behind his truck, it had begun to rain. Huge, dark thunderheads shadowed the landscape and had driven the working archaeologists out of the ruins and into their tents. Others stayed under cover in the main work area and busied themselves labeling bones. Tarps had been lain over the burial and secured.

With Carl's and Pete's help, Ruby rigged a tarp over the front of her Plymouth Coupe so she could work on the engine. She hung a lantern from the open hood and engrossed herself in the task of fixing the wire harness.

Ruby welcomed the rain. Although she wanted to keep digging, to keep unearthing the civilization that lay beneath their feet, she knew it would be good for her to rest. And she needed her car in working order.

Pete came up from behind and peered under the hood. "Yates is going into town for a while," he said.

"What does he want us to do?"

"He said to use the time as we like. Carl and Cynthia are documenting the bones from the ancient burial."

Ruby looked over toward the sinkhole and pitched her voice low. "No indication anyone's come across what we found?"

"Nope. They marked it off as a hazardous area. Don't think anyone's going to be exploring down there."

"That's good. I guess . . ." She couldn't be sure. She still wanted to tell the police, even though she'd promised Pete she'd give him time.

"How's the car?" he asked.

"Slow going. I've got a terrible headache." She instantly regretted her words. He'd apologized already, and she really didn't mean to belabor the point, but she was sick of the pain.

"Don't you think you should be resting?" Pete asked.

"I'll rest later." She shrugged.

He leaned over the car. "This engine is amazing. It's so clean."

"Thanks." Ruby untied the bandana from around her neck and swabbed perspiration from her forehead. The rain had made the air muggy and stifling.

"You've got a little grease on your chin," he said.

She wiped the cloth over her face. "Gone?"

"No." He took the bandana from her and started toward her chin. She pulled away. "I'm not going to hurt you," he said, sounding a little wounded himself.

"I don't know why I flinched. Just a little edgy, I guess."

"I promise I won't whack you again." He grinned.

Ruby narrowed her eyes at him, but let him wipe the grease smudge off her chin. She couldn't help but look into his eyes as he concentrated. Nice eyes. Really nice. He finished and tossed the bandana onto a table next to the car.

"Hey, don't. Give it back." She swiped the bandana off the table.

"Sorry," he said. "I didn't think you'd want it back now that it's dirty."

"Well, you thought wrong." The bandana had been Matthew's. It was her prized possession.

"Okay." He held his hands up in surrender.

"I'm sorry." She shouldn't have snapped, but the bandana was all she had left of him. She tied it around her neck again.

"Are you sure you don't need any help?" he asked. She glanced up at him and saw from the look in his eyes he was sincere. He really was trying to help. But she wanted to be alone. Working on her car had always been a meditative experience for her. It took her out of herself and provided instant gratification. A feeling of accomplishment. Making order out of the chaos of her life.

"I'm sure." She bent herself over the engine again and held her breath, waiting for him to leave.

She heard him walk away and exhaled. She took hold of the bandana and held it up to her face, breathing in the scent of the memory that haunted her. The same memory she hoped would haunt her forever.

Dr. Yates returned from town in a good mood. He even asked Ruby if she felt better.

"I'm glad you weren't hurt too badly," he said with a hint of a smile.

She would be happy, too, if she were in his shoes. Discovering the burial site could answer the age-old mystery of why the Anasazi died out, or fled the area, over two thousand years ago, if the find was Anasazi. Perhaps now his resentment of her would ease, and he would see her as a colleague instead of an enemy. Ruby felt even more encouraged when Dr. Yates invited them all to celebrate at the cantina that night, with dinner and drinks on him.

Pete offered her a ride into town, but she opted to drive herself, anxious to see how the car ran.

By the time she walked in to the cantina, the others had already been there long enough to order a round of drinks and several baskets of chips. Spike must have just finished a joke, because he laughed uncontrollably while Carl sputtered his beer on the table. Laughter filled the cantina, and the group seemed on their way to a good and boisterous drunk.

All except Pete. He sipped his beer casually, watching the others toast themselves and Dr. Yates.

A chair sat empty between Spike and Pete—obviously saved for her. When the group saw her enter the bar, they all called out her name in cheerful greeting. Ruby took the seat between Spike and Pete. Pete lifted his bottle of beer in her direction and Spike wrapped his burly arm around her torso, squeezing the air out of her lungs.

"Delgado! Have a drink with me. We're celebrating." Spike finally let go of her.

"I'll have a soda," she said, straightening her blouse.

"A soda? You can do better than that."

"No, really, I can't."

Spike growled in a playful way, squeezing her again. "Come on."

"She said she doesn't want a drink." Pete's voice was flat.

Spike lifted his hands in surrender. "Okay, okay, calm down, Marshall. Just havin' a little fun."

Ruby put her hand on Pete's arm. "Pete, it's okay. He didn't mean any harm."

Spike chuckled. The sound was gravelly, and yet warm. "No harm, man. No harm. Just want to make sure she's taken care of, has a good time."

Ruby swallowed at the awkwardness of the situation as Pete took a swig of his beer.

"How'd you meet Dr. Yates?" Ruby asked Spike, needing a diversion.

"John and I go way back. Fought in the war together. He saved my life once, and then I saved his. That bonded us, you know? We've been doin' each other favors ever since. I'm helping him with this dig, and he's helping me stay alive financially." He chuckled again. "I guess I'm pretty much unemployable. John's the only one who'll put up with me."

"You two seem so very different," Ruby admitted.

"That's an understatement," Spike said. "But, we've seen and been through a lot together."

"So, you've worked together for some time?"

"Yep. Since he came back from Peru."

"Peru? He had a dig there?"

"Well, sort of . . ." Spike looked at the table. "I shouldn't have mentioned it. Sore subject." He scratched at his scar. "It was tough coming back from the war. John had his education to fall back on, but I didn't finish high school, so it was odd jobs here and there. It's been hard to make ends meet. I can cook, though. John tracked me down a few years ago, and I've been cooking for him and his crew for quite a while now. John's always been there for me, and I'll be there for him." He downed a shot of tequila, wincing.

Ruby could smell the tequila, the tangy allure of it. Maybe

she could have just one. What harm would it do? The waitress passed by, and Ruby waved a hand at her.

"I'll have a . . . ginger ale, please."

The waitress nodded, and before Ruby could question her decision she turned back to Spike. Lowering her voice, she asked, "So, tell me. Why does Dr. Yates dislike me so much?"

"John's a hard man." Spike grabbed a chip and munched on it noisily. "Don't take his bein' quiet personally."

"Is he always so rude?"

The waitress returned with her soda.

"Look, I don't know what's eatin' him," Spike said. "All I'll say is that everyone's got problems, and we all handle them differently. I know John hasn't been exactly hospitable to you, but don't let it bother you."

"I can try." Ruby sipped her ginger ale.

"You're all right, kid." He winked at her and downed another shot.

By the time dinner was served everyone, with the exception of Pete and Ruby, had consumed enough alcohol to be downright sloshed. Once or twice Ruby caught Yates' eye, but he quickly diverted his gaze. Pete had been silent the whole night.

"Don't feel like celebrating?" she yelled over the noise, ducking her head at the last minute to avoid a loaf of bread spiraling in her direction.

"Not really," he said, leaning toward her.

"What gives?"

He shrugged. "Just a lot on my mind. I think I'm going to take off."

Ruby looked at the others having a great time, laughing, talking. "I'm right behind you."

They walked out into the coolness of the night. The single exterior light on the building illuminated the light rain misting around them, making the air sparkle. Thunder rumbled in the distance.

"See ya'," Pete said as he headed toward his truck.

Ruby had parked further away from the building, and strained to see her way to her car in the darkness. Once there, she hopped in and turned the key. The engine chugged, sputtered, started, and then promptly died.

"Oh no . . ." she said, trying again. Nothing. "Damn."

"Problem?" Pete was standing at her open window.

"Thing won't start again. I must have missed something."

Ruby got out of the car and flung open the hood. The darkness of the moonless night prevented a quick diagnosis.

"It's pretty late," Pete said. "Let me give you a ride to the site. We'll come back in the morning and figure it out."

"I hate leaving it here," she said.

"It'll be fine. You'll see. C'mon, I'll give you a lift."

CHAPTER 4

Tiny raindrops, coming down harder now, hit the windshield as Ruby and Pete drove in silence down the bumpy, muddy road.

"Yates seems pretty excited about today's findings. He didn't throw me even one dirty look tonight," Ruby said.

Peter just stared at the road ahead. All night he'd been silent, gloomy, almost morose.

There's nothing worse than a moody man.

Ruby was about to say something sarcastic to lighten the mood when Pete swerved to the left and slammed on the brakes. The truck slid to a slippery stop off the road and into a small ravine.

"What the hell?" Ruby yelled.

"There was something in the road. Something big," Pete said, looking into the rearview mirror.

Ruby looked out the rear window and saw a large figure lying in the road. "Is it a coyote?"

"Too big for a coyote. We better take a look." Pete put the truck into reverse and backed past the object, turning to shine his headlights on it.

They both jumped out of the truck and ran toward the

figure. Pete got there first and knelt next to it for a closer look. Ruby caught up, rain streaming from her hair into her eyes. She looked down to see a man, face-down in the mud, covered in long, stiff cactus spines—cholla cactus spines. A rope had been wound around him, holding the poisonous spindles against the man's torso.

"Oh shit." Ruby clamped a hand to her mouth.

"Can you hear me?" Pete asked the man.

A stifled moan came from the man's swollen lips.

Now on her hands and knees Ruby crept toward him, and then, sitting cross-legged, gently lifted his head and rested his cheek on her thigh. The man's breath came in ragged gasps as he struggled for air. She brushed his soggy hair off his forehead and saw that this was no man, but a boy, seventeen years old at the most.

"Let's get this cactus off him." Pete started to untie the ropes.

Within seconds the rope no longer bound the cactus, but it still stuck, the needles embedded into the boy's skin.

"We need to get him to the clinic." Pete grasped one of the branches but jerked his hand back. He sucked on his fingers.

"Cholla is barbed," Ruby said, rain pouring down her face. "What do we do? How do we move him?" If it weren't for the shallow rise and fall of the cactus spines on the boy's back, Ruby would have thought he was dead.

"We need to get this cactus off of him. Wait a minute," Pete said. He ran to the truck and came back, pulling on gloves. He placed his protected hands around one of the thin branches and carefully pulled. The spines, deeply embedded, wouldn't give. He pulled harder. The boy groaned.

"Damn it," Pete whispered.

Ruby knew pulling the branches slowly would be unbearable. "You'll have to yank them out fast," she said, her stomach lurching at the thought of it.

Pete fixed his grip around one of the branches and tore it off the boy's back. The boy screamed, arching his back in agonized pain. His head slumped into the mud.

Ruby bent over him, lifting his face off the ground, and again stroked the dirty, wet hair from his forehead. "I'm sorry. I know it hurts. We are here to help you." She didn't know if he heard her or not, but he definitely didn't respond. "I think he's passed out," she said to Pete.

"At least he won't feel anything then, or remember it." Pete began pulling the branches from the boy's skin in rapid motions. The unforgiving barbs at the end of the needles created more damage coming out than they had going in, and Ruby bit back tears. The needles had left his back and arms bloody, bruised, and torn. But there was something else on his back. She leaned closer.

"Pete, look. What's that?" As soon as she asked, a horrifying thought struck her. "Are those *lash* marks?"

"Looks like it."

She blinked hard, trying to process the image. "I can't believe what I'm seeing," she said. "Can you?"

Rain dripped from Pete's curls onto his forehead and nose. "Well, believe it."

"What do you mean?"

"Later. Help me lift him."

They pulled the boy's limp, partially naked body to a sitting position.

Pete squatted next to him and put one of the boy's arms around his neck. He then grasped him around the waist and lifted the boy to his feet. The boy slumped against him.

"Look at his arm." Ruby pointed to the boy's right upper arm, swollen and oozing with pus and blood. "Could be a snake bite." She unbuckled her belt, pulled it from her pants and then wrapped it around the boy's bicep, a few inches above the bite mark, cinching it tight. "If this is a snake bite it might be too late to tourniquet, but it's worth trying. We've got to get him to the clinic *now*."

Pete shook his head. "Not the clinic. I'm taking him to Los Campos. There's a hospital there."

"But that's over ninety miles away."

"Yep. We've got to go."

"Pete, let's just take him to Dr. Mendenhall. That arm worries me. He could have been bitten by a rattlesnake, and if that's the case we don't have much time."

"I'm taking him to the hospital." Pete shifted his weight to get a better hold of the boy's waist.

"Don't be ridiculous, Pete. He needs help *fast*."

"Are you coming, or am I going to leave you out here in the rain?" He hoisted the boy over his shoulder, carried him to the truck, and waited for her. She had no choice. She hurried to the truck, opened the door, and helped Pete fold the boy's body onto the seat. Ruby climbed up and scooted in next to him, pulling his body toward her to support him.

She took off her jacket, balled it up, and placed it under his neck to keep his head steady. She placed her hand on his forehead, checking for fever.

"He's burning up."

Pete removed his coat as well, and tucked it around the boy's wet and shivering body.

Then he hurried into the driver's seat. "Let's go," he said.

CHAPTER 5

R uby stood at the window of the boy's hospital room, her nails bitten to nubs. He lay asleep on his stomach, tubes and IVs sticking out of his body. She hoped they'd gotten him there in time. God only knew how long he'd lain in the road with the needles biting at his skin and poison coursing through his veins before they'd found him.

Who'd tied the cactus to him? And why?

She'd heard about ancient religious sects that practiced self-flagellation and self-torture, like Opus Dei. Could this young man be associated with them, or a sect like it? The factions she'd heard of used their rituals more symbolically, performed them to cause discomfort but not destruction as she'd seen on the boy.

Pete reached around her and offered her a cup of coffee.

"Thanks," she said, still wet and chilled. The steam from the coffee warmed her face.

"Any change?"

"No."

They could only see one side of the boy's gray and hollowed face. To Ruby, he looked like a corpse—it reminded her of what she'd seen in the cave the other day. A chill zipped down her spine.

"I hope he makes it," she said under her breath. The hospital stirred memories—helplessness, uncertainty, fear. She hated the sterile, sickly-sweet smell. The recollection settled on her like a thick, relentless fog. The last time she'd left a hospital, she'd left without Matthew. Never again to see him alive.

Pete stood nearby, silently sipping his coffee.

"We took a risk driving him this far," she said.

He shook his head. "I couldn't take him to Mendenhall."

"I know his clinic is small, but time could be a really important factor here. Especially if he has a snake bite."

"Mendenhall is not the man to deal with this." Pete held his coffee cup under his chin as he stared at the boy.

She narrowed her eyes. "Why?"

"I don't trust him."

Ruby recalled the photo of Dr. Mendenhall shaking hands with a Nazi official. Would he be worthy of anyone's trust?

"Why? Does it have something to do with the war? The fact that he's German?" She didn't want to mention the photo just yet.

He gave her a sideways glance, as if surprised she would mention such a thing. So he did know more about Mendenhall than he was saying.

"Maybe," he said. "I've heard rumors."

"Rumors? What kind of rumors?" Getting information out of this guy was like trudging uphill in knee-deep sand.

"Some of the men in the village thought he was conducting experiments on them. Medical experiments."

"Do you believe them?" Ruby asked. It sounded preposterous.

Pete shrugged. "The villagers here are very suspicious of modern medicine. Like Dr. Mendenhall said, they prefer their own remedies—or to visit a curandera, or medicine woman. Problem is, the closest curandera is in Mora. About sixty miles north of here.

"But you insisted that *I* see Dr. Mendenhall."

"I knew he wouldn't hurt you."

"How did you know that?" Ruby wished Pete would just stop with all the secrecy. It was infuriating.

"You're a gringa—white, one of his kind."

"You're not serious."

He arched an eyebrow at her.

"I'm half-Castilian," she informed him.

Pete gave a derisive snort. "You don't look it, don't talk it, don't act it. You may have Castilian blood in your veins, but you certainly don't own it."

"You don't know anything about me." Anger, sharp and familiar, started to rise in her chest.

"I can tell. *We* can tell."

"And who is *we?*" Ruby couldn't believe the nerve of this guy. He sounded as condescending as Dr. Yates!

"You know, *we* of Mexican descent."

"We? With a name like Marshall? Doesn't sound very Mexican to me. Sounds like the name of one of Dr. Mendenhall's *kind.* Unless, of course, your name's actually Medina."

His jaw flexed. "I'm getting more coffee." He turned and walked away from her.

Hypocrite. Ruby leaned her forehead against the window and thought about Mendenhall's '*kind*' and the photo she'd seen of him shaking hands with the Nazi. The self-proclaimed superior race. Genocide. As much as she hated to admit it, maybe Pete had a point. Perhaps Dr. Mendenhall did have a bias against the people of Las Montanas.

She turned her attention back to the boy, letting her gaze wander over the mess of torn flesh on his back. The pain must have been unbearable.

When Pete returned with fresh coffee, she decided to let the previous conversation go.

"Who would do something so cruel?" Ruby said softly, touching her fingertips to the glass. "And what was he doing wandering around in the rain at night?"

"After someone brutalized him." Pete's voice cracked with emotion. She turned to him.

"You indicated you might have seen this before. Where?"

"I never said that." He avoided her eyes.

"You did."

"I don't know what you're talking about," he deadpanned.

Ruby glared at him. She couldn't believe he had the nerve to lie to her face—just as he had before with the bodies.

"We have to get back to the site. It's almost two," Pete said.

"Why are you lying to me? Again? What's going on here?"

"I can't talk about it." He finally looked her in the eye.

"I'm not leaving," she said. "I want to know more about this boy and what happened to him. I want to know if he'll be all right."

"This boy is none of your business."

"He most certainly is." She rounded on Pete, sick of his patronizing behavior. "We saved his life. What if he has no family, no one to care for him?"

"He has a family."

Ruby's mouth dropped open. "You know this how?"

"I just know."

"That's right, you know everything," she snapped. "About random corpses, about this kid, and apparently my entire professional dossier. But you're not talking, at least not to me. It's all a big damned secret."

Pete's jaw clenched again, and she could see the muscles pulse in his face.

"Don't you care about what happens to him?" She grabbed his arm, swinging him around to face her. "We found him. He is our responsibility."

"No, I don't care, and he is *not* my responsibility. Nor is he yours." He crumpled the paper cup in his hand. "I'm leaving. Are you coming with me?"

Ruby crossed her arms, holding her coffee cup closer to her face. "No."

Two doctors came from behind the metal doors into the Emergency Room and started past them. Ruby stepped in front of them.

"Excuse me? I'm Ruby Delgado, and this is Pete Marshall." She tilted her head toward Pete. "We're the ones who brought in that boy," she said, pointing.

"I'm Dr. Phillips." He offered his hand, and Ruby grasped it.

"How is the boy? Is he going to be okay?"

"We'll know more in a few hours. He did suffer a rattlesnake bite. I think we caught it in time, but his condition is so weak he's having trouble hanging on. The wounds on his back are infected, and he has a fever. There are also signs of a virus, perhaps influenza. His injuries are pretty extensive. We just have to wait and see if he pulls through." The doctor paused a moment. "Do you know him?"

"No," Ruby said. She looked at Pete, who remained infuriatingly silent.

"Did you happen to get his name?" the doctor asked.

"He was unconscious when we found him," Pete said. Another lie.

A nurse appeared from the corridor. "Doctor, there's been an inquiry on the boy. His name is Nicolas Baca. We're looking for medical records now."

"Nicolas, huh?" the doctor said. "Thanks, Jean."

With a swift, military-like turn, the nurse left as quickly as she'd come.

Nicolas. The name echoed in Ruby's head like a gong. She felt her knees give way, and she grabbed Pete's elbow for support. She felt so weak. She probably should have heeded Mendenhall's advice and rested for the last couple of days, but how could she with the discovery of the ancient burial? She had to power through. She hadn't wanted to give Yates any more reason to dislike her.

"Miss?" The doctor moved toward her, concern on his face. "Are you all right?"

"I'm fine," she said, shrugging it off. "Just tired, I guess."

"It's late. Why don't you get some rest? Nicolas isn't going anywhere tonight."

"We were just leaving," Pete said, taking hold of Ruby's arm. "Thanks, Dr. Phillips."

ತಲ್ಲಿ

Ruby only slept a few hours that night. The alarm woke her at six-thirty.

Dreams of Matthew and Nicolas had merged and intertwined. She couldn't tell where Matthew began and Nicolas ended. She dressed and crawled out of her tent to find that she was the last one up. Pete was sitting alone at the campfire, eating breakfast.

"Hey," she said, stifling a yawn.

"Hey."

She watched him for a few moments, trying to come up with something to say. But in the face of his stony silence, she couldn't think of anything.

"Ruby," Spike called to her, waving her over with a spatula. She walked to the mess tent and followed him inside.

"Mornin'," he said. "How about some of my special *huevos caliente*? They're guaranteed to wake you up."

"Sure."

Pete came into the mess tent and stood next to her, apparently waiting for a second helping.

"Where'd you two run off to last night?" Spike asked. "We didn't see you when we left the cantina."

"Well—"

"Her car had broken down again. I gave her a ride back here," Pete cut in. The lies just rolled off his tongue. Ruby bit her lip.

"Where's the car?" Spike asked.

"We left it at the cantina," Ruby said, eyeing Pete. He held his plate out for Spike, who loaded it up. Then he went back outside to eat.

One of the crew started to help himself to the tray of eggs.

"Hey!" Spike called out. "I got twenty people to feed and you've been up here three times already. Go away."

The man glowered at him and stalked off.

"How about some of those eggs?" Ruby asked.

Spike obliged, and Ruby sat down to eat. Just as she finished her breakfast and started on another cup of coffee, Yates called an assignment meeting. Cynthia and Carl were to finish cataloging the bones found at the northern end of the site, several of the crew were to excavate another grid unit in the southern end, and Pete and Ruby were to work in a new area in the east end that had been only partially laid out with a grid.

Pete quickly grabbed his equipment and headed out before Ruby even finished her coffee. About five minutes later, she gathered her things and joined him. He was taking photographs of the area they were to work in. The ground sloped to a deep recess and Pete was taking close ups of the strata.

"Where do we start?" she asked.

"There are pottery shards all over this area. It must have been a kitchen or some kind of storage facility. I'll work here; you work over there." He pointed to an area covered with two or three dozen small-to-medium-sized boulders.

"Doesn't look like anything's been cleared over there," she said.

"Those stones need to be moved out of the way so we can finish gridding it."

"You're saying I have to move all those stones?" she asked. He had some nerve, all right.

"That's what I'm saying." He put his camera in his satchel.

"By myself?"

He raised a brow. "Can't handle it?"

She shook her head at him. "What is the matter with you?"

"Nothing," he said nonchalantly, as if he had no idea what she was talking about. "What do you mean?"

"Your attitude."

"There's nothing wrong with my attitude. I'm just busy."

Ruby sighed and stood tapping her foot a while, unsure how to bring up last night. "I wonder how Nicolas is doing."

"He'll probably be fine," Pete said, absorbed in his task. He'd pulled a trowel from his satchel and had started to work at the earth with delicate scraping motions.

"I sure hope so . . ." She took a deep breath. "I still can't believe how we found him, the cactus, the lash mar—"

"I wouldn't worry about it," he interrupted. "You'd better get busy; you don't want Yates to see you standing around." He grabbed a pair of gloves from his back pocket and threw them at her feet. "Here, you'll need these."

They were the same gloves he'd used to pull the spines out of Nicolas' back. The bloodstains had turned black. He stopped scraping and looked up at her. "Listen," he said, his voice softening. "We'll probably never know exactly what happened to Nicolas or how it happened. You just can't let it get to you. We did a good thing last night. But now we have work to do."

Ruby bit her lip, letting his words sink in. She hated to admit it, but he was right. She needed this dig, this work, on her résumé. This was her opportunity to finally get her education and career back on track. It was her opportunity to move forward, to get away from the past— from all the heartbreak and sorrow.

She turned and walked toward the pile of rocks.

CHAPTER 6

From the corner of his eye Pete watched Ruby go, and then breathed a sigh of relief. Finding the boy, Nicolas Baca, last night was the absolute worst thing that could have happened on the heels of finding the skeletonized bodies. Nicolas had obviously joined the Brotherhood. He was about the right age.

Pete's brother Ricardo had joined when he was sixteen. His father was still a member. Pete had never been interested. Blind faith in anything had never sat right with him, even when he was younger. His lack of religious devotion had caused problems between him and his father, and the more his father insisted that he join the Brotherhood the more he dug his heels in and refused. When Ricardo died, he knew he'd made the right decision. And now it was too late for Ricardo.

Keeping information from Ruby was getting harder by the minute. Things seemed to be spinning out of control, and Ruby was on top of it like a . . . well, a ferret. The name people called her behind her back suited her well.

He could guess with almost absolute certainty what happened to Nicolas Baca. He'd seen the blood and the bruises before, but he'd never seen anyone in such bad shape. Continuing to work, he resolved that he would just keep putting Ruby off as long as possible and focus on the work until he had time to think everything through. He had agreed to her imminent deadline, but . . .

ॐ

A couple of hours later, when he finally looked up to the lip of the slope from where he'd been working, Ruby's boots were inches from his face. He'd been so absorbed in his thoughts and in his work that he hadn't heard her approach. His gaze went up the length of her.

"Finished." Her cheeks glowed pink, and smudges of dirt dotted her chin and forehead. The red bandana hung loose and rumpled around her neck. Wild brown curls framed her face, sticking to her skin. "You know—" she sat on her haunches "—you're scraping away too much of the strata there. We won't be able to see where the soil changes. You should use a brush instead of that trowel."

He looked at the trowel in his hand. She was right . . . God, he hadn't even noticed.

"Here. I'll help."

Ruby sorted through the satchel of tools, and found a pick and two brushes. She tossed one to him and then jumped down into the recess. She was so close to him he could smell her hair—clean, like citrus. As she worked Pete found himself sneaking glances, noticing the dewy perspiration on her skin, the length and darkness of her eyelashes. From what he could tell she wore no makeup, and certainly didn't need any. Suddenly she straightened, took the bandana off, wiped her forehead with it, and tied it around her neck again.

"You wear that thing every day?" he asked.

"Always." She bent down over the wall of the recess again, working the soil with the brush. "So, when are you going to tell me about Nicolas Baca?"

The question startled him. He thought he'd gotten her off that subject.

"Don't know if there's anything to tell."

"I haven't been here in Las Montanas very long, but I'm from a small town. Everyone knows everyone, and everyone knows everyone's business. I'm sure it's not much different here."

He stopped working and focused on her narrowed eyes. "He lives here, in Las Montanas."

"I gathered that. And you know him."

"I know *of* him."

"Who is he? Why did someone do that to him? Does the village here have some kind of medieval penal code?"

He pointed his index finger at her. "Don't judge what you don't know."

"I'm not judging!" She threw her hands up into the air. "I'm just . . . confused. After the bodies, or skeletons or whatever it was we found, and then this kid . . . Can you really blame me? And then your suddenly negative opinion of Dr. Mendenhall. Why now?" She sighed. "You seem to know a little about all these things, but you're stonewalling me. I've kept your secret. Haven't I proven you can trust me?"

He snorted. "You haven't proven anything except that you ask a lot of questions, Ferret."

Her upper lip twitched. "Don't call me that. I hate that."

He tossed down the brush and rubbed the perspiration from his face with the back of his hand. How was he going to keep her away?

"Look," she said, "I'm just worried about the kid, that's all."

"Why do you care so much about someone you don't even know?"

Her mouth dropped open. "Just because I don't know him doesn't mean that I'm devoid of human compassion. You *do* know him, and yet you don't seem to care. Why is that?"

"Hey, we've done our good deed. It's over. I'm sure he'll be fine." He wanted to stop talking about this. He wanted to work

—in silence. He continued brushing the earth with small, even strokes. He thought he saw a shard poking through the dirt.

"I need to know he's okay," she said.

Pete stopped and looked over at her. "Are you one of those people who always needs a cause?"

"No," she asserted. "It's just . . . well . . . Nicolas. . . Oh, you wouldn't understand."

"Understand what?"

"Why would I tell you anything?" She raised her chin at him, her doe-like large eyes narrowing with skepticism.

"Then don't." He shrugged and bent over the wall again.

"You wouldn't understand because you've never been responsible for anyone's death."

He pivoted to face her. She avoided his gaze, staring at the mountains.

"If you had then you would know the constant, all-consuming weight of guilt. The pain never goes away. It's like a giant rock crushing the life out of you. But this boy, Nicolas, I realized that . . . maybe . . . if I could help him it might ease some of the pain, you know? Maybe gentle the memories." She kicked at a pebble. Then she looked directly into Pete's eyes. "It's killing me."

"What—" Pete started, then stopped. He had no idea what to say. "I mean, who?"

"My son. Matthew." She turned her back to him.

Pete leaned his hand against the wall. He'd never considered that she might have been a mother. He'd never thought about her past, her family or her childhood—only her work, her success.

She turned back to face him, her eyes filled with pain.

"He was six years old. I took him everywhere. I wanted to teach him everything I knew: engines, rock climbing, martial arts, caving, archeology. He was so smart. He was five when I taught him how to climb. One day . . . *that* day . . . we climbed higher than he'd ever gone before. I'd heard of some petroglyphs in a cavern high on the mountain. We had almost reached it. He was tired, but I wanted to get there. I knew other people had heard of these drawings, but I had to get there first. Instead of turning around like I should have, I pushed him to go further. When we finally reached the cavern it looked a little unstable, but I ignored my instincts. He had to rest, and we settled in. Within minutes, I felt the floor tremble. An earth tremor. Just a small one, but it was enough to . . . The wall gave way, and we were—"

She stopped, took a deep breath. "I could hear him crying, but I couldn't do anything. Part of the wall had landed on my legs. I couldn't move. The next thing I remember, I was in a hospital bed. I asked for him again and again, but I kept losing consciousness. When I was finally stable, they told me he'd been crushed." Tears filled her eyes, though she was blinking them back. "Sometimes, I still hear him crying . . ." She turned away from him again, her entire body stiff. She put a trembling hand to her mouth.

"I'm so sorry," he said. What a horrible thing to have endured. "How long ago?" he quietly asked.

She straightened. Sniffed. Wiped her face with the bandana. Then she turned around to face him. "Four years on March twenty-fifth. God, how I hate that day. Sometimes I wish I won't live to see the next one. I miss him. I want to be with him again."

Pete knew what guilt and despair felt like, and he knew there was nothing he could do or say to make it better for her. Grief was a private hell, and no amount of consoling and comforting would help. She would have to find her own way through it.

"I'm sorry," he said again, and meant it.

She nodded. "I'm just starting to learn to live with it, you know? Right afterward, I was suicidal. A year later, I started drinking—heavily. I moved to an abandoned Hogan on the Navajo reservation because I wanted to be alone, isolated from everything and everyone. God, I was a mess. I just wanted to be numb, you know?" She pressed her lips together.

Yeah. He knew . . .

"But I don't want to be numb anymore. I want to feel. I'm just not sure I know how."

He cleared his throat, uncomfortable with this rush of personal information. It seemed to tumble out of her. He wasn't quite sure what to do or say. "You need to forgive yourself."

She laughed. "Right. Not possible. He was my son, Pete. My responsibility. My *life*."

He studied her face. She looked way too young to have a six-year-old son, especially four years ago. He worked the math in his head. She'd had to have been nineteen or twenty when she had him. And no mention of a husband. That was another story, for sure. The obsession with Nicolas Baca made more sense now —a kid in danger. And as much as he wanted to deny it, Nicolas *was* in danger.

He watched as she ran her hand along the top edge of the depression in the wall, mounding the loose dirt together. She gathered some of it in her fist and let it fall to the ground, the wind catching particles of it and blowing them into the air. He reached a hand toward her, thinking to comfort her, but pulled back when she fingered the red bandana at her neck.

"He gave me this on his fifth birthday. He liked to give gifts on his birthday, instead of receiving them. He was very special, and I, well, I screwed up. That's why I have to help Nicolas. Do you understand? Someone tried to kill that boy."

He did understand. If only he could tell her his story, his pain. They had much in common but, unlike her, he couldn't find the courage to tell his tale.

"Help me to help him," she said. "Tell me all you know about Nicolas Baca."

He looked into her eyes and felt he could see all the way into her heart. He realized it wouldn't be hard for him to get lost in those eyes—and quite possibly her heart—and want to stay lost. She had shared her deepest pain with him, imprinting it on him like a brand. He didn't like how it moved him. He didn't want to feel touched by her and her story.

"I can't," he said.

She held his gaze and then folded her arms across her chest. With that protective motion her eyes lost their tenderness, their dewy sadness, and turned to smoldering granite stones filled with bitterness. They burned through him, all the way to his soul.

"Then damn you to hell," she said before climbing out of the trench.

CHAPTER 7

Ruby decided she would go back to the hospital to see Nicolas on the next break Yates gave them. And if she couldn't, she'd wait and find him in the village. If he had survived.

She walked toward some of the Mexican crewmen who were digging or moving boulders, taking them to piles away from the marked-off units. The urge to join them, to dig, hit her hard. As she approached them, several of them eyed her, talking amongst themselves in Spanish, and no doubt wondering what she wanted.

Two of them ignored her and snapped their cameras, documenting the unearthed areas, while others dug and scraped the loose sand away from the floors of the ruins, which lay several layers down. She picked up a shovel and started to dig with them, ignoring their remarks. If they only knew she understood every colorful word. They spoke of the inappropriateness of her being out here with them—a frail woman, a student, someone who had the luxury of being able to use her brain to make a living rather than doing hard labor. She could hear the disgust in their voices, and she could understand their resentment. This work belonged to them, not the students.

But she didn't care. Not now. She just had to dig.

One man, the one working closest to her, moved much slower than the others, slower than even she moved. She'd just begun to perspire with the afternoon heat, but this man was drenched with sweat, his skin gray and pasty-looking. A pale ring surrounded his thick lips.

Too many cervezas at the cantina last night, she guessed. She remembered the feeling of a cruel hangover: like someone drained all your blood and replaced it with lead.

Her shovel hit something hard then, and she scraped the earth and sand away from it. A large boulder was buried beneath several layers of earth. Roughly the size of a large watermelon, it would have to come out. And as much as she wanted to, she couldn't move it herself.

"Hey," she said to the sweating man.

He turned bleary eyes in her direction.

She motioned him closer. "C'mere."

Dragging his shovel, he shuffled over.

"*¿Me ayude con esto, por favor?* Help me with this, please?" she asked, pointing to the rock.

He thrust his shovel hard into the earth and slowly began to loosen the rock. It started to break away from the dry, hard dirt that had kept it encased for so long.

After a few minutes the man faltered, losing his balance.

"*¿Que es?*" Ruby asked. "What is it?"

"*Nada.*" He wiped perspiration from his brow with the sleeve of his sweat-soaked work shirt. Strangely enough, gooseflesh rose on his arms. He worked on the rock again, with Ruby helping this time. Slowly, they freed it from the ground. When the man bent over to pick it up he fell forward onto his face, unmoving.

"Hey!" She shook his shoulder. "*Señor!*" Bending down, she turned his face away from the dirt. His skin was as hot as fire.

"Someone help!" she shouted to the other workers.

One of the younger men reached her first. Tall, wiry thin,

and shirtless, he had his T-shirt wrapped around his head into a makeshift turban. He pointed to his friend lying on the ground, accusation in his eyes.

"*Se callo.* He collapsed," Ruby said. "He seems to have a fever. I think he's sick."

"*¿Huberto, que te pasa?*" the man said, bending down to address the unconscious man. He rolled Huberto over, then lifted him up with superhuman strength and hefted the limp body over his shoulder.

"*¿Como se llamo?*" Ruby asked his name.

"*Carlos. Tienemos que ir al Dr. Mendenhall.*" He wanted to take him to Dr. Mendenhall's clinic. She agreed he needed medical help but, remembering what Pete had said, she wasn't sure. Together, Carlos, carrying the prostrate Huberto, Ruby, and some of the other workers walked toward the camp, toward Dr. Yates' Airstream.

Yates stepped out. "What's the problem?"

"This man collapsed," Ruby said. "He's burning with fever. We've got to get him to a doctor."

"Dr. Mendenhall," Carlos said.

"Perhaps the hospital?" Ruby suggested.

"No. Carlos is right. Mendenhall can handle this," Yates said. "Don't be long."

Hesitating, Ruby looked for Pete. She couldn't see him anywhere.

"Take the truck," Yates said, nodding toward a red Ford with peeling paint and a cracked windshield. He tossed the keys to Ruby. "There's an old mattress in the storage tent you can put in the truck bed."

Ruby nodded and motioned for Carlos to follow her. Pointing at one of the onlookers, she told him in Spanish to get the mattress. He ran to the tent and emerged, dragging the stained, lumpy mattress. Together with some of the others, they arranged it in the bed of the truck.

Carlos carefully lay the sick man on the pallet and held his head steady.

"I'll go with him. I will stay with him in the back," he said in Spanish. He unwrapped the T-shirt from his head and pulled it on over his sweaty, chestnut-brown chest. Ruby hopped in the truck, peeled out in the dirt, and headed for the clinic.

⊚⊰⊚

Ruby, nervous and antsy, paced the small waiting room while Carlos slept in one of the metal chairs. Within half an hour, Dr. Mendenhall came out.

"How is he?" Ruby asked.

"He's pretty sick."

"Will he be all right, though?"

Carlos woke up and jumped to his feet.

Dr. Mendenhall shrugged. "I don't know."

"You don't know? B—"

"*¿Qué ocurre con él?*" Carlos asked what was wrong with him.

"It looks like the flu."

"Is it serious? Can he go home?" Ruby asked.

"Yes, but he needs to be monitored," Dr. Mendenhall said. "These viruses can turn bacterial in a heartbeat. Flu can also create other complications, especially given his age."

"Does he need medicine?" Carlos asked in startlingly good English.

"I'll give him something for his congestion and aspirin for pain and fever," the doctor explained.

Ruby thought of the man with the cough who came in the last time she was at the clinic. "Dr. Mendenhall, that man who came in when I was here, did he have the same illness?"

Dr. Mendenhall raised his eyebrows. He seemed surprised that she remembered. "It was similar, but not entirely the same."

"Did he recover?" she asked.

"He—" The doctor lowered his eyes and scratched at his prickly beard. "Daniel passed away last night."

"You mean, people are *dying* from this virus?" Ruby asked, goose pimples raising on her skin. Had Daniel's body been thrown into yet another unknown pit somewhere? What about his family? Would there be a funeral?

"Daniel had a rare strain. Add to that, he was in poor health due to his alcoholism. I couldn't help him."

"How contagious is this virus?" Ruby asked.

"It's hard to say."

She clenched her jaw. "Dr. Mendenhall," she said more forcefully, "how many people have fallen ill from this virus?"

"You have many questions today, Miss Delgado." Dr. Mendenhall took off his glasses and rested his hand on his hip. His lips twitched.

She stood taller. "I'm concerned. This seems to be serious. Have you notified anyone about this? Perhaps the Center for Disease Control?" She tried to suppress the panic in her voice.

"Daniel is the only one who has died, and I told you he was in poor health. It isn't unheard of for elderly or sickly people to die of the flu. And as for your question about notifying someone, the CDC handles matters on a much broader base than this. Las Montanas is too sparsely populated for this to be of concern. Now, if you don't mind, I'm sure your friend in the examining room would like to go home."

Ruby didn't know what to say next. He had sufficiently shut her up. But something here didn't measure up.

"There's nothing more I can do." Dr. Mendenhall shrugged.

"I see." Ruby couldn't shake the unsettled feeling, but at this point there wasn't much more she could do. She looked to Carlos. "Let's get Huberto and go."

Carlos directed her to Huberto's home. Once they ensured he was settled with his family Ruby took the opportunity of having both Carlos and the truck at her disposal, and they drove to the cantina to pick up her car.

Once back at the site, Ruby went to Yates' trailer. He came out before she could knock on the door, a cigar between his teeth.

"How'd it go?" he asked after removing the cigar.

"The doctor said he has some kind of flu. I guess there have been a few very bad cases in the area."

"Hmm." He exhaled, the smoke billowing around his head. "I hope it's not too contagious. I'd hate to lose more of the crew. Is this fellow going to be able to return to work soon?"

Ruby blinked in surprise. "Dr. Yates, he was so sick he keeled over. Another man died from this."

Where was his compassion?

"I don't mean to be callous," he said, placing the cigar between his teeth again. He sucked on it so hard his cheeks caved in. He exhaled—this time, right in her face. "But you obviously don't realize the importance of this project, Miss Delgado."

Perhaps she'd overstepped her bounds. Finally Yates had started to be civil to her, and now she had to go and get confrontational. She remembered her purpose for being here and decided to back down.

"Dr. Yates, I do understand the importance of the project. I was also concerned for the man."

"We have to keep focused on the project. Don't let trivial mishaps cloud your mind. I need your talents." He turned and climbed the steps back into the trailer. The screen door slammed with a thwack, making her flinch.

She sighed, reluctantly admitting he had a point. Distraction would do her no good. She needed to focus on her work and concentrate on learning how to be the best archaeologist she could be. But she wouldn't stop worrying about Nicolas Baca, fighting for his life in the hospital. His doctor said he also suffered from flu-like symptoms. Could it be the same virus? Had Nicolas seen Dr. Mendenhall before?

So many questions, and really none of it had anything to do with why she was in Las Montanas. Once again, she had allowed her dream to be put on hold by things and events she had no control over.

CHAPTER 8

All the rocks in her assigned unit had been photographed and removed. Now Ruby could focus on finding the small, thin pottery shards that littered the different layers of strata. Along with the shards she found animal bones, hair, remains of leather garments, and other items considered refuse. This had obviously been some sort of trash pit. She concentrated hard, her fingers filtering through the tiny artifacts. She didn't even see Cynthia and Carl approach her.

"You're still out here?" Carl asked. "It's almost quittin' time, girl."

Ruby looked at her watch. Seven-fifteen. "I missed some time when I took Huberto to the clinic."

"Yeah, we heard about that," said Cynthia. "Is he going to be okay?"

"Bad case of flu." She shrugged. "Guess time will tell." She stood and stretched, her muscles sore and tight from squatting for so long.

"We've come to say goodbye," Carl said.

Ruby's brow furrowed. "Goodbye? Where are you going?"

"We applied to open a field school in the Yucatán last fall,"

Cynthia explained. "And today we got word that our application was approved! We have to be there in three days."

"Wow! That's fantastic." She hugged both of them, but her gut squirmed with subtle disappointment. They had been kind to her, and she hated to lose them. That assignment would be hard to turn down, though. "But what about the burial site?" Ruby asked. "Doesn't Dr. Yates need you to continue?"

Cynthia nodded. "Yes, but he understands the importance of this for us. And we've got a good start on cataloging most of the findings here. It won't be hard for the rest of the group to finish." She smiled. "Before I forget to ask, are you going to the press conference?"

Another furrowed brow. "What press conference?" Ruby asked.

"Dr. Yates is going to be interviewed tomorrow morning in Albuquerque," Carl said. "He leaves tonight. He gave everyone the weekend off. You should go."

Funny, no one said anything to her. "I don't think so."

Ruby recalled her own press conference: the click of the cameras, the glare of the flashes, the stupid questions. Not her cup of tea. Besides, this was Yates' moment. News of her finding the Noche Triste treasure hadn't been completely forgotten, and she didn't want to upset his moment—upset *him*—by stealing any of his thunder.

"Well, you'll be on your own for dinner, then. Yates has given Spike and the rest of the crew the night off, too. You'll be here alone," Carl told her.

"Why don't you go with them?" Concern filled Cynthia's voice.

"I'll be fine, you guys. I can think of worse things than having an evening to myself. I really don't mind."

Carl put his arm around Cynthia. "We've got to go, honey. We've got to make it to Texas by morning."

"You hang in there." Carl hugged Ruby again. "You're doing a great job. Don't let anyone tell you otherwise."

"Thanks. And good luck. If you have any openings in Yucatán in the future, call me. I'd love to work on a site there."

"You're the first on our list," said Cynthia.

Ruby watched them walk toward their half-loaded car. They seemed so happy. She almost envied them their new assignment, but then reminded herself she'd always wanted to work with John Yates and learn more about the Anasazi.

🌀

The coolness of the chamber chilled her skin as she crouched against the earthen wall. Something scratched at it and squeaked.

A rat.

Its ropey gray tail snapped back and forth, and then the animal skittered into a hole in the wall. A shaft of sunlight penetrated the cave, illuminating the decayed, deformed, oozing bodies. Another beam of light hit the top of the human heap, revealing the terror-stricken features of their faces.

Something glittered on the wall. She shifted to see the sun's reflection bouncing off a metal object. Curious, she was drawn to the shimmer, but she'd have to climb the hill of the dead to cross the cavern. Staring at the bodies, she thought she saw some of them move. She could almost hear their moans. A whimpering came from beneath the pile—a small, weak sound.

A voice called to her for help. "Help me! Help me, Mommy!"

"Matthew!" Ruby screamed aloud, sitting up in her sleeping bag. She shimmied out of her bag and pushed open the tent flaps to emerge into the brightness of a full moon.

She raced across the camp, hardly aware of the shrubs and ground cover tearing at her bare feet. She crashed through the rope surrounding the sinkhole, lifting the spikes from the ground with her body weight. She stopped, winded and gasping for breath, staring into the pit. Voices called out to her. Men's voices. Groaning, begging, weeping. Above them all, the little boy's voice. Her boy's voice. Matthew.

"I'm coming. I'm coming," she said, sitting at the edge of the hole. She extended her feet into the blank space, preparing to jump in, when something in her snapped. Blinking hard, she scooted away from the opening. A chill fingered its way down her spine as whimpering cries filled her ears again.

Wasn't it just a dream? A dream about Matthew trapped under those bodies, buried alive? She dreamed of him almost nightly, but never like this. And as far as she knew, this was the first time she had been sleepwalking.

But I am awake.

The sound came again, a distinct cry of some sort from below the earth. A real cry. Not a dream.

The cry rang out again. Wailing. Could it be someone alive down there? She shuddered. She should go down there and see. But how would she get back out? She closed her eyes to think, and it came to her. She ran back to her tent, this time aware of her tender feet. She picked her way carefully, wincing in pain. Once inside, she yanked out the goathead thorns from her stinging feet and pulled on her socks and boots. She grabbed her climbing equipment, including ropes, carabiners, spikes and a mallet, and stuffed them into her pack. She stepped into the harness and tightened it around her waist and thighs, checked the carabiners, grabbed her pack, and ran back to the sinkhole.

She drove a stake into the ground with the mallet, one end of her rope tied to the stake, and then listened for the cry. Nothing but crickets. A faint breeze stirred her hair. She *had* heard something, hadn't she? She waited, straining to hear.

It's happened. I've finally gone crazy.

The cry came again, this time weaker.

"That's real," she said out loud.

She rechecked the harness and then threaded the rope through the carabiner. Facing the spike with her back to the hole, she squared up her feet at its ledge. Pulling the rope taut, she tested her weight against the spike and began to lower herself down. Once she'd cleared the top of the sinkhole she eased her way down farther and then hung free, her hands holding the rope above her. As she continued down the stench of decay made her gag, but she fought the reflex.

The whimpering started again. She felt in her back pocket for the small flashlight she'd put there, hoping it wouldn't drop into the pile of—

Don't think. Just do.

Avoiding the bodies, she tilted her legs upward to start herself swinging. Once she cleared them, she released the rope and landed at the side of the pile. One of her boots stepped on something hard.

An arm bone, with bits of leathery flesh on it. Was it an ulna or a radius? What did it matter?

She gasped, clapping her hand over her mouth. Crouching and holding on to the wall, she waited to hear the cries again. Her stomach churned, every instinct telling her to get the hell out. Once she'd calmed herself, she unclipped from the rope and set her pack on the ground.

She pulled her bandana from around her neck, opened it up, and tied it over her nose and mouth. It helped block the stench, but not much. Sweat broke out on her forehead and upper lip, and she tried to control her trembling limbs.

Something shuffled in the dark. She swept the cavern floor with the flashlight beam until it rested on a pair of watching eyes. The thing yelped and then panted. *A dog?* Moving the beam she tried to study the creature, but all she could make out were glowing, golden eyes. The light hit on the back wall of the cavern, and the disorienting feeling of déjà vu slammed into her. She tilted her flashlight at a higher angle, above the eyes, and the beam of light rested on something metallic. She swallowed hard. She'd seen this in her dream, too.

Focusing again on the eyes, she slowly inched her way around the bodies so she wouldn't startle the creature. Reaching the other side of the cavern took some careful sidestepping.

The creature growled, and Ruby froze. She could see the outline of its head and its ears.

A coyote! He must have fallen into the sinkhole, attracted by the smell. But why did he just sit there staring at her?

Moving the flashlight around, she noticed what looked like a viga, or wooden support beam trapping one of the coyote's paws. She aimed the light above her. More vigas.

This underground cavern had not been carved from the ocean a millennium ago. It had been created by man. It looked like a mine, but there had never been mining in this part of New Mexico. Perhaps it was once part of the ancient dwelling. A storage basement or old kiva?

The coyote growled again and then whimpered. His right forepaw was wedged under the beam, too. "It's okay, fella. I'll get you out." Her light danced around the dark cavern. "Somehow."

The flashlight's beam caught the reflection of the metal object on the wall again, but now she could see a silver rosary draped over a wooden crucifix, roughly the size of her hand. She slowly edged closer to it so she wouldn't frighten the coyote, and she touched the rough-hewn wooden figure. The crudeness of Christ's ill-proportioned and misshapen body reminded her of a child's stick drawing.

The expertly crafted silver rosary twinkled in the light. The beads looked handmade, each one varying in size and shape, but all highly buffed and polished. She reached out again and tugged the wooden cross from the wall. She turned it over and studied the back. The wood had been sandpapered smooth. No hook or nail hole marred its surface. Likewise, no nail or hook marred the cavern wall. How, then, had the crucifix been suspended?

She pushed it up to the wall then took her hand away. It fell to the ground and landed face-down in the dirt. She tried again, only to get the same result. How had it been supported?

A cry from the coyote startled her. The beam lay at her feet and simply lifting it would release him. But she had no idea how heavy it was. And if she could lift it she'd then be alone in the cavern with a wild animal, and who knew how it would react?

She needed a weapon of some sort, just in case. Flashing the light around her feet, she noticed a long, clean femur bone. It looked older than the other remains. The thought of touching it made her skin prickle. Handling the bones of the ancient dead usually didn't bother her, but these . . .

Slowly, she reached down and took hold of the bone, feeling its coolness in her hand. She couldn't hold the flashlight, carry the bone, lift the tie, *and* defend herself all at the same time. The coyote sighed and put his head down on the ground, as if impatient with her deliberation.

"You won't hurt me, will you?" she asked, her voice shaky.

She stuffed the crucifix into her shirt pocket and lay the bone within easy reach, should the coyote decide to attack. She knelt and placed her hands around the beam, gripping it tightly. Never moving her eyes from the coyote she lifted the beam, feeling the strain in her back. Once the weight came off his paw he jumped backward with a yelp, and then sat, holding his paw off the ground.

She frowned. "Hurts, doesn't it, pal?"

The coyote stared at her, panting. Then he stood and crept toward her, placing some weight on his injured foot and limping.

Leaning forward Ruby picked up the bone, and the crucifix fell out of her pocket. The coyote stopped and cocked his head. He craned his neck forward, moving his snout toward the wooden cross. He opened his mouth and snapped for it, but he missed. Ruby raised the femur above her head and took the crucifix up in her other hand. The coyote let out a guttural growl and bared his teeth at her.

"Nice coyote . . . Don't attack me." She slid the crucifix back into her pocket, and the animal growled again.

"You want this?" she asked, pointing at it. "Why would *you* want it?" He yelped at her and then turned, hobbling on his foot, and disappeared into the wall.

How in hell had he done that?

Still clutching the bone, Ruby inched her way toward the wall where the coyote had vanished and noticed a mound of dried thicket and tumbleweeds stacked against it. Toward the bottom of the pile of weeds, faint moonlight pooled on the floor. Another entrance. The coyote must have crawled through there.

Stepping closer, she could see the scrub had been strategically placed, blocking the small opening. She tried to pull it away but cringed when its thorns sank into her fingers. She put her bleeding thumb to her mouth and sucked on it.

Kicking the prickly bracken with her boots, she managed to get most of it away from the wall. When she squeezed past the remaining thorns, though, her shirt caught and ripped. She pushed on as the entrance became a tunnel, sloping upward. Ruby continued shuffling forward in a hunched-over position, the ascent making her breath come faster, until she saw an opening partially covered by a huge boulder.

She must be pretty far from the cavern with the bodies now, and fear that she wouldn't be able to fit through took over. Still, she forced herself forward. She squeezed into the opening, easily making it through, and her head popped out into the moonlit night. She wriggled free of the hole to find the coyote sitting about fifty feet away.

"You again? I thought you'd have run off by now."

He cocked his head. It was then that she noticed a jagged scar on his brow, just below the ears. The fur around the scar had grown back oddly, making it look like a giant cowlick. The coyote tipped his head in the other direction.

She kept the coyote in her periphery while she scanned the area. The tunnel had led her only a hundred feet away from the roped-off sinkhole. How could the crew have missed this opening? Besides, the area around the boulder looked freshly dug.

She peered closer at the earth and noted the claw marks. "You did this," she said to her new friend. "You must have smelled the decay. You hungry?"

She sat for a moment, thinking. This was ridiculous. Those bodies should be reported. She fumbled in her shirt pocket and pulled out the crucifix and rosary. These artifacts and the possibility that the cavern could be part of the ancient, possibly Anasazi, dwelling changed everything. As an archaeologist, she had to notify Yates of this find. And as a decent human being, she had to notify the authorities. She couldn't keep the secret any longer. Tomorrow, she would report what she had found.

She sat at the mouth of the opening a while longer, feeling the slightest hint of peace creep into her mind. The coyote, ears pricked, had lain down and continued to watch her as if waiting to see what she would do next. About to walk back to her tent, Ruby realized she'd left her pack in the cavern. She dreaded going back in, but she couldn't leave the gear behind.

She lowered herself into the tunnel, and her coyote friend let out an ominous howl. She peeked up over the side of the hole just in time to see him, head tilted back, as he howled into the darkness. Then he stopped, caught her gaze, and ran away.

"You're no fool," she muttered. *Unlike me.*

She once again faced the bodies. She tried to inhale some courage before carefully picking her way around them. Forcing herself to look at the dead, her fear and disgust dissolved into a sudden sense of profound compassion.

She turned on the flashlight and searched for the rope she'd used to lower herself in. That's when she noticed something else in the wall: a doorway framed with railroad ties, partially covered over with mud. Unless she shined the light directly on them, the railroad ties blended with the darkness.

To get a closer look she would have to climb over the mass of decaying bodies, and the thought sent her stomach turning. She couldn't do it. It was time to get out. But why would someone close up a doorway? What was behind it?

What is *this place?*

Pete had mentioned something alluding to a cover-up when

his brother died. If she reported what she'd found, would it merely be covered up again?

She took a deep breath, steeling herself for the loathsome task of climbing over the carnage. She tried to ignore the lumpiness of the bones beneath her boots. She swallowed hard and focused on the doorway. Becoming more and more nauseated by the second, she tied her bandana tighter around her face.

Once she was over the rotting mass, she took the femur bone and scraped away at the wall. It crumbled easily under pressure. The soil was dry and smelled old, like blood and sweat.

When she'd chipped away a hole wide enough to fit through, she stopped digging. Grabbing her flashlight from her back pocket, she shined it into the darkness to find yet another cavern. Four hard, wooden, rectangular objects lined the far wall.

Mustering all the nerve she could, Ruby hoisted herself up onto the ledge of the hole and attempted to crawl through. Instead, she cartwheeled and landed heels over head in a lump on the ground. The flashlight fell and rolled away. She got to her feet and clung to the wall behind her. When the flashlight stopped rolling, the beam shined on the bottom corner of another wooden object. She rose slowly, brushing the dirt from her face with trembling fingers, and reached for the flashlight. She grabbed it and shined it on the object. It was a crude altar.

Three rows of railroad ties, approximately three feet in length, led to another railroad tie that served as a kneeler. Two-by-fours held up a small flat surface where one's arms could rest in prayer. Looming above the kneeler, a foot or two away to the left, hung a large dog-eared and yellowed poster of Christ hanging on the cross. On the right was a hand-carved crucifix, much like the one she'd found earlier. Rosaries of all colors and sizes, dried desert flowers, and several circular objects made from thorny branches adorned the little shrine. Several dust-coated candles sat on the armrest next to a box of matches.

The altar was old, yet the poster, candles, and matches were all modern. She turned the beam of light on the four rectangular boxes at the back wall. The beam hit on a dusty metal clasp on one of the boxes. She went over to it and reached out to open the clasp. She pulled it to open the box, and the box shifted.

Ruby gasped, stumbling backward. She ran into the altar, knocking down the candles. The box creaked open more, and something tumbled out onto the dirt. Another partially decomposed body. Ruby stifled a scream.

Three other coffins stood upright against the wall. More bodies. Ruby's knees buckled, and she struggled to support herself. The air turned thick and heavy, suffocating her.

The body lay before her—stiff, shriveled, and partially skeletonized. Its hair was dark brown, almost black, and half decayed away. Kneeling down, hands shaking, she used the femur bone to push the body over. It was nearly weightless. Black bloodstains seeped into dead eye sockets that left hollow, gaping holes. Its jaw, slack from the weight of gravity, hung open in a rictus of terror. Ruby took a closer look at the head and noticed something atop it.

Thorns . . . A crown of thorns.

Her gaze drifted down to the bloody gouges at the wrists and ankles. This person had been crucified.

The roof of the cavern seemed to sink down on top of her. The tomb closed in, and the air grew heavy. She felt faint and dizzy, and almost gave in to unconsciousness when she heard breathing. Ragged, hurried, restless breathing.

With renewed strength, she stumbled over the altar and threw herself into the opening she'd made in the wall. When she pulled herself out, the flashlight slipped from her hand and rolled into the heap of bodies. The cavern went dark until her eyes adjusted to the faint shimmer of moonlight coming through the sinkhole. She clambered over the bodies, waving her hands in front of her to find the rope she'd left dangling through the sinkhole, but couldn't find it. She frantically swished at the air and strained to see in the dim light. The rope had vanished.

The other opening. Get to the other opening.

Ruby climbed over the bodies again, focusing on nothing but the other entrance. Where was the pool of moonlight she'd seen coming through the brush?

With her hands stretched out in front of her, she searched for the small tunnel and found it. Crouched low, she moved through it. Where was the damned moonlight? Scrambling, her hands traced the tunnel walls. She felt the upward slope of the ground when she began to ascend. Still there was no opening, no moonlight.

She banged her head on the ceiling and yelped. Reaching above her, she pressed at the hard surface. It wasn't dirt; it was rock.

What the hell?

Clawing at the earth, she could feel the edges where rock met dirt. She leaned into the tunnel wall, her heart hammering in her chest. The large granite boulder must have been moved over the opening. But how? Why? By whom?

She hurried back to the sinkhole, afraid that at any moment she'd crash into someone or something in the dark. Brittle bones gouged at her when she again passed through the pile of corpses, no longer caring.

Get me out of here! Please! Someone! Anyone!

A faint thudding came from above. Footsteps. She looked up at the opening and saw someone there. Someone holding something large and square, like plywood.

"Hey! Help! Get me out of here!" she called.

But the plywood just covered the hole, sealing her in.

"Stop!" she screamed. "Let me out!"

She stared at the corpses again, all sensation in her limbs fading, her body going numb. Her mind went blank, and she sank down into the darkness.

CHAPTER 9

R uby woke, spitting dirt out of her mouth. She coughed and sputtered, and pushed herself to sitting. Faint light surrounded her. She struggled to her feet.

"Hey!" she shouted. "Who's up there? I need help!"

"Ruby? Ruby, is that you?"

She never would have thought she'd be so happy to hear that voice. "Pete! Get me out of here!" For a brief moment, she hoped he hadn't been the one who had trapped her down there.

"Hold on!" he called back to her. "I'm coming!"

In seconds, her green climbing rope snaked down before her eyes. Pushing against the wall, she stood up again and attached the rope to her harness with the carabiner. She grabbed her pack.

"Okay, I'm ready!" She gave a gentle tug on the rope.

Lifting her off her feet, Pete slowly pulled her up. When she reached the ledge of the hole, she found the strength to crawl out before collapsing on the ground.

The clean night air greeted her with its crispness, and although it was unbearably cold out she'd never felt anything so welcoming in her life. She lay unmoving, face-down on the cold, hard earth. Earth that smelled of only dirt and not decay.

Pete's warm hands grasped her shoulders, and he helped her up. "My God, Ruby. What happened? What the hell were you doing in there? I saw the board over the hole and—"

Her head rested in the crook of his shoulder, and he gently brushed her hair away from her face.

"I . . . I . . ." Tears welled in her eyes. "Someone . . . Someone buried me . . ."

"Buried you? What do you mean?"

"Obviously, someone tried to trap me in there. With that," she pointed at what looked like a pallet with plywood nailed on top. I heard someone—"

"Oh God. You're shaking," he said, wrapping his arm around her shoulder.

"I'm so cold. And I feel sick." She forced down the urge to vomit.

"Let's get you back to camp."

Ruby shrugged him off and pulled at her shirt. "I've got to get out of these clothes. Death . . . They smell like death."

"Let's get you warm first."

Ruby's knees turned to mush, but Pete caught her before she hit the ground. "I have to get this smell off me." She pulled hard, ripping the buttons off her blouse, revealing a white cotton T-shirt underneath.

Pete took the blouse from her and tucked it under his arm. She sank again, leaning heavily against him. He gathered the rest of her equipment, and they shuffled toward camp. She couldn't seem to get her feet under her, and her knees kept giving out.

"I can't walk. I feel so sick, so dizzy."

Pete dropped the equipment and lifted her off her feet. He carried her the rest of the way to her tent. Once there, he set her down and covered her with her sleeping bag.

"I'll make you something warm," he said. "Coffee?"

"Ugh. I can't get warm. Aren't you cold?" she asked, her teeth chattering.

"I think you're in shock. C'mon." He helped her to her feet and picked her up again.

"Where are we going?"

"Yates' trailer."

"I don't want to see him." She couldn't have him see her like this.

"He's not there. He's in Albuquerque for the weekend. It's okay."

She exhaled in relief, now remembering what Cynthia had told her.

When they reached the Airstream, Pete leaned her against the shiny surface to get the keys out of his pocket. He opened the door and helped her climb the two metal steps into the interior. He set her on a long, covered bench next to a table and wrapped her sleeping bag around her more tightly.

"I'll make coffee," he said.

"Is there tea?" she asked.

"Yep. Does that sound better?"

Ruby nodded, and glimpsed the clock. Five-thirty. Almost daylight. How long had she been down there? Pete clanged some pots and pans about, and then struggled to light the burner.

In a few minutes, the water came to a rolling boil. He set two steaming cups of steeping tea in front of her. "You should feel better after this."

"Thanks." She sipped, burning her lip, but the hot liquid felt good going down. After a few swallows the chill melted out of her, and her trembling subsided.

"Ruby, what were you doing down there?"

"I found another chamber. There were coffins, four of them. I opened one and . . . a body fell out. Pete—" She focused on his eyes. "—it looked like it had been crucified. This isn't some radiation experiment gone bad. It's something else, something more."

"Wait, wait." He placed his warm hand on her cold one. "Slow down."

"I'm telling you it's something really weird. Something religious. There was an altar, crowns of thorns, candles, but it had all been sealed up. I don't think anyone's been down there for a while. But someone was down there with me today, I heard this heavy, ragged breathing, and they somehow got out and then buried me." She shuddered, remembering the feeling of suffocation. Tears sprang from her eyes. "Someone tried to kill me."

Pete put his strong, warm arm over her shoulder. "Did anyone see you go out there? Do you think you were followed?"

"No. I thought I was the only one there." Ruby sniffed. "I haven't told anyone about the bodies."

"I know you haven't."

"But Pete, we have to tell someone now." She pulled the crucifix and rosary from her pocket. "I found these down there. That place must be some kind of . . . I don't know . . . shrine to the dead. And who knows where those bodies, or skeletons are coming from. There could be some kind of sick killer on the loose. We can't be silent any longer."

He closed his eyes for a beat, then said softly, "You don't understand, Ruby."

"What's to understand? Someone tried to *kill* me." A wave of dizziness caught her off guard, and she put her fingers to her temples.

"You okay?" He placed his hand at the back of her head, steadying her. His touch was tender, caring.

"I'm really tired."

"You should get some rest." He stood and slid the table away from her. "You've been through a lot. We can talk about this later. I'm going to go get your equipment."

"I don't want to go to sleep," she said, her words sounding slurred even to her ears. "What about the others?"

"They've all gone. A weekend off is a rare thing for Dr. Yates. I don't think they'll be back until Monday, but I'll wake you in a couple of hours."

The trailer spun again. Too weak to argue anymore, Ruby lay down and closed her eyes. Her arms and legs felt heavy, immobi-

lized with fatigue, and as soon as her head hit the cushion she
was out.

⊗⊱⊚

When Ruby awoke, daylight streamed through the window of
the trailer. She guessed it to be around nine in the morning. Pete
sat kitty-corner from her, his head on his arms, sleeping. She
stretched and untangled herself from the sleeping bag. Now it,
too, smelled of death. She stumbled toward the back of the
trailer in search of the bathroom.

When she found it she hurried inside, peeled off her clothes,
and threw them outside the bathroom door before closing it
behind her. She stepped inside the micro shower and turned on
the water, pulling the curtain behind her. A fresh bar of soap
beckoned, and she lathered up. She rinsed and lathered again,
then washed her hair. She tilted her head toward the stream of
water and opened her mouth, letting the spray clean away the
acrid taste of decay. She and Pete would have to refill the tank
before Yates returned. No conditioner for her errant curls, but
that didn't matter. At least she was clean. Not only that but
having slept, she could think about last night's events more
clearly.

The body that had fallen out of the coffin *had* been crucified.
Ancient religious sects came to mind again. She knew that at
Easter some of them performed the Passion, complete with a
mock crucifixion. The Chosen One would be secured to the
cross with ropes for a few hours. If left up too long, he would
suffocate. The act was ritualistic, symbolic. But nails and a crown
of thorns? It seemed extreme.

She turned the water off, opened the curtain, and searched
for a towel. A small cupboard provided several. Wrapping one of
them around her she scanned the small room, aware she had
another, more pressing problem. No clean clothing. She'd die
before she put the old clothes back on. In fact, she couldn't wait

to burn them. And Pete was right outside the door, sleeping. Maybe she could sneak by without waking him and make her way to her tent.

She opened the door to find Pete standing just outside, holding her clothes. Crimson warmth crawled up her face, and a sinking feeling hit her stomach.

Pete stared at first, then diverted his gaze. "Sorry, I didn't hear the shower and wondered . . ." He held up her clothes.

She wrinkled her nose. "I can't put those back on. But I *needed* a shower. Do you think Yates will mind?"

He smiled. "Yeah."

She and Pete both laughed. How different things would be if it were Yates standing in front of her right now. She could just see the outrage on his face. She was probably the last person he'd want in his shower.

"I'd better get dressed," she said.

"Oh, right."

But he didn't move. His eyes lingered on her skin, and she could almost feel their caress. A tingle raced down her spine.

"Can I, uh . . . Can I get through?"

"Sure. Sorry." He stepped back but she had to squeeze past him, her shoulder brushing his chest. "I can get you fresh clothes from your tent," he offered.

"Thanks. That would be great." She ran her hands through her wet curls.

This time *he* had to squeeze past *her*, and he casually put his hand on her waist. Her heart flipped at its warmth, and instinctively she pulled the towel tighter around her.

"Be right back," he said with the hint of a smile.

Once he was out the door, she walked into the kitchenette. She opened the small refrigerator and practically salivated when she spotted a half-round of cheese on a simple white plate. Next to it, olives, smoked oysters, and some kind of pâté waited to be devoured. Yates had taste, for sure. She rummaged through a cabinet and found saltwater wafers. Perfect.

She sat at the table, mounded a more than generous portion of cheese onto one of the crackers and popped it into her mouth, savoring the flavor. It'd be better at room temperature, but she didn't care. It tasted glorious. She had heaped just as much cheese onto another cracker when Pete opened the door and walked in. She covered her mouth, embarrassed he'd witnessed her gluttony.

"I was hungry," she said, her mouth still full.

"I can see that."

"I won't eat much. He'll never notice."

"Right." Pete grinned, sitting opposite her, watching her eat.

"You're staring." Her skin heated under his gaze.

"You look different."

She let out a small, uncomfortable laugh. "Well, my hair's wet and I'm half-naked."

"I know." A smile spread across his face.

She rolled her eyes. "I'll get dressed." She put down the cracker, stood and, clutching the towel to her body, scooted past him. She grabbed the duffel bag he'd brought from her tent.

When she re-emerged completely dressed she picked up the dirty clothes off the floor and held them at arm's length, gagging inwardly at the recollection of what she'd seen and smelled in the sinkhole. Without hesitation she tossed the clothes outside the trailer, all except her red bandana. Instead, she took it to the kitchen sink and ran it under a flow of water, poured a glob of dish soap on it, and scrubbed it clean.

Pete started on the cheese and pâté, and even opened himself a beer.

Ruby finished washing the bandana, squeezed the water out of it, and opened it up to dry. "It's a little early for that, don't you think?" She nodded to the beer.

He shrugged. "It's been a long night."

"I'll say." Truth be told, she'd love a beer right now.

"Want one?" Pete held one out to her.

"No." She crossed her arms and leaned against the sink. "So tell me, why'd you come back to the site so early this morning?"

"I told you. I wanted to check on the sinkhole. Make sure no one had done anything with the bodies. I have to say, the pallet over the hole made my heart race. Someone knows we've been in there." He joined her at the counter and nudged her aside. He leaned over the sink, turned on the faucet, and splashed some water on his face.

"I know you don't want anyone to know about those bodies because you think you have some lead on what happened to them, but I think it's about more than just Dr. Mendenhall. We have to report it. *Now.*" Ruby held out a small dish towel for him.

He stared into the sink, his face dripping. "Not yet."

"Someone tried to kill me down there. This isn't just about you, Ricardo, and your theory anymore. It's also about me. I want to know who tried to bury me alive out there."

"I understand. But we can't say anything yet." He took the towel from her.

"Why not? Why? Why? *Why?*" She knew she shouldn't come unglued, but she was tired of this game. *His* game.

He shook his head. "They won't be any help."

"Who won't?"

"The authorities, the sheriff. I've tried."

"So you *do* think there's a cover-up of some kind." She couldn't keep the sarcasm out of her voice.

"You don't know what you're talking about, Ruby," he snapped. "They're involved. They have to be."

"You're saying this is some kind of religious conspiracy?"

He shot her a look. "I didn't say anything about religion."

"Oh, come on! You should see it down there—altars, rosaries, a crown of thorns on an actual crucified body. Are there any religious cults around here?"

He held the towel to his face, as if hiding behind it, but she still saw him clench his jaw. After a few moments, he turned to her and placed his hands on her shoulders. He looked into her eyes. "Okay Ruby, you win. You're right. It's not just about me anymore. You're involved now, too. More than you know." He sighed. "They won't let up on you now, either. You know too much."

"But I don't know *anything*!" She threw up her hands. "What are you talking about?"

"I can't tell you. It would just put you in more danger."

She slammed her fist on the counter in frustration. "God, Pete!"

"I promise I'll tell you everything I know, but not now. Just give me some more time. Please."

She sighed, looking into his face. Why was she buying this crap? What made him so damned convincing? She supposed it was because he'd seemed so concerned about her. She was so confused.

"Only if you answer some questions for me," she said.

"If I can." He released her shoulders and put his hands in his pockets.

"You still think Mendenhall is involved," she said for clarification.

"Yes."

"What about the religious icons? What do you think they mean?"

"The people here are devout. The rosaries, altar, the crucifix all mean something. I'm just not sure what yet."

"And what about the crucified body?" A shudder ran down her spine. "Do you know anything about that?"

He shrugged. "A few years ago, one of the village men started to bleed—from his head, his side, his wrists, his ankles. Everyone called it a miracle."

"The Stigmata?" she whispered. She knew from her studies that there had been many cases of the so-called Stigmata throughout history. Stigmatics, mainly members of Catholic religious orders, show some or all of the wounds inflicted on Jesus, according to the Bible, during his crucifixion. They intermittently bled from their wrists, feet, or their side, between their ribs. Some even displayed wounds to the forehead similar to those caused by the crown of thorns. St. Francis of Assisi was the first recorded stigmatic, and St. Padre Pio of Pietrelcina was later afflicted. However, over eighty percent of recorded stigmatics were women. Most cases turned out to be hoaxes, but some had remained unexplained.

"That's a newsworthy event," she said. "Was it reported?"

"After many town meetings, the village decided to keep it a secret. Most people don't want reporters and cameras here. They have a simple lifestyle, and they want it to remain that way."

"Surely not *everyone* wanted it kept secret."

"No. A few disagreed. They wanted it reported to the archdiocese in Santa Fe. Some even got violent about it."

"Violent? What happened?"

"There was a riot in the village. The people who incited the violence were overcome by the others. They were taken away. Just disappeared."

Ruby raised her eyebrows at him. *Disappeared? Maybe into an underground hell?*

"Do you think they were killed?" she asked.

"*Something* happened to them."

Ruby's mind was flooded with questions, her previous fatigue suddenly gone. "Who were they? Do you know exactly?"

"No. I was in Arizona with Dr. Yates. I only heard about it later."

"And what happened to the man with the Stigmata? How did he die?"

"Suicide. He couldn't handle what was happening to him."

"Was there a funeral? Do people know that he's down there?"

Pete shook his head. "He had no family. Suicide is a mortal sin. His taking his own life shattered all their hopes of him being some kind of Holy Man. They started to believe that he'd faked the Stigmata—done it to redeem himself, sort of as a penance."

"For what?"

Pete gathered up the food and placed it back in the refrigerator. "There was a rumor going around that he'd molested some of the boys in the village. People started to avoid him, talked about him behind his back. If he got people to believe that he was blessed with the Stigmata, maybe they'd change their opinion of him."

"Do *you* think he faked it?"

He scoffed. "Yep. I don't believe in miracles."

Ruby had to admit she didn't, either; although she used to. Way back before her life had spiraled out of control. She furrowed her brow, trying to organize her thoughts. "How was Dr. Mendenhall involved with this particular case? The supposed radiation experiments—how do they fit in?"

Pete leaned against the counter again, his hands resting on the countertop, elbows bent. "Mendenhall serves as the assistant coroner. My guess is that the village wanted the man autopsied, just to make sure the Stigmata was a hoax, and then left the responsibility of disposing of the body to Mendenhall."

"And the good doctor had the perfect resting place? A hole in the ground?"

"I've told you too much." Pete stiffened. "I should go. Get back to work. The others could show up at any time."

"I'll come with you," Ruby said. "I want to hear more."

"I'll tell you more later. Just give me some time to get this figured out. Besides, I don't want you to—"

She looked into his face expectantly, the scar on his chin distracting her for a moment. "You don't want me to, what?"

"I don't want you to get hurt again." His eyes softened as he looked into hers.

"I appreciate that, Pete. Really." She felt her face flush. "But I'm not going to stop looking into this. I'm invested now. Someone tried to kill me."

"Just sit tight for a while." His eyes pleaded with hers. "Let's get more information first. Be patient." Pete reached over and patted her shoulder before walking out of the trailer.

Ruby let out a puff of air, frustrated. Master West, her martial arts master, had always told her she needed to have more patience. Things hadn't changed since her time with him almost a decade ago. But would patience save her this time, now that her own life was at risk?

CHAPTER 10

After she cleaned up her mess in the trailer, Ruby took her sleeping bag to her tent and tossed it inside. Hands on hips she looked around the site, wondering what to do next. She could get back to work, even though Yates had given everyone the weekend off. He might appreciate her putting in the over-time. She wrinkled her nose at the thought, absently laying her hand on the red bandana at her neck. It was still wet, and felt cold and itchy against her skin. But she wouldn't take it off. It was a constant reminder of Matthew. Of how she messed up, and how she would do penance for his death for the rest of her life.

She thought about what would have happened had the tables been turned, and she was the one who died. Or if he were alive now, and whoever it was who had trapped her down in that cavern had been successful in killing her. Matthew would have been left alone.

Thinking of Matthew reminded her of Nicolas—alone and injured in the desert, in the rain. Did he have someone to care for him?

She wondered if he'd been released from the hospital. Or was he still ill, languishing alone? Did he suffer from the same virus as Huberto? The one that killed Daniel? Had he been a patient of Dr. Mendenhall's, too? The only way she could free herself from all the nagging suspicions was to find out the truth.

She remembered the expression on Pete's face when he had pleaded with her, and the way his eyes lingered on her in the trailer. Could he be falling for her? Or did he just want to charm her into not asking any more questions? Why wouldn't he tell her anything else?

She tapped her hands on her knees. No, Pete couldn't be entirely trusted. He lied. He had no concern whatsoever about Nicolas Baca. He'd gone so far as to knock her unconscious! And his ideas about Dr. Mendenhall . . .

An idea struck her then. Master West had some pretty close connections with some of the martial arts instructors in the FBI. Maybe he could help her get information on Dr. Mendenhall.

Ruby hadn't spoken to Master West in a couple of years—not since Matthew died. In his attempt to save Ruby from her alcoholism, her brother had contacted Master West when she was at her worst. He'd come all the way to Los Caballos from Albuquerque to see her, but she'd refused to talk to him. She didn't want him to see her in her half-mad state, in her shame. She'd wanted to be numb forever at that point. Would he even speak to her now?

She could use the pay phone at the cantina, but there was the matter of her car . . . The stupid thing still needed to be fixed. To ask Pete for a ride would be out of the question. She needed distance from him. He confused her.

Resolved to fix the car, she stepped out of her tent and into the brilliant sunshine. But not before grabbing her trusty transistor radio.

When she finally got a look under the hood, with Elvis Presley singing 'Blue Suede Shoes' in the background, she saw the problem with the engine clearly. *The alternator. How did I miss that?*

She grabbed her tools from the trunk and then settled in under the hood. She didn't have a permanent solution until she could get new parts, but she had ideas for a temporary fix. The sound of another engine distracted her, and she straightened up to see Pete taking off in his truck.

Good. She could finally have some peace and start to work on things *her* way. First she'd see what she could find out about Mendenhall, and then maybe she'd have time to go to the hospital in Los Campos to check on Nicolas Baca and still be back before Yates returned. He hadn't turned up yet. Maybe he'd decided to hang around in Albuquerque.

When she was satisfied with her work on the car, she crossed her fingers and turned the key. The engine roared to life on the second try. She stashed her tools and the radio in the trunk and then drove to the cantina.

Afraid the car might not start again, she kept the engine running when she hopped out to use the pay phone. She fumbled with the correct amount of change and slipped the coins into the slot on the phone. Her hand shook as she punched the numbers. Would he speak to her? She tapped a fingernail against the receiver while the phone rang. When he answered, she was caught off guard. She'd half-hoped he wouldn't be there.

She told him everything that had happened since she'd arrived in Las Montanas, and he agreed to look into Dr. Mendenhall for her. Relieved, Ruby thanked him and told him to leave a message at the church rectory in Las Montanas and she would call him back.

One difficult task down. She headed back to her car.

One equally as difficult coming up.

🙙🙖

"Excuse me," Ruby said to the wiry-thin nurse sitting behind the circular counter. "Can you tell me which room Nicolas Baca is in?"

The woman eyed her from over the top of her cat-eye glasses, which were too wide for her narrow face. She leafed through some papers on a clipboard. "He was released yesterday."

"Oh, then he must be doing a lot better." Ruby tapped her fingernails on the counter. "Do you know how I can get in touch with him?"

"What's your relationship to the patient?"

"I'm the one who found him and brought him in."

"Honey, even if I had that information I wouldn't be able to give it to you."

Ruby cleared her throat. "Is Dr. Phillips on duty?"

Rolling her eyes, the nurse shuffled more papers. "He's on duty, but I don't know where he is. You might check the medical library. It's one of his favorite places to take his break. You won't be able to get in, but you can wait for him outside if you want."

"Where—"

"Third floor."

After asking a number of hospital personnel, she finally found the library. The door's sign read STAFF ONLY. She tried the knob. Locked.

"Pardon me," someone said from behind her. She turned to see a tall, lanky man with graying hair. Stepping aside, she watched him pull out some keys and insert one in the doorknob. He caught her gaze and stopped mid-turn.

"Sorry," she said, turning away. He quickly opened the door and slithered inside. Ruby shoved her foot into the open entryway just as the heavy door settled upon it. Good thing she wore her boots today.

Clenching her teeth, she carefully pushed the door open only wide enough to squeeze through. Would she remember what Dr. Phillips looked like? What would he do when he saw her? She hovered, straining her neck to see around the stacks of books and countertops. Not able to see much from her vantage point, she eased toward one of the large shelves and moved down the aisle beside it. She walked up and down four other aisles before she saw him hunched in a small cubicle, reading papers in an open manila folder.

"Dr. Phillips," she whispered.

He turned, first smiling at her and then narrowing his eyes.

"Dr. Phillips, I—"

Alarm spread across his face. "Who are you?"

"I'm Ruby Delgado. I'm the one who brought Nicolas Baca in the other day."

He stood up, placing his hands on his hips. "How'd you get in here? I'm afraid you'll have to leave."

"Please, just tell me if Nicolas Baca recovered from the virus."

"I can't disclose anything about a patient without his express consent if you are not immediate family."

"Please, I need to know."

"I'm sorry," he said. "You really do have to go. I—" A woman's voice crackled over the loudspeaker above their heads. "Dr. Phillips, please report to the ER. Dr. Phillips to the ER."

"And now *I've* got to go. I'll walk you out." He gently captured her elbow and ushered her toward the door.

"Fine, just tell me about Nicolas. Who picked him up? His family? Was he still sick? Did he mention how he'd been hurt?"

Once out in the hallway again, Dr. Phillips trained his eyes on hers. "It's against hospital policy for me to discuss a patient with anyone but family. I'm sorry. I can't help you. Now, I really have to go."

Before she could say anything else, he was gone. Ruby headed for the elevators, lost in thought and disappointed at having driven all that way for nothing. At least she had Master West looking into Mendenhall's past. She stared at the dull tiles as she walked, no longer as hopeful as she'd been after talking with Master West.

The elevator dinged, and she lifted her head just in time to see Pete walk into it. "Pete!" she yelled. She raced to the elevator, but the doors rolled shut before she got there.

What was he doing at the hospital? She scanned the hallway and then flew toward the stairs. She ran down three flights, and when she reached the ground floor she stopped, looking both ways down the corridor. Pete slipped through the exit doors. She ran after him and scanned the parking lot, but he was gone.

She checked into a motel that night in Los Campos. She didn't want to go back to the site, although she'd love to drill Pete about his hospital visit.

Time away from the site—and from Pete—would give her a chance to inventory the past few days and reflect on the bizarre events and oddities she'd witnessed in that short period. The sinkhole, Mendenhall and Pete's theory of medical experimentation, Nicolas Baca, and the man in the coffin with the signs of the Stigmata all took up space in her head.

She had a clear picture of all these things but couldn't piece any of them together. Her stay in Los Campos would also give her the opportunity to purchase a new alternator for her car and fix it once and for all.

Late the next morning, she left the motel. She had purchased a generator and fixed the car. It was running like a champ. Now if she could just get some information on Mendenhall, she'd be done with the distractions for a while. If Master West found out that Mendenhall's past was as evil as she feared, she'd go to the authorities with or without Pete's consent. Her work and her life were too important for her to be harboring secrets she'd had nothing to do with. It had been a long time since she valued her work and her own life. It felt good. And it was ridiculous she'd let this secret of the bodies go on so long.

❧

Ruby arrived at the church rectory in the early afternoon. The short, rounded adobe building stood nestled in a grove of cottonwood trees, adjacent to the Church of St. Mary Magdalene. The church was a much larger structure with two steeples on each side of it, both topped with robin's-egg-blue turrets.

A plump woman with dark eyes and salt-and-pepper hair opened the door. "You must be Ruby. I'm Rosita. Pete told me about you. I'm so glad you're here." She smiled. "A large envelope arrived for you just a few minutes ago."

"An envelope?"

"*Sí*. Won't you come in for some lunch? I've made tamales. Dr. Yates' students always love my tamales."

Ruby stepped through the threshold, into a small foyer filled with the spicy aroma of freshly cooked posole and red chili. "No, I can't, really. But I appreciate you accepting the package for me."

"Come in, I'll get it for you."

Ruby stepped inside the door, and Rosita slipped away before she could ask about Master West's phone call.

"Just let me get some tamales for you to take and I'll get your envelope," Rosita yelled from the hallway.

"Oh, no; that's okay. I'll eat . . . later," Ruby said to an empty hallway.

A man entered from another doorway and, taken by surprise, Ruby flinched. From the white tab he was inserting into the clerical collar of his black shirt, she guessed he was the local priest.

"I'm sorry to have startled you," he said. He was tall and fit, with a shock of black hair peppered with white streaks above each ear. "I'm Father Martinez." He held out his hand.

"Ruby Delgado." She took his hand, and as she looked into his eyes an uneasiness washed over her. She lowered her gaze, grateful to hear Rosita's footsteps returning.

Rosita walked back into the foyer, with a brown paper bag in one hand and a manila envelope in the other. She studied Ruby with the eyes of a concerned mother.

"You are skin and bones. Promise me you'll eat these tamales." She handed the bag to Ruby and then turned to the priest. "This is Ruby, one of Dr. Yates' students."

"I've just met her, but her reputation precedes her. I've heard all about Miss Delgado. The finder of the treasure of the Noche Triste."

Ruby forced her lips into a faint smile, not quite knowing how to take this declaration. She rolled the paper bag tighter.

"Enjoy the tamales," Rosita said with a generous smile, handing her the envelope.

"I will. Thank you so much." Although impatient to look at the contents of the envelope, Ruby was touched by the woman's concern. Rosita reminded her of Juanita Ramirez, her old friend who also had the strange urge to mother her.

Back in the car, she set the brown bag of tamales in the seat next to her and opened the envelope. Inside, she found three photocopied reports and a note in Master West's handwriting.

Here's your information. This guy sounds like a real piece of work.

She sifted through the reports. All three were about radiation testing in the last few years in Los Alamos, New Mexico. A black-and-white photo showed the lead scientist of the project, Dr. Wilhelm Mendenhaus. It was Mendenhall. Ruby's heart began to race as she read on. Apparently, when he'd been discovered testing subjects without their knowledge, he claimed he was working for the U.S. Government. Government officials denied his allegations. He was sent to a remote site in New Mexico and assumed another name.

Was he doing experimentation for the government again?

The sound of a vehicle skidding to a halt jolted her from the reports. She looked up to see Pete's truck.

"Man, am I glad to see you," he said through the cloud of dust he'd just created. "We've got to get back to the site."

"Why? What's going on?"

"Yates is back."

She shoved the reports into the envelope. "I thought he wasn't going to be here until Monday."

"The press conference was canceled. Some local politician's son got married and the media jumped on it like vultures. Yates' find suddenly became less than newsworthy."

She stared at him blankly, the information from the reports still racing through her mind.

"Come on," Pete said. "We have to go. Yates is in a mood."

He put the truck into gear and sped away, leaving her in another cloud of dust *and* a cloud of confusion. The most important thing to her was her work, but in her hands she had evidence that Dr. Mendenhall might be continuing his experiments on unsuspecting people and killing them in the process. She'd made up her mind: she would tell the authorities, Pete be damned. This was far more important than his secrets or her career.

CHAPTER 11

The stillness and heat of the late afternoon gave Las Montanas the feel of a ghost town. Ruby drove slowly down the main street, focusing on the crumbling buildings flanking the street. There was a strange beauty in the primitiveness of the village canopied by gnarled and knotted cottonwood branches.

Pea gravel crunched under the tires, and a warm breeze blew in through the open window. She braked to avoid a lazy pig and two chickens crossing the street. She grinned, guessing there was a joke in there somewhere. While waiting for the pig's laborious crossing—the chickens had already disappeared—she spotted a patrol car parked in front of a small building. She pulled up in front of it.

Ruby considered what she would say to the sheriff when she went inside. She lay her hand on the manila envelope that contained the articles Master West had sent her. Pete's certainty that the sheriff was somehow involved in the cover-up of the mysterious pile of bodies made her uneasy, but she had to trust that law enforcement would do the right thing. How he reacted to the information she was going to give him would clue her in to whether he was involved or not, though. She decided the articles would be better used as evidence later.

After she parked the car and tucked the manila envelope under the driver's seat, she hopped out and headed for the building. She opened the rickety screen door, and it whined and creaked on its hinges then clanged shut once she stepped inside.

Fluorescent lighting overhead flickered in the dark. A barrel-chested man of Hispanic descent dressed in a khaki uniform came through the back door, holding a coffee cup.

"Are you the sheriff?" she asked.

"Yes." He casually sat on the corner of the desk, put the cup down, and clasped his hands over his lap. His brass name tag read J. GALLEGOS.

"I, uh . . . I'm here to report . . . I found some bodies."

He tilted his head slightly. "Oh?"

"Yes," she said, raising her chin. His casual demeanor at her words surprised her. "I'm an archaeologist working with Dr. Yates over at the—"

"I know who you are. What can I do for you?" he asked in a heavy Spanish accent.

She swallowed. Of course he knew who she was. Everyone in this town did.

"Out at the site, I fell into a sinkhole and landed on top of a pile of . . . partially decomposed bodies, some skeletons. Later, when I—"

"Later?" His eyebrows shot up. "Why didn't you report this when it happened, eh?"

"Well, I . . . uh . . ." Heat crept up her face. "I wasn't sure what I'd seen."

"You landed on a pile of bodies, but you weren't sure what they were?" He folded his burly arms across his chest. "You seem all nervous. Sit down. Tell me everything." He pulled up a metal folding chair and motioned for her to sit. "You want some coffee?"

"No, thank you." She sat down in the chair, and he resumed his perch on the edge of the desk, facing her.

"I did know what they were, but I was knocked unconscious and . . . didn't remember . . . right away." She wished she sounded more convincing, and less crazy.

The sheriff blinked. Why did he not seem the least bit surprised?

She swallowed, hard. "As I was saying, later I found *another* cavern, adjacent to the one I fell into. There were other corpses, bodies, in various stages of decomposition, but they were stored in coffins."

Sheriff Gallegos took another sip of his coffee. He gazed at her expectantly.

"There were four coffins," she added.

He slid a notepad across the desk toward himself and scribbled something on it. Then he crossed his arms, resting them on his sizable belly. "*Gracias*, Miss Delgado. I'll look into it."

"We also— I mean, *I* also found someone in the road who'd been brutally abused. I have no idea if these things are related, but his name is Nicolas Baca. I took him to the hospital in Los Campos a few nights ago."

Sweat glistened on the sheriff's brow, and his hands shook slightly as he added more notes on the pad.

"When I saw the coffins, I heard someone in the cavern with me," she continued. "Whoever it was tried to bury me alive. But Pete found me."

At the mention of his name, Gallegos lifted an eyebrow. "Pete?"

"Yes, Pete Marshall."

Ruby thought she detected an expression of derision cross his face.

"All very interesting," he said. "Thanks for bringing this information forward. We'll check it out."

She stared at him. "That's it?"

"Yeah." He stared back at her, his face still emotionless save for a slight twitch of his closely cropped mustache.

"Okay." Pete's notion of the cops being a part of the so-called cover-up clanged in her head. Maybe there was something to that. Ruby stood up and Sheriff Gallegos did, too.

"I'll get the door for you," he said with a smile, indicating for her to step in front of him.

Ruby walked to the door, and Gallegos opened it for her. She left the building, the screen door slamming shut behind her.

The sun had not yet descended on the horizon, but the clouds in the sky were streaked with crimson, lavender and gold. Fragments of conversation from the café down the road floated on the breeze. The rustling of leaves in the trees hummed all around her.

She got into her car, replaying her conversation with the sheriff. The only detectable reaction he'd shown was when she'd mentioned Pete. She probably shouldn't have brought up his name. Had she put him in danger? A knot formed in the pit of her stomach. He would be angry with her for reporting the dead, but she'd needed to do something. Besides, in truth, she barely knew Pete. He could be the biggest liar of all.

When she arrived back at the site, she parked her car and headed directly for the mess tent to refill her canteen and check her assignment on the bulletin board. She was startled to see Dr. Yates standing just inside the entrance of the tent.

"Ah, just the woman I want to see," he said. The words were friendly, but the delivery wasn't. She knew she was about to catch hell for returning so late.

"Sorry I'm late, I—"

"Not here. Follow me." He strode past her and out of the tent.

Ruby followed him as he made his way toward his trailer.

When they reached the awning, he motioned for her to sit in one of the director's chairs. She declined, choosing to stand.

"I just received a visit from one of Sheriff Juan Gallegos' deputies on patrol," he said.

Ruby's heart thumped in her chest, but she raised her chin, not about to be cowed by this news.

"Seems that when you fell into that sinkhole, you landed on some bodies."

"I did." She nodded.

The vein at Yates' temple throbbed, and his face turned an unpleasant shade of pink.

"For some reason, you failed to mention this to me."

To stall, Ruby shifted her weight from one hip to the other—not sure how to begin or what to say. "I was knocked unconscious," she said. "I only remembered seeing the bodies later. And then I went down there again, and I found more bodies—one that looked like it had been crucified."

An uncomfortable silence rose as Yates pulled a cigar out of his shirt pocket, clipped the tip, and then lit it. "But you still didn't bring it to my attention."

"No, but I see that I should have," she fibbed. "You know about it now, though, as do the authorities." She paused. "I think we should stop excavating until this situation is resolved."

Yates exhaled smoke in her direction. She choked back a cough.

"This is *my* project, Delgado. *Mine*. You find so much as a fingernail, I want to know about it. How dare you keep something like this from me? And you sure as hell shouldn't have gone to Gallegos."

"Why not? He's the legal authority out here, isn't he? Someone tried to kill me down there, Dr. Yates."

"This is federal land. Gallegos has no jurisdiction. If you feel you are in danger, you are free to leave anytime." He sat, resting his elbows on his knees. He held the cigar between his teeth and took another drag on it.

Ruby's mouth dropped open. He really didn't care that her life was at stake. *Bastard.*

His patronizing words made her blood pulse in her ears, but she wouldn't give up that easily. "Then let's report it to the Feds."

"I intend to, but you stay out of it."

"But I found the bodies," she protested. "Me and—"

"Marshall." Yates leaned back in his chair, crossing one leg over the other.

She nodded. "Don't you think they'll want to speak with us? Don't you think they'll want to know that someone tried to kill me? What about the safety of the others? Can you guarantee that nothing will happen to them?"

"No one's out to get you or anyone else on this site. You were just the one who got in the way," he said, disturbingly casual about it. "Like I said, if you want to leave go ahead. If you decide to stay, then just do your work. I'll handle this mess."

"Dr. Yates, I think I know who did this—"

Yates leaned forward, his gaze penetrating hers. "I don't want to hear your half-baked theories, Miss Delgado. You've done your part by reporting the bodies. That alone could directly compromise my findings. You will make no mention of this to anyone else, and you will focus on the work or I'll throw your overcompensated ass off this project so fast you won't have time to blink. You're costing me time and money. I won't put up with that any longer. Are we clear?"

"I had to report those bodies, Dr. Yates." Her voice was softer now, but he didn't seem to be warming.

"Are. We. Clear?" he ground out.

Ruby blinked at the threat in his voice. Anger rose inside her like bile, and she dug her fingernails into her palms.

"Tomorrow I want you to supervise the excavation of unit four-seventy-five. There'll be a tractor and scraper to handle the heavy work. Then I want the soil picked through by hand and screened. You'll have a crew of about seven. Is that understood?"

All she managed was a tightlipped, "Yes."

CHAPTER 12

Late that afternoon, everyone retreated to their tents to escape the heat. Ruby went to the mess tent in search of a cold Coca-Cola. She wasn't disappointed. She chatted with Spike for a while, hoping he would give an opinion about the bodies in the cavern, but he wouldn't talk about it. He did tell her where Pete lived, though, which she was grateful for. She needed to speak with him. She had to tell him about going to Gallegos, and she needed to know what he had been doing at the hospital. Had he gone there to check on Nicolas? And if so, why didn't he mention it to her?

Spike had said to park at the cantina. She followed the path to a cluster of small homes and spotted it. A tall coyote fence surrounded his little house like a fortress.

A pinkish glow lit the mountains as the sun began to set. Cicadas buzzed in the cottonwoods, and the sound filled the still-warm air. Ruby found a gate in the tightly constructed wall of wood and opened it. Behind the fortress walls lay a dying flower garden and a small, thirsty lawn.

She knocked at the front door. Hearing no movement behind it, she knocked louder. Pete finally opened the door, barefoot, his hair disheveled and his shirt tail only partially tucked into his jeans. He looked as if he'd been sleeping.

"Did I wake you?" Ruby asked.

At first he looked shocked to see her, but then he left the door open and retreated to the pine bed where he'd apparently been napping. Ruby stepped down three or four inches into the house and onto a beautiful chocolate-colored floor. She was familiar with the crafting of these unique floors. A mixture of adobe mud and ox blood gave it a rich hue, and hours of hand buffing gave the floor a soft, dull glow.

With his arm flung over his face as he lay on the bed, Pete ignored her while she poked around the house. Splotches of clean, blank wall stood out where pictures had hung. Only a few framed black-and-white photos remained. One in particular drew her attention. A young Pete—about sixteen, she guessed—and a much taller boy stood arm in arm, leaning against a Chevy pickup. Their faces radiated the cockiness of young men and the happiness of those who hadn't yet faced grief. A brother or cousin, she assumed, due to their similarity in expression and posture. Maybe this was Ricardo. There was mischief in Pete's smile, and his hand rested on the tousled-haired head of the older boy. His grin dripped charisma, and deep dimples creased his cheeks. His eyes sparkled with life. She hardly noticed the scar on his chin that was now so evident.

Pete had changed a lot since that picture.

She turned and looked at him on the bed. He hadn't moved. Had he fallen asleep again?

"Are you sick?" she asked, concerned.

"No. Tired." He pulled himself up to a seated position and swiveled to rest his feet on the floor.

No, he wasn't tired. It was something else. She watched him for another moment. "You're drunk."

"Maybe," he mumbled. "So what?"

"We need to talk, Pete."

He stood, shuffling into an adjoining room. She heard water

running. He must have gone into the bathroom, since the kitchen was in the opposite direction. It held only the basics: a small sink, a few tables that served as storage for dishes and cups, a refrigerator that matched the sink in size, and a worn and battered gas stove. The room smelled like stale beer.

After a few minutes, he returned. He'd slicked back his hair and tucked his shirt into worn jeans. He'd even put on shoes.

"What were you doing at the hospital earlier?" she asked.

He glared at her from under heavy brows. "If anyone has any explaining to do, it's you. You went to Gallegos."

She sighed. "I'm sorry. I had to. Yes, I reported the bodies, but I didn't divulge the new information I have."

He shoved his hands in his pockets. "What information?"

"I have a friend of a friend at the FBI. I asked if he would do some research on Dr. Mendenhall. What he found was more than interesting. I think you're right. I think he's been doing medical experiments on the people of Las Montanas. Radiation experiments. For the government."

He sank back onto the bed and ran his hands through his damp hair.

"Why didn't you say anything to Gallegos about this?"

"I wanted to see how the local authorities handled it. If you're right and they're involved, it'll be obvious."

He shook his head, his gaze directed at the floor.

"You didn't answer my question about the hospital, Pete. Were you checking up on Nicolas?"

"Yes," he said, his eyes still trained on the floor. "Did you mention Nicolas to Gallegos?"

"Yes."

Pete's face blanched. "Did you mention me?"

"Yes."

"Well, then." He slapped his thigh. "The cat's really out of the burlap now. Gallegos will find a way to shut us down. You've compromised the dig."

She crossed her arms. "Yates said that the site is on federal

land and Gallegos has no jurisdiction. He can't shut anything
down. Why are you lying to me? Have you been lying to me all
along?"

He leveled her with a look so penetrating she wanted to
flinch. "You have no idea what you've done," he said, his voice
low, almost a growl. "Why didn't you listen to me? Why didn't
you give me more time?" A wet curl fell onto his forehead.

"I had to. It's been hanging over my head like a thunder-
cloud. At least I got the ball rolling. Now we'll wait and see what
happens. And the sooner something does happen, the sooner
this will be over. We might even find out how Ricardo died."

He shook his head, his lips pressed together in a thin line.
"You have to go." His tone was curt, dismissive. "I've got things
to take care of."

"But—"

"Tell Yates I'll be out first thing tomorrow." He met her gaze,
and for a brief moment she saw his pain in those dark, soulful
eyes, and it nearly broke her heart. Yet she had no idea why. He'd
lied to her, encouraged *her* to lie, and was *still* lying.

"Come on, Pete."

"See you tomorrow." He went over to the door and opened it,
waiting for her to leave.

She walked out of the house, into the neglected garden. The
door slammed behind her, startling her. With a frustrated sigh,
she made her way to the gate nestled within the coyote fence.

❧

Pete walked to the small fridge in the kitchen and pulled out
another can of beer from his second, near-empty, six-pack. The
metal popped as he used the church key to open it, and in one
big gulp he swallowed half the contents.

Why wouldn't she leave it alone?

When he'd told her about Mendenhall, and the rumors of
medical experimentation, he'd been reaching. He'd only heard

rumors about it. He knew Mendenhall hadn't killed Ricardo or the others in the coffins. Someone in the Brotherhood had. He knew it, he just couldn't prove it. Yet.

What she had found when she tumbled down onto those bodies was a secret burial ground for the Brotherhood. The bodies in the coffins were obviously the bodies of the Cristos—the chosen ones within the Brotherhood. Ricardo.

The Brotherhood had existed in Las Montanas for over three hundred years. But in the past several years they had become more covetous of their members, and their solidarity was more important than anything—even their own families. Now, he guessed other members of the Brotherhood, those not of the chosen, were also buried down there. Perhaps José, who died from emphysema, or Mateo who succumbed to cancer, or Martín, who was killed in a car accident.

But the cavern Ruby found couldn't be their only burial place. There had been a Cristo named every year for centuries. It was rare that a Cristo died during the Passion, the reenactment of Christ's crucifixion every Good Friday—until five years ago. All five had died as a result of the ritual.

Pete stared out into his yard, thinking of Ruby. As annoying as she was, she made him feel things he hadn't felt in a long time—loneliness, protectiveness, desire, frustration. He'd tried to avoid her, lie to her, even hurt her, but he couldn't make her go away. He hated that he loved the way she caressed the red bandana that hung down on her chest. He hated that he felt her pain and wanted to make it go away. He hated that she was becoming a real problem.

When Yates had come to him and told him Ruby had reported the dead, he felt as if someone had punched the air from his lungs. He knew he didn't need to explain to Yates why he himself didn't report it; Yates knew about the Brotherhood. Passionate about preserving culture at all costs, Yates must have assumed Pete would keep quiet for the same reasons.

His eyes rested on the framed picture of his family hanging

on his kitchen wall. His sisters, Marguerite and Sophia, had been just babies then. They'd come later in his parents' marriage. Now fifteen and twelve, they'd grown into fine girls. He hadn't spoken to any of his family since Ricardo's memorial service, but he'd seen the girls in town.

Pete's thoughts drifted back to that day. He had stood outside the house, next to the car he and Ricardo had shared. He hadn't been able to bear to be in the house, celebrating his brother's death. He could hardly contain his anger and his sorrow, and sharing food and drink with the others in the village would only have been a mockery of his feelings. He had wanted to be alone.

"Why are you not rejoicing, Pedro?" his father had asked, coming up behind him.

"My brother is dead."

"Your brother is more alive than ever. He is seated with God at this moment. He is watching you, loving you. You must not grieve."

Pete whirled around to face him. "Ricardo was young. He had so much to live for. He wanted to get married, have children. He told me so. We talked about it many times."

"Ricardo had a higher calling. He was chosen, and now he is where he should be—with God."

Pete remembered staring into his father's eyes. How could he have been so blinded by a farce? His brother had died far too early in the crucifixion. Obviously, something had gone wrong— yet again. Why hadn't anyone else seen it?

"Bullshit," Pete had said, never taking his gaze from his father's face.

"Pedro, do you blaspheme your God?"

"I blaspheme *you*, old man," he growled. "Ricardo was not chosen by God to die. It wasn't his time. He trained for months for this so-called honor, and yet he died within ten minutes. Someone *killed* him."

"I will not listen to such talk." His father's face clouded with fear and rage.

"You *will* listen," Pete said. "I refuse to accept Ricardo's death as one of 'natural causes, or illness' and I'm going to find out what happened."

Pete had watched his father's face fall. He suddenly looked very old. "I have one son who has left this earth to live with God," he said, his voice steady. "But my other son, my Pedro, is the one who is dead to me."

The words stung, even just remembering them. Pete had fought tears that threatened to humiliate him. His father had turned and walked slowly back into the house like a man who truly grieved. But he hadn't been grieving Ricardo; he had been grieving Pete.

Now, looking at the photograph, his eyes drifted from the girls to his mother and father. How could his father not have mourned the death of Ricardo, his favorite son? He had offered no comfort to anyone in the family, just had hidden away for days in the morada. Ricardo had been murdered, and he'd done nothing.

When Pete took the matter into his own hands he had been cast out of the family, practically cast out of the village. Thankfully others were more sympathetic than his family, and he had been able to continue living in Las Montanas. But he had not been able to deny the looks of betrayal and angry sneers of many of the village men, nor the notion that he was dead in his father's eyes.

Pete flung his half-empty beer can at the photo. The glass shattered and the frame hung precariously from one corner, the faces of his family staring back at him.

He sank into one of the kitchen chairs. There was only one way he could take control of the situation. And in doing it, the matter would be out of Ruby's hands. Ironically, he'd need her help him do it, and that would mean telling her everything. He just had to figure out how.

❀❀❀

Dust clung to Ruby's sweat-streaked face as she and one of the Mexican crewmen shook one of the large earth-sifters back and forth between them.

Things had been quiet at the site since she'd reported the bodies to Sheriff Gallegos three days before. Too quiet. Nothing had happened, and no one had come. Neither Dr. Yates nor Pete had spoken to her, and the other students seemed to be staying away on principal. Lord only knew what they had told them about her.

She motioned for her partner to stop, and they set down the sifter. Two or three bones, some teeth, and a few pottery shards littered the top of it.

"Let's take a break," she said in Spanish. "We should probably drink some water."

Winded, Ruby placed her hands on her hips while she caught her breath. She looked over at the sinkhole. Yates had said this was federal land. He should have reported the find to the federal authorities, as he said he would, but clearly Yates, like Pete, was a skilled liar.

It seemed it was time to call Master West again.

CHAPTER 13

Two days later Ruby led Dr. Barton Thurber, the state epidemiologist, and his team of four to the sinkhole. After getting some advice from Master West, she had made a call to the state epidemiologist's office. Dr. Thurber, a big man, close to six and a half feet if she had to guess, looked as if he hadn't missed many meals. He had a head of thick brown hair, and his beard was nearly as full. His four colleagues pulled ropes and carabiners from their large black bags and strapped belts over their khaki jumpsuits.

Within minutes, Dr. Yates and the rest of the group came running over.

"What's going on here?" Dr. Yates bellowed, his face red with fury.

"This couldn't wait any longer," Ruby said, hands resting on her hips.

"You have no right—"

Another car sped down the road and then stopped near Dr. Thurber's vehicle in a cloud of dust, interrupting Dr. Yates' tirade. A man wearing a jaunty fedora with a camera strapped around his neck hopped out.

"Who is this?" Ruby asked Dr. Thurber.

Dr. Thurber gave her an apologetic grimace. "Probably a reporter. We can't leave the lab without at least one of them following us. I'm sorry."

"We can't have a reporter here," Ruby said. "We can't compromise the site."

"You're damned right we can't," Dr. Yates said, stepping up to the man.

"I'm going to have to ask you to stand back," Dr. Thurber said to the gathering crowd of students and workers. "We don't yet know what we're dealing with here." He assisted his team with their gear, and two of them prepared to climb down into the hole.

"What in the hell have you done?" Dr. Yates asked Ruby between clenched teeth. "Do you know what this means? The project, *my* project, will be totally overshadowed by this . . . this dog and pony show you've arranged."

"Dr. Yates, I—" She hadn't meant for it to come to this, with the reporter and all. "After I went to Gallegos, I thought he'd handle the situation. When I told *you*, you said you would take care of it, but *nothing happened*. I couldn't let this go. Not when lives are in danger."

She looked over at Pete, who looked back with venom in his gaze. He turned and walked away.

"You've really screwed up now," Dr. Yates said to her before following Pete.

Ruby closed her eyes, biting her lip. She probably had screwed up, but how could she let this go on any longer? She couldn't let her ambition—or anyone else's for that matter—endanger the lives of others. She'd done that before, and it had cost her the most important person in her life—her son. She opened her eyes and looked around at the other students and workers. Each one avoided her gaze and silently walked back to their posts.

The epidemiology team took about two hours and forty-five minutes to gather the bones and bodies and place them in body bags. After the last one was removed, Dr. Thurber crawled out of the hole.

"I need you to come down here, Miss Delgado," he said. "Put on one of these coveralls, would you?" One of his team members handed her the boxy outfit and helped her into it. He then handed her a surgical mask and helped her tie the ends at the back of her head. It seemed silly; she'd already been exposed to whatever they thought was down there.

Once Ruby was appropriately covered, with the harness safely buckled around her waist, the team lowered her down into the cavern after Dr. Thurber. When she touched down on the floor of the cavern, the doctor loosened her ropes.

"Where did you say the coffins were?" he asked, his voice muffled by the mask.

She looked down at the barren earth below her. Without the mass of decaying corpses, the cavern seemed so much bigger. She walked toward the opening into the other cavern and peered in. Everything was gone—the coffins, the altar, all the other paraphernalia. "I don't understand. It was all here. Did you see the one with the crucifixion marks?"

He shook his head. "I didn't see anything like that."

She couldn't believe it. Someone had seen to it that the bodies in this room were removed. But who? Oh, this was worse than she'd ever imagined.

"I don't understand. They were right there." She pointed.

"I don't know what to say," said Dr. Thurber. "But we'll work with the skeletons we have. If anything else turns up, you can reach out to me directly."

She nodded, still dumbfounded.

"Now, let's get out of here." Dr. Thurber pulled on the rope, signaling his team to pull them back up.

Once they resurfaced and removed their coveralls, Ruby handed him the envelope that Master West had sent her with the information about Dr. Mendenhall. "Dr. Thurber, I don't know what happened here, or what happened to the other bodies, but this might help." Her voice wavered slightly, and she hoped he hadn't noticed.

"Thank you," he said, shaking her hand. "We'll keep you posted. We might have a quarantine situation on our hands, so you'll hear from us soon."

She helped them finish loading up their van and then watched as they drove away.

⚜

Three days later Ruby squinted as she stared at Yates' silver trailer, which shined brilliantly in the sun. The metal and glass looked hostile next to the earth tones of the high desert and the ruins that were once homes and gathering places.

The door to the trailer opened, and she flinched with surprise when Spike came out. She'd been expecting Dr. Yates to come thundering at her, ready to throw her off the project. While she'd been down in the sinkhole with Dr. Thurber, Dr. Yates had driven away from the site and no one had seen him since. She was sure he would've been back by now. But even without him, Ruby and the others continued to work the burial site. Pete wouldn't speak to her, and the others only made polite conversation.

As Spike approached her, she tried to read his expression. His face remained stoic, as always.

"Is he in there?" she asked.

"He's over in that ruin," he said, pointing. "He wants to see you. Told me to tell you to wait here for him."

"I bet he wants to see me," she muttered.

"He's pretty riled." Spike dropped a heavy hand on her shoulder. "I'll be at the cantina if you need to talk after."

She forced a smile. "Yeah. Thanks." She wondered if Dr. Yates had somehow had the bodies removed. But why not all of them? She shuddered. Maybe he'd been responsible for the deaths. Maybe Pete knew about it. But why not remove all of the bodies? She couldn't make sense of it.

Ruby slumped into one of the director's chairs as he walked away. How long would she have to wait for Dr. Yates to come over and tell her she was through? Maybe she should go pack her bags right now.

He probably wouldn't have been as angry if the reporter hadn't come. She'd never intended for that to happen. Dr. Yates had been right: this kind of sensationalism—murder in a small town, bodies massed in a grave—overshadowed the more humble story of one more ancient burial site. But she couldn't let the absurdity of this secret go on any longer.

A high-pitched ringing sent her heart into spasms. It sounded like an alarm clock coming from inside the trailer. She scanned the area Spike had pointed to, looking for Dr. Yates, but she couldn't see him.

The incessant, metallic noise continued, driving her inside the trailer. She had to make it stop. She went to the bedroom and found the clock. Fumbling with it she dropped it to the floor, its shrill sound echoing in her head like a violent mantra. She picked it up, turned it over, and finally silenced it. She took a deep breath and set it back on the dresser. Her eyes landed on a photograph sitting on the shelf above his desk. It was a picture of Dr. Yates, a white woman, and a native woman holding a baby.

Ruby sat on the worn, flattened cushion of Dr. Yates' rickety desk chair. She pictured him sitting here, hour after hour, poring over his work.

She got up to look out the window. Barely visible, near the back wall of the far ruin, she saw Dr. Yates' hat bobbing. How long would he make her wait? Running her hands along the smooth surface of the desk, she sat back down. The thought of Yates having something to do with the bodies niggled its way into her mind again. Maybe proof of some kind was right here. In this office. This desk. It didn't seem likely, but . . .

She studied the long, narrow drawer before her, and then she slowly opened it.

Order reigned inside with pencils, pens, a stapler, and paper clips resting neatly in a wooden organizer. Feeling brave, she opened one of the side drawers. Inside she found stationery, envelopes, a letter opener, tape, and stamps. The drawer on the other side held files. She looked out the window again and saw that Dr. Yates hadn't moved from where he'd been before. She ran her trembling fingers along the tabs of the manila files, and stopped on one labeled UNIVERSITY OF NEW MEXICO, GRANTS AND FUNDS. Pulling the file out she let go of the cover flap and the folder fell open, littering the floor with papers.

"No, no, no!" she said under her breath. How would she ever get them back in order? She piled the papers together but stopped when she saw a piece of UNM stationery. A letter addressed to Yates. The subject line read: *In regard to further funding for the Anasazi project.* Her eyes skimmed the body of the letter:

We regret to inform you that funds from the private sector have been withdrawn from your project. An investigation into our past files uncovered an ethical breach of conduct. Although the investors feel that you are not legally at fault for the situation in Peru, ethically, there is a problem. Please understand that the government grant still stands, and you may continue with the project in Las Montanas, New Mexico, but the additional funds you requested have been denied.

She stared at the letter, then at the drawer. Funds from the private sector withdrawn? An ethical breach of conduct? What the hell happened in Peru?

A noise at the door startled her and she quickly shoved the papers back into the file, slid the folder back into place, and eased the drawer shut.

Dr. Yates entered the office, removing his hat. He glared at her. "What are you doing at my desk?"

"The alarm clock was—"

"Let me get straight to the point," he interrupted. "You cannot remain on this project." He put his hat back on and wiped the sweat from his face with a pristine white handkerchief.

Her breath caught. "Dr. Yates, please let me explain."

"There is nothing to explain," he said brusquely. "You're dismissed."

His eyes were hard and cold, and she knew there would be no convincing him to change his mind. He hadn't wanted her here from the beginning, so now, after this, how could he ever be persuaded to let her stay?

He pulled a newspaper out from under some files on the desk. That was her cue, she guessed.

Ruby stood to go, but he motioned for her to sit back down. He tossed the paper in front of her. "Read it," he said. "Out loud."

Ruby gulped and then read. "ARCHEOLOGICAL DIG SITE UNCOVERS POSSIBLE MURDERS – A mass grave was discovered in an underground cavern near the village of Las Montanas. Local authorities, fearing foul play, called for the state epidemiologist to investigate. It was thought the victims were pawns in a medical experiment; however, no evidence has been found to support that assumption. Sources report that all the victims died of natural causes. Some of the bodies showed signs of the Stigmata, or markings of the crucified Christ. The archbishop of Santa Fe has stated that the matter of the Stigmata will be investigated."

Ruby raised her eyes to meet his. His narrowed at her. "There was no mention of a team of archaeologists or an ancient burial site. Our discovery will never compare to this sensational story."

Her suspicions of Dr. Yates being the murderer suddenly vanished. Why would he do something to compromise his own work?

"Dr. Yates, I didn't intend . . . The reporter twisted it all around."

"Do you have any idea what you've done? This is an outrage." His face flushed red. "Now, if you'll excuse me." He pointed to the door.

Ruby stood up, as rigid as a fence post.

"Get out," Dr. Yates said. "I'm revoking your scholarship."

Her eyes widened. "You can't do that. You don't have the authority." The shock of his words struck terror in her. She couldn't lose her scholarship. It was her second chance. She had to divert him, get him to talk longer. Somehow she had to persuade him to change his mind.

"I do have the authority, and by God I'll use it." His steely gaze bore into hers.

She took a deep breath, desperately trying to control her emotions. "You have made it no secret that you resent my finding the treasure of the Noche Triste. Revoking my scholarship would only show professional jealousy. Then the whole world will know just what a damned jerk you are."

She could see his rage reach the boiling point. She'd crossed the line, but what did she have to lose?

"How dare y—"

"Maybe they'll also find out what happened in Peru," she cut in. "Just what *did* happen in Peru, Dr. Yates?"

The veins in his neck visibly pulsated. "That's it! Get out! I'll make sure you never work in this field again."

"It's a big world, Dr. Yates. You can't control my career."

"Get out!" he bellowed again.

She tilted her head, not doing as he'd demanded. "What were you hiding out there? What happened in Peru that would make you turn a blind eye to murder right under your nose?" He might not be the murderer, but he knew something. Why would Sheriff Gallegos send him a message the minute she left the police station? "The body I found in the coffin was someone who had wounds in their hands and feet. I've been told there was a man here who had suffered from the Stigmata. Or maybe it just looked like the Stigmata. Maybe he was *crucified*, Dr. Yates. But that body wasn't down there when Dr. Thurber arrived, was he? Did your friend Gallegos see to that?"

"I told you to leave," he said between gritted teeth.

She stood her ground. "Have you heard about Nicolas Baca?"

"Who? What are you talking about? Get the hell out *now*!" Dr. Yates slammed his fist on the desk.

She hesitated a moment, just to show she couldn't be intimidated by his fit of temper. Then she walked past him, left the trailer, and headed straight for her tent.

There, she threw her gear and clothing into her duffel bag, tears streaming down her face. After taking a quick look around to make sure she hadn't forgotten anything—but not really caring if she had—she stepped out and headed for her car. She left in a flurry of tears, skid marks, and dust.

Where she was going, she had no idea.

❦

The gloomy, musty cantina would be the perfect place for Ruby to lick her wounds. She kicked at the napkins and empty cigarette pack that littered the floor under her table and looked around the space. Wrought-iron fixtures hung from dusty, cobwebbed chains, and the glass housing for the bulbs were so grimy the lights cast an eerie yellow glow. Thick curtains kept out the daylight. She looked for Spike, but he wasn't there.

At the bar an old man slept, drink in hand, saliva dripping from his mouth. In a far corner, three men talked loudly. A few nights ago, the place had seemed festive and friendly. Funny how one's mood could color everything.

The darkness and filth felt right for her current state of mind. The overweight bartender stood with his hands on the bar, watching her, but didn't turn his back on the rowdy men in the corner.

Ruby stared at the two shots of tequila sitting on the table in front of her. The toxic aroma took her to a faraway place, a place of obscurity, a place where she could forget her troubles. She longed to be there. She could almost feel the alcohol burn down her throat.

She'd come so far. She'd been sober for two years, and for what? This?

She laughed out loud, and the men in the corner stopped arguing to stare. She glanced over at them. They probably thought she was crazy. *No, boys, just a screwup.*

Their conversation resumed, but their eyes still lingered. A few years ago, when she was training in martial arts, she would've been able to take any one of them down inside of thirty seconds. She studied her hands, wondering if she could still do it. She couldn't be sure.

She reached toward one of the glasses and twirled it with her fingers. The liquid dripping from it made a ring on the scratched table top. The comfort was so close . . .

She stared into the glass, reading both her past and future in the two ounces of tequila, when something moved into her line of vision. Legs. Legs in jeans. Muscular legs.

She raised her eyes to see Pete standing in front of her. "What do you want?" she asked.

He took a chair, turned it backward and then sat down, straddling it. He leaned his arms across the back. "Nothing," he said with a shrug.

"Why are you here?"

"I was looking for you."

She sniffed. "Save the tongue-lashing for someone who cares, would you? I've had about all I can take today."

She studied his powerful forearms and her gaze traveled across his smooth, muscular chest. Slowly her gaze passed over his neck, chin, lips, and nose. Their eyes locked, and she became vaguely aware of a heat arcing between them.

"What are you doing here, Ruby?" His voice was softer than she'd ever heard it.

"I'm thinking about getting stinking drunk."

She lifted one of the shot glasses to her face, about an inch from her mouth. The smell of the tequila practically making her dizzy.

"Don't," he said.

"Why not?"

"Because you really don't want to, and you know it."

Her hand trembled, and she watched liquid coat her fingers.

"Put it down, Ruby."

Her hand stopped shaking, and she raised her eyes to his. "Why do you care?"

"I want to show you something," he said.

She lowered the glass and very deliberately put it down right next to the other glass on the table. When Pete reached for her face, her heart flipped. He stopped at her neck and untied the knot of her bandana. He slipped it off and gently wiped the tequila from her dripping fingers before setting the bandana on the table.

"What is it you want to show me?" she asked.

Leaning his hands on the back of the chair, his legs still straddling it, he stood up. "You're going to have to come with me to find out."

He started out of the cantina, and Ruby followed. She was almost out the door when she realized she'd left her bandana, and her heart stopped. "Wait." She turned back around, grabbed the bandana from the table, and held it tightly in her fist. She eyed the two still-full shot glasses on the table. She hesitated, staring at them, tasting them in her mind, and then turned and followed Pete outside.

CHAPTER 14

The cool air outside nipped at her skin. When they reached his truck, Pete put on a leather jacket and tossed Ruby a denim one. His smell lingered on it, and she wrapped it tightly around herself and got in the truck.

They rode in silence. She watched as his hair swirled freely around his face in the light breeze from the open window. Beneath the mussed locks, his expression was hard. They sat close together, her arm occasionally brushing against his. She scooted closer to the door.

"So, why aren't you furious with me?" she asked.

"Who says I'm not?"

Outside, a low cloud hovered above them. Lightning flickered and streaked behind the mountains. A deep rumble followed. They took the winding road up around the hillside, and the truck jerked and jolted on the bumpy gravel. In the distance more of the spiked, spidery legs of a lightning storm darted through the sky. The air smelled electric and damp, and the tension between her and Pete was palpable.

A puzzling smile parted his lips as he looked over at her. Did he feel this unbelievable heat between them, too? After the truck climbed up another steep, bumpy dirt road, he stopped about two hundred yards from a dimly-lit adobe structure that backed up against a hill, camouflaged by pine trees. Tiny windows near the top of the perfectly rectangular building glowed yellow.

"What is this?" Ruby asked.

"A morada," he whispered. "C'mon."

She climbed out of the truck and studied the surroundings in the dim moonlight. More lightning flashed. It lit the trees and the gray, silver-flecked boulders on the hill above them. Goose bumps rose on her skin, and she hugged the denim jacket closer to her body.

He motioned for her to follow him farther up the hill. Sounds of human chanting floated on the breeze. Was it singing? Was this morada a church of some kind? The wind picked up and swirled her hair in her face. It whistled through the large trees and moaned through the valley. Pine cones plopped to the ground, having been loosened from their boughs with the strength of the breeze.

Pete slid behind a gnarled, stooped tree, and she followed. Tiny raindrops fell on her face. She watched him closely, her anticipation rising. The stubble of his beard glistened in the moonlight.

"Wait here," he said.

He ran, crouched low, toward the rough wooden double doors of the morada. Prying one of them open about an inch, he peered in. He motioned for her to join him. When she reached the doors, he moved aside so she could view the interior of the building. He pulled her so close, she could smell the leather of his jacket as she was scrunched up against it. His hand on her arm was firm and warm.

Through the crack, Ruby saw the bare backs of several men. They knelt on the floor, their bodies swaying gently. The chanting continued, and a strange slapping sound accompanied the voices in the small, stuffy room. Ruby squinted to see better.

In unison, each man flung a small whip with leather tassels

over his shoulders, striking his own back. Blood rose to the surface of their skin and ran in tiny rivulets down toward their waists. She pressed her brows together, remembering the marks on Nicolas' back. But the marks on his back had been larger, made from something bigger than these small whips.

One of the men fell forward and collapsed onto the floor. No one stopped their ritual, they just continued as if they weren't aware of him.

Hundreds of candles flickered in the small structure, giving it a golden glow. The flames lit up the Santos—wooden canvases with rustic depictions of saints, that adorned the walls behind the altar. The smell of sweat and blood came forward in a rush of hot air. Ruby pressed her face closer to the crack. In front of the men, at the altar, a large man wearing a black hood emerged.

Pete nudged her. "See that man over on the far side, near the front? The one with the black hair and white mustache?" he whispered.

She strained to see. "I think so."

"That's my father," he said.

Her eyes widened. She instantly saw the similarities: the strong jaw, full lips, dimples, and the thick dark hair, though the father's was peppered with gray. She turned to Pete, read the torture on his face. She could see he hated watching, hated being there. Reading his expression, her heart ached for him. This caused him pain. She looked away from him and back to the men and their ritual.

Two men, one on each side of the altar, began to turn the cranks positioned next to them. Within in a few moments, they'd hoisted the body of a man into view; the man was suspended solely by his arms. His head rolled back and his mouth moved, but Ruby heard no words.

The hooded man approached the suspended man, a long bullwhip coiled in his hand. He snapped it toward the suspended man, and a piercing crack filled the room. The limp body flinched.

Ruby's breath caught in her throat. Unable to watch, she turned her face away while the crack of the whip filled the air again. Her eyes met Pete's. His long lashes were rimmed with moisture.

"What *is* this?" she asked.

"This? This is hell."

❧

Pete had shoved himself away from the wall of the morada and ran toward the truck. Ruby caught up with him a few minutes later, breathless. Rain pelted them in large, furious drops. Pete, his soaked hair hanging in loose waves around his face, opened the passenger door for her and motioned for her to get in. When they were both inside they sat quietly, listening to the rain as it hit the metal roof.

Pete's face, partially lit by the glow of moonlight through the low cloud cover, registered his anger. He opened his mouth to speak but then shut it. Could he not find the words? Or did he still not trust her?

"It's time you knew about what you found in that cavern," he said.

"That would be nice." It was about time.

"What you found was a burial place for the Redeemers."

"What are the Redeemers?" she asked.

"Those men. In there," he started. "The Redeemers are a secret brotherhood."

She didn't respond right away. There was so much she wanted to know, but she worried that if she overwhelmed him with questions he'd clam up again. "What about the coffins I found?" she asked after a beat. "Are they associated with the Redeemers?"

"Yes," Pete said, tapping his index finger on the steering wheel. "Members of the Brotherhood are buried together in a secret place so they remain together. There's a bond that follows them even into death. But the coffins are reserved for the Cristos."

"I've heard of secret societies in other parts of the world, but I've never heard of the Redeemers."

"They're secretive about their lives and rituals. My mother doesn't even know about most of it. It was a rule in our house that we didn't discuss it." Pete ran his hands over the steering wheel. The rain was coming down in furious torrents now. "They flog themselves for the sins of others."

Ruby nodded ever so slightly. An image of Nicolas flashed in her mind but she stayed quiet, letting Pete continue.

"I never liked the fact that my father was a Redeemer. It took him away from us, made him hard. Unrelenting. Fanatical. I didn't buy into his kind of religion, even as a boy. I always thought it was weird, but in the last few years it's gotten really weird," he said. "Even more secretive. The rituals have become more intense. Extreme, as you saw in there."

"Then it needs to be stopped," Ruby said.

He shook his head, water droplets falling from his hair onto his leather jacket. "You don't understand. How can this be stopped?" He looked at her, no anger in his eyes. Only helplessness, despair. "Certainly not the way you want to do it. By getting those state officials out here you've undermined their entire culture, a religious practice that's existed for hundreds of years. You've exposed them, and now they'll retreat even deeper into secrecy. If I'm correct, they'll do anything to protect themselves. And I'll . . . I'll never know how my brother died."

Her brow furrowed in confusion. "Ricardo?"

Pete nodded. "He was a Cristo."

Her heart broke for him, for Ricardo, for their poor mother. But she had to ask . . . "Nicolas Baca?"

"He's this year's Cristo." Pete anxiously rapped the knuckle of his index finger against the steering wheel.

"But there were other bodies in there. They couldn't have all been Cristos."

"No. They weren't."

"But they seemed to have recently died. Why?"

"I don't know." Pete lay his head back against the headrest. "I don't know. I thought I knew, but now . . . Everything is so messed up."

She swallowed. "Because of me? Because I called the state epidemiologist?"

He looked her square in the eyes. "Yes."

Ruby turned to the window. Rain blurred anything she might see outside as it pounded the truck. "Do you want me to leave Las Montanas?" she asked. "Because I don't think I can now. If Nicolas Baca is going to succumb to the same fate as those I found in the coffins, I can't leave knowing that I didn't do something to stop it."

"If you had asked me about leaving a few days ago I would have said yes, that I wanted you to go, but now . . ."

"Now?" she pressed.

"No. I don't want you to go."

She turned back to face him, surprised by his answer. "Why not?"

"Now that this has been uncovered again, I'd like for you to help me find out how Ricardo died."

Ruby smiled, amazed at her own thoughts, her own emotions. She'd hoped he would say just what he'd said—that he wanted her to stay to help solve the crimes and prevent another, but what she really wanted was for him to tell her that he wanted her to stay because he wanted *her*. It had been a long time since she felt anything for a man. Since before Matthew. His father was a one-night stand, and when she had contacted him he wanted nothing to do with her, or his child. So, she'd closed off that part of her heart. But now, with startling clarity, she felt it opening up once again.

Ruby and Pete decided she should stay at the rectory, and together they headed over to talk to Father Martinez. Rosita was the one to open the door, though. They explained Ruby's situation.

Rosita flung out her arms and pulled Ruby into a tight embrace, welcoming her to stay for as long as she needed. She quickly showed Ruby where she could leave her things and then nudged her toward the kitchen.

After she had some dinner with Rosita, Ruby made a phone call to Dr. Thurber's office. She wanted more clarification on the bodies in the cavern. What could have killed them? Her thoughts kept coming back to the photograph of Dr. Mendenhall. Could there be some kind of truth to the rumors of his performing some kind of experimentation on the men, and maybe even the women of Las Montanas? People like Huberto, and potentially Nicolas, were still dying for some unexplained reason, and she needed to know more.

She tried to press Dr. Thurber, but he abruptly said he couldn't discuss the subject further and hung up on her. Shocked at the abrupt click, she held the receiver from her face and then set it gently back onto its cradle. She couldn't be certain, but she thought she heard fear in his voice.

This thing obviously seeped out beyond Las Montanas. But how far? And where had the bodies in the coffins gone?

Nicolas' tortured body—cactus spines embedded deep into his skin—flashed in her mind again. She shook her head to clear the image, and returned to the room Rosita had made up for her. She climbed into bed and, exhausted, fell asleep the moment her head hit the pillow.

She didn't wake up until after ten the next morning. The reality of losing her place at the University, and possibly her career, was starting to sink in. The loss left her feeling empty, but the emptiness had a weight to it, similar to the one she'd been carrying around since Matthew died. She struggled to get out of bed. When she finally did, she shuffled toward the kitchen in search of coffee in her baggy T-shirt and shorts. She didn't have to check a mirror to know dark circles hung under her eyes and that her hair was a tangled mess.

The smell of coffee pulled her into the small, warm room, alive with the aroma of breakfast. Rosita stood at the gas stove. Ruby was surprised to see her cooking breakfast so late. She figured everyone would already be busy with their duties for the day. Yet the table had three place settings. Ruby took a chipped mug from the cabinet and poured herself a cup of the strong black coffee.

"May I help?" she offered.

"No, no. You rest," Rosita said over her shoulder.

Ruby nodded, still too exhausted to argue, and sipped her coffee.

Father Martinez walked into the kitchen, yawning. The priest, too, looked like he'd had a rough night. His pockmarked face looked haggard, as if he hadn't slept well.

"Miss Delgado," he greeted her, sounding surprised.

"Father."

"She is going to stay with us for a while," Rosita told him over the running water in the sink.

He sat opposite Ruby. He wore a gray V-necked sweater and faded jeans. His dark eyes raked Ruby's face, and she lowered her gaze. "Certainly," he said. "Any way we can help. What does Dr. Yates have to say about this?"

"We had a . . . difference of opinion," she explained. "We both thought it best that I leave." Her humiliation ran too deep to say more.

"This business with the federales and those bodies . . . the reporters . . . Is that why?" he asked in heavily accented Spanglish.

She swallowed, looking into her coffee cup. "Yes."

"Tricky business," he said. "But what else could you do, no?" He lifted a shoulder.

She looked into his eyes, surprised at his response. "Well yes,

Father, what else could I have done? I went to the sheriff, and he did nothing. I couldn't keep quiet about something like that, though I didn't mean to cause so much trouble." Her words tumbled out, sounding like a confession. Staring into the priest's eyes she felt herself pulled, compelled to talk, to reveal herself.

"I understand," he said, then turned to Rosita. "The archbishop's people will be here tomorrow to investigate this business with the Stigmata. Be sure to have the place presentable. We'll need a few extra beds."

"*Claro que sí.* Of course," Rosita agreed without looking at him.

Ruby studied the priest. She wondered how far she could press him for information. "Father Martinez, what do you know about the Stigmata?"

"In what way do you mean?" he asked, brows raised.

"I mean, is it possible? Does it happen? *Has* it happened?"

"It is possible. In fact, it seems there is a case of the Stigmata in the village. Manuel Medina bleeds from his wrists and ankles."

Medina. Pete's father.

"Does he really . . . bleed?" she asked. "Is it all the time?" Pete had never mentioned the Stigmata when talking about his father.

"Perhaps," the priest said, sipping his coffee. "Although I have not seen Manuel in that state. And no, in most cases it is not all the time. Historically, it happens when the afflicted is at prayer, or having just received the Eucharist, or perhaps when they have received a vision, or a message from God."

"Do *you* think it's real, Father?"

"We cannot determine what's possible and what isn't, eh? Only the Father knows that." He rose from his chair, coffee cup in hand. "The Stigmata is a gift, an acknowledgment of one's faithfulness. We cannot merely ponder the possibility of its existence. Instead, we must believe that it does exist." He smiled at her and left the room.

She watched him go, noticing his powerful, masculine walk.

She fixed her eyes on his broad shoulders flexing underneath his sweater, wondering what had kept him up last night.

◈

After she showered and dressed, Ruby drove out to the clinic to see Dr. Mendenhall. She wanted to come right out and ask him about the rumors. To ask him if he'd performed any kind of medical experimentation on the people of Las Montanas. If he had he would probably deny it, but she just needed to see his expression when she asked; to see if she could read anything in his face.

No one was present in the waiting room when she dinged the little bell at the window. When Mendenhall appeared behind it, she gave him a tight smile. He didn't seem moved. It was silly to draw this out, to make inane small talk. She'd get right to the point.

"I need to know the truth, Dr. Mendenhall. About the rumors of experimentation."

He crossed his arms over his chest. "Guilty as charged," he said.

Ruby blinked. She'd never imagined he would admit it.

"But that was several years ago. And no one has died from those experiments. To my knowledge, at least."

"Oh." Still stunned she stared at him, not sure what to say next.

He waved his hand, beckoning her to come through the door. Should she follow him? The place was deserted. But she had her martial arts background to fall upon, should he try anything. When they reached his office, he motioned for her to sit in one of the client chairs at the front of his desk. He walked around to the other side and sat down. He grabbed a coffee cup off the desk and held it between his hands. "You are a bright woman," he said. "An observant one."

Ruby looked down at her hands in her lap. "I'm not so sure about that."

"I am." He raised his brows. "That's what makes you dangerous."

Ruby lifted her head to see him smiling at her. He put the coffee cup down. "When I conducted those experiments all those years ago, I believed I was doing something good. We'd developed the first atomic weapons and needed to know how the radiation emitted from them affected people. It was all in the name of progress, of science. But now I realize the pain I caused to those unknowing test subjects, so I'm trying to make up for it. Doing my penance, so to speak."

Ruby knitted her brow. "I don't understand."

Dr. Mendenhall steepled his fingers. "At one time, I could have had any position I wanted in medicine. I was one of the most prominent physicians of my time. But when I was charged, and I was indeed charged with the crime, the government betrayed me. I went to prison. The knowledge of what I'd done to those people chipped away at my heart like an axe chipping away at stone. I wanted to make up for my transgression. So when I was released I changed my name and set up my practice here in Las Montanas, where several of my test subjects were from originally. I've devoted my life to studying them. I'm looking for defects that my work may have caused."

Ruby's eyes widened. "And? Are there?"

The doctor closed his eyes and nodded.

"Like what?"

"Immune deficiencies, deformities, retardation—" His face tightened. "—other things."

"What about this virus that seems to be circulating around here, Dr. Mendenhall? Do you know anything about it yet?"

"Not enough, but it's funny you ask . . . You got officials down here on the pretext that the government was still involved in radiation experiments on humans. And ironically enough, I believe you're not far off the mark."

"Really?" she asked, struggling to believe he was agreeing with her, when she'd accused *him* of the experiments in the first place. "But how?"

"Scientists have started conducting experiments in biochemical warfare. These desolate, remote desert areas are the perfect laboratories, if you will. It isn't done with the intent of infecting humans, but on occasion mistakes are made—the weather changes, winds shift, or animals are infected, causing breakouts of diseases such as anthrax, rabbit fever, Q fever."

"So what do these diseases do?" she asked.

"Primarily they attack the upper respiratory tract and can, in many cases, lead to pneumonia. If not treated the lungs will fill with fluid, thus 'drowning' the patient." Dr. Mendenhall pushed his glasses up on his nose.

"Is that what happened to Huberto? The man I brought in from the site? And the man who was in here when I first came in —after I found the bodies?"

"I really cannot discuss their cases with you," he said, apology in his voice. "But maybe I can answer other questions you might have."

She wondered about Nicolas. Had he contracted pneumonia?

"If these viruses start in animals, how do they get transmitted to humans?"

"It depends on the disease, but some possibilities are fleas, feces, insect bites. And sometimes it's even airborne, like with anthrax."

She nodded. "So you think the virus in the village is a result of some government experiment gone bad?"

"It's possible, but I don't know enough about it yet to be certain," he said. "And believe me, I'm working on it. These experiments, if that's what is happening, are wrong." He closed his eyes for a moment before continuing, his voice softer. "I know that now."

"I wonder if any of those bodies in the sinkhole had any of these diseases," Ruby said, thinking out loud.

Dr. Mendenhall smiled and took his feet off the desk.

"Who knows how long some of those bodies had been down there in that cavern. The decay in some of them had to have been advanced, so it would be difficult to tell. Perhaps the epidemiologists just didn't want to alarm the public. We're always the last to know."

Ruby realized the truth of his words. Not very comforting, but unfortunately he was right.

"What do you think of this Stigmata, Dr. Mendenhall? There has been mention of it here in the village. Have you heard it mentioned?"

"Of course," he said. "I suppose the condition is possible. But in most of the cases, it's a physical disorder caused by or aggravated by the emotions of the individual."

"So it can be psychosomatic?" she asked. "Why would it be so prevalent here, though, and not in big cities?"

"This is a deeply religious community—very old-world, very superstitious. It is also isolated from the *real* world of modern theories and practices. The behavior of these people can be odd, seemingly irrational, and unconventional. The Stigmata is entirely possible, especially in a place like this. The Stigmata has also been known to manifest itself in the minds of the insane, the mentally ill, the psychotic. This, mixed with religious fervor, gives this kind of phenomenon the distinct possibility of existing."

Ruby thought on his words, thought of all that they'd discussed, and something occurred to her. "Dr. Mendenhall, could the intake of large doses of radiation cause psychosis?"

The doctor raised his hands, steepled his fingers again, and tapped his forefingers on his pursed lips. He smiled at her. "As I said, you're an extremely bright woman, Miss Delgado."

CHAPTER 15

Father Enrique Martinez sat on the edge of the bed, studying the items on the small table in front of him. The single burner he'd plugged into the wall slowly heated, and the pot of water made a tinny rumbling sound as it threatened to boil.

The portrait of Jesus stared at him. The Savior held up two fingers in a blessing. Try as he might to deny it Martinez knew he'd been cursed instead of blessed, cursed with secret urges and desires. Unthinkable vices. Weakness.

The hypnotic, sorrowful eyes of Christ burned holes into his soul. The hypocrisy of his life and his work ate at him like rust-eroded metal. Who was he to lead men? Who was he to wear the vestments of the holy? He had fooled them for so long, but his faith burned with such vigor he thought he could make them see, make them understand what he understood. Yet men had died, and the responsibility fell to him. He'd never intended to introduce death to the men of Las Montanas, but he had. And they kept dying.

Guilt festered inside him, threatening to eat his soul, but he had to remain strong. He had to show them he could protect them from evil, from themselves. It was his duty.

His hands shook, even clasped before his chest as they were. The addiction seemed to be getting worse. He never imagined a year ago, when he vowed to quit smoking, that it would be so damned difficult. But then again, everything in his life had been difficult from the day he'd been born. Abandonment at the age of four by his mother into the hands of an abusive, alcoholic father had taught him only one thing: he was worthless.

Oh, how he craved a cigarette. He wanted to feel the smoke fill his lungs, burning his insides, sending the rush to his blood vessels. And the pain, he wanted that, too—the pain of the smoldering ember sinking into the flesh of his arms and legs. His penance was the only thing that could chase away the evil in him.

A knock at the door made him jump. He stood, smoothed his pants with sweaty palms, and opened the door.

"Manuel," he said, relieved. "You don't know how glad I am to see you."

The old man smiled, his white mustache lengthening with the movement of his mouth. He handed the priest the tobacco leaves.

"I know it is a lot to ask of you, to keep my little secret," Father Martinez said, his voice low. He opened the box and inhaled, the smell of the tobacco thrilling his senses. The deep, pungent odor made his blood surge through his veins in anticipation of the rush.

"*Sí,*" said Manuel. "I had trouble quitting myself, but I was able to do it."

Martinez mustered a smile that he hoped looked sincere. "How long has it been?"

"Ten years. Although at times I could sure use a smoke, even still."

How well the priest understood those feelings. The doctor had told him he'd damaged his lungs almost irreparably, but he had to stay alive so he could save the others.

Being a priest meant being like God. People all too often

didn't understand that priests were human, too; that they didn't possess God's strength. Every man has his failings. Suddenly, he wanted Manuel to leave. He needed to commit his secret deed in private.

"Manuel, the archbishop is sending some people out this evening. They want to see you, and they want to question that woman, Ruby Delgado."

"I know, Padre." Manuel sighed heavily and lifted his arms, wrists exposed. They were smooth and clear, and showed no signs of his affliction. "I cannot make it happen, Father. It comes when the Lord sends it."

"What will you tell them, Manuel?"

"The truth, Padre."

Martinez sighed. This had become an ugly business. The Delgado woman had meddled in affairs that didn't concern her, and because of it his work could be sabotaged. The archbishop coming to Las Montanas would create additional problems for him, as well. Something needed to be done about her.

"Gracias, amigo," the priest said, eager for his friend to leave him in peace.

Manuel nodded and left the room, closing the door behind him.

Martinez stared down at the tobacco. So much trouble for such a self-destructive habit. But wasn't that the reason he craved it so? As much as he craved a cigarette, and the searing pain the smoldering tip would cause—inflicting harm on his body made him feel better. It took away the *real* pain. He couldn't risk smoking, even when away from the rectory. Rosita would smell it on him in a second and give him no end of grief about it, so he had to resort to this silliness. He watched the water bubble furiously.

I'm not really killing them, the voice echoed in his head, startling him.

It was back—the voice that spoke to him from the dark, the voice that preyed on him day and night, and in his dreams. It was the voice of Satan himself, the evil one enticing him to do his work.

Martinez put his fingertips to his temples. *Go away,* he thought, wrestling with the temptation to summon the voice again.

I'm giving them the gift of eternal life, to sit next to the Holy Father. It is no sin.

He shook his head. Why wouldn't it leave him alone? He must control it. He must be strong enough to prevail over this madness. It was his duty, his life's work.

To watch them hang there, the blood seeping from their outstretched arms, their bound legs, is gratifying. It makes me feel . . . powerful . . . worthy.

"No! Shut up!" Martinez shouted into the empty room.

He grabbed the heated pot, poured the water into his cup, and then twirled the spoon furiously, trying to make the tea bag steep faster. He pinched a small amount of the tobacco leaves between his fingers and placed them in his mouth. Instantly, his salivary glands went into overdrive. How he hated the taste of the vile stuff. He sucked and then spit, repeated the process, and then took the odious substance from his mouth and washed the residue down with the boiling hot tea. It scalded his mouth and throat; he could practically feel the blisters forming, and he smiled.

Yes. Pain. Redemption.

Between the caffeine and the nicotine, his body came alive. He could feel the rush of his capillaries as they constricted—that familiar, comforting rush. Strength. Everything would be fine now. The voice would stop ringing in his ears.

In death they are free.

"Yes. Free."

Staring into the leftover water still boiling in the pan, he thought about his mission and how it conflicted with the ideals of his predecessor, Father Alvarez. The old man had called him a hypocrite. Not in so many words, of course. The benevolent

Benito Alvarez would never come right out and say what he thought. Didn't Father Alvarez understand his desire to redeem the world of its sin?

The people of Las Montanas—the Redeemers—had taught him so much. They showed him their piety, their worth in the eyes of God. The fight against evil bore constant struggle. Had Father Alvarez had no struggles? If he had not, then how would he know the meaning of true sacrifice? He had been a coward.

Calmed by the effects of the nicotine and absolved by the burning of his mouth, Father Martinez folded his hands and bent his head in prayer.

❦

Pete sat in the café and sipped the burnt coffee in front of him. Josephina, the pretty and robust wife of the café owner, had brought him a cup. She made the worst coffee he'd ever tasted, yet the place never lacked customers.

He sat in the booth in the farthest corner, his favorite spot. Here, no one would bother him with their indifference. They were never outwardly rude to him, but he remained an outcast to the people of Las Montanas. Ever since he had started his investigation into Ricardo's death, they had treated him like a stranger. Most of the time he didn't care, but today he did.

"More coffee, amigo?" Xavier Piedras, the café owner, asked Pete, holding the glass pot over his mug.

"No, thanks." He feared his stomach couldn't handle any more of the vile stuff.

A loud boom of voices distracted him from his thoughts, and he watched Sheriff Gallegos enter the café. The burly, self-assured man filled the doorway. He nodded and tipped his hat to the patrons, an arrogant smile wide across his face. The customers greeted him with friendly hellos and respectful nods. Gallegos's eyes found Pete, and he began to walk in his direction. Pete stiffened.

The sheriff removed his hat and boldly sat directly across from Pete in his booth. Pete looked out the window.

"Buenos dias, Pedro."

He returned the greeting with a disdainful look. Gallegos had been particularly cruel to Pete at the time of Ricardo's death. The sheriff of Las Montanas had a mean streak, and though most people claimed to like him they really feared him. But not Pete. All he felt for the sheriff was contempt.

"I heard you're a hero," Gallegos said, cracking his knuckles one by one. "You took the Baca boy to the hospital, no?"

Josephina appeared at the table to take Gallegos' order. "The usual?" she asked. Gallegos nodded. Pete met the sheriff's gaze when Josephina scurried off to the kitchen, shouting the order to Xavier.

"You had no business interfering, Pedro."

"He was dying," Pete ground out.

"He wouldn't have died."

"He'd been bitten by a rattler; his arm was the size of a tree trunk. We saved his life."

The sheriff nodded. "If you say so."

Josephina brought the sheriff's meal, and he began to eat. Pete watched through narrowed eyes.

"You speak to your papa lately?" Gallegos asked with a mouthful of food.

The sheriff knew he hadn't. The whole village knew he and his father didn't speak anymore. He just wanted to goad Pete.

"No. You?" Pete returned the question, knowing full well that Gallegos had.

"Sí. If I didn't know better, I'd say he misses you."

The words struck the pit of Pete's stomach.

"He sees you working with that professor," Gallegos continued. "I think he wishes you would come back home to help him with the farm. He's getting old, Pedro. He needs his son to carry on the family business and the legacy."

Pete nearly scoffed. "Legacy?"

"The Redeemers. Ricardo, your papa, his papa, and his papa before him have all been members of the Brotherhood, no? The tradition needs to be carried on, *Hermano*."

Pete clenched his jaw. The familiarity with which Gallegos spoke to him about his family made his blood pressure rise. It was none of his business.

Gallegos wiped his mouth with a paper napkin, then threw it onto the plate of his unfinished breakfast. "You think about it." He got up and placed his hat back on his head, throwing money onto the table. "And Pedro, stay away from the gringa. She'll destroy the Brotherhood. They were on the news, *Hermano*. She's trouble. And you don't need that kind of trouble," he said, his words tinged with a threat. The sheriff gave him a surly grin and walked away, waving goodbye to the other patrons.

Josephina returned to clear the table. "You okay, Pedro?" she asked with a hand on her hip. "You look kinda tired."

He gave her Gallegos' money and some change for his own coffee. "Yep, that's it. I'm just really tired."

He wished insomnia was his only problem.

❦

Ruby lay staring at the ceiling, waiting for sleep. She'd counted every knothole in the vigas above her and still she couldn't calm her mind.

She got up and pulled on shorts, not bothering to change out of the T-shirt she'd worn to bed. The cold, hard floor chilled her feet, sending shivers up her legs. She fished through her bag for a clean pair of socks and a sweatshirt, and pulled them on. Maybe a glass of milk would help her sleep.

Careful not to make any noise, she slipped out the door. She passed through the sitting room and into the living room. A book of matches sat next to a large devotional candle. She lit it, bathing the room in a golden glow. Santos and other religious portraits hung on the walls, watching her with painted eyes. As she looked at them, the warm atmosphere of the room suddenly became oppressive and eerie. Her skin crawled.

She hurried to the kitchen, poured milk into a small plastic glass, and drank it down. She walked back through the living room, debating whether or not she should go back to bed. A stack of books, piled high on a small table, sat near the fireplace, and she decided to wait until she started to get drowsy. Curious, she began to go through the books.

An old, worn Bible caught her attention. Bound in leather and printed with faded gold letters, it looked like an antique. A dog-eared piece of paper stuck out of the center. She picked up the Bible and read the passage on the wafer-thin leaf. It was from John's gospel—Jesus' prayer to His Father, the night before His crucifixion:

After saying this, Jesus raised his eyes to heaven and said: Father, the hour has come: Glorify your Son So that your Son may glorify you; So that, just as you have given Him power of all Humanity, He may give eternal life to all those you have Entrusted to Him.

And eternal life is this: To know you, the only true God . . .

She stopped reading. *Glory. Eternal life.*

Her own lack of faith hit her squarely in eyes and nearly knocked the wind out of her. Wasn't that what she feared—no eternal life? No afterworld, no salvation? She realized the weakness of her faith, how weak it had been her entire life. Being raised Catholic and attending Catholic school didn't make one faithful. Faithfulness came from within. From conviction. Sadly, she didn't have that.

Her grief over Matthew was still very raw. She was so angry. Angry for not having the power to save him. Angry for not following her God-given gift of intuition. She'd known the cave was unstable. Every limb in her body shook with that knowledge, but she hadn't heeded her own instincts. She'd ignored them because her boy was exhausted. She took a calculated risk and lost.

Now her instincts told her something else, that something evil lurked in this village and Nicolas Baca could be the next target. This time, she wouldn't ignore her intuition.

She set the Bible aside and turned to biting her nails, thinking. She watched the candlelight flicker, and after some time her eyes began to close.

The sound of a door opening startled her out of the light doze. She heard deep voices. It sounded like two men.

She recognized Father Martinez's voice immediately and thought the other voice sounded familiar, too. Sheriff Gallegos, maybe? Without hesitation she returned the Bible to its place, blew out the candle, and crouched low between the sofa and coffee table. She strained to hear their words through their harsh whispers.

" . . . so he's been released . . ."

" . . . will be well enough soon . . ."

" . . . mustn't waste time . . . Easter approaches . . ."

She held her breath in the hope of hearing more clearly. They spoke of Nicolas, she was certain.

" . . . reported it. Won't be any more trouble . . ."

They said goodbye, and Ruby heard footsteps coming toward her. She crouched lower in her hiding place. The footsteps moved steadily in the direction of the front door. She heard the door open and raised her head slightly, just in time to see the sheriff leave. She quickly slipped back to her room.

It seemed as if she'd just fallen asleep when she woke to a hand pressing on her throat and a blinding light shining in her eyes. She gasped for breath, her eyes widening, only to be seared with the painful light.

"Get up," a deep, raspy voice whispered.

She struggled to free herself from the man's hold. She started to scream, and the hand moved from her throat to her mouth.

Inhaling deeply through her nostrils, fighting for lost oxygen, she tried to comply with the intruder's demand.

"I said get up," he growled. The man pulled her to her feet with an effortless tug. He stood behind her, her head coming only to the middle of his chest. One of his hands covered her mouth, the other jabbed her in the back.

Something ripped, and before she knew it he'd secured tape over her mouth. What was happening? What was going on?

He held her arms hard, his fingers sinking into her biceps. A yelp came through her nose. His grip moved down to her wrists, and he bound them with the tape. She thrashed her body about, trying to wriggle out of his grasp. He covered her eyes with something and tied it behind her head, blindfolding her. She yelped again, and this time something hard smacked up against her ear, sending stars exploding in her head.

He shoved her, pushing her out of the room and down the hallway. A door creaked as he opened it. She faltered and balked, not trusting her legs without her sight, but he kept pushing. Cool air hit her bare legs, and she heard a car door open. She struggled against his grip and tried to get away, but he grabbed her around the waist, lifted her off her feet, and threw her into the car.

With a stifled cry, her nose smacked into the stiff vinyl seat. Where was he taking her? What would he do? Her mind buzzed with questions and images, like the static of a radio. Then the door slammed against her feet, jamming her kneecaps up into her thighs. She groaned.

The man's weight jostled the car when he got in. The engine started, and she was forced backward immediately as the tires bit into the dirt. Warm liquid—most likely blood—trickled down her nose and made breathing even more difficult. Her heart hammered in her chest, and she could feel the pulse of it racing in her ears. She couldn't move! She couldn't break free. The coolness of the air mixed with her fear, and her body flew into spasms she couldn't control. Even her eyes, pressed down hard by the blindfold, began to hurt. A rush of white stars filled the darkness.

The car jumped and jolted as it sped along. She imagined all sorts of horrible terrors that would come when the driver stopped. Would she be beaten? Raped? Killed? Who could be so threatened by her, or despise her so much, that they would do this?

She tried to slow her heart rate. She needed to focus, to pay attention to everything around her and listen for clues. She sensed there was only one other person in the car with her, but she couldn't be sure. The world had turned upside down without her vision.

After what felt like hours the car skidded to a halt, throwing her forward. She rolled onto her back and fell against the hump in the middle of the floorboard. Pain radiated from her spine, down through every limb. The back door opened, and powerful hands circled her arms and dragged her to the ground. She fell with a thud. She rolled to face the voice, not wanting him behind her.

"If you know what's good for you, you'll leave this village," the voice said. "If you can get out of here alive."

Ruby listened as the man's footsteps move farther and farther away from her. The car started then peeled out, grit and dust flying about and burning her face.

CHAPTER 16

D riving out to the dig site, Pete continued to think about his conversation with the sheriff in the café. He had a hard time believing that his father wanted him to carry out the legacy of the Brotherhood. His father hadn't spoken to him in two years. But why else would the sheriff tell him that? Perhaps the Brothers wanted to lift the shadow that had fallen on the Brotherhood and bring the Redeemers back to full unity. Tradition dictated that all males of a Redeemer family belong to the Brotherhood, just at different levels. The first level was that of the initiates or novices; the second was Brother of Light; the third, Brother of Blood; and the most revered and most esteemed rank, given only to one man every year, the chosen one —the Cristo.

Because his father and Ricardo were Redeemers, Pete's absence from the Brotherhood upset the balance.

This was the belief of the Brotherhood, of the entire community of Las Montanas, really. For months he'd been wondering why this sect of the Brotherhood held so much importance in the community. Perhaps the men of this sect, living in such a poor and provincial community, needed a sense of purpose. And that purpose was to sacrifice themselves for the sake of others. Or it could just be elitism of the highest order, like the KKK or the Nazis. Either way, he couldn't imagine himself "carrying out the legacy" of his brother and father.

Yet, to be accepted back into his family . . .

Whether he admitted it to others or not, he missed his family. If he explored the idea of joining the Brotherhood, perhaps he would be able to find out what happened to Ricardo and the other Cristos. He would have to show remorse and humility for shaming his family and the community, though—it's the only way they would accept him.

He turned off the road and headed toward the site, tapping his finger on the steering wheel, letting his thoughts organize themselves. In order to join the Brotherhood he'd have to undergo initiation, including the self-torturing rituals. He shook his head; he didn't think he could go through with it.

But he could take time off from the dig to investigate . . .

He pulled truck onto the site next to Yates' and went in search of the professor. Pete found him working in the burial site, placing slivers of material into glass jars.

"Good morning, Mr. Marshall." His voice sounded uncharacteristically chipper.

"Morning."

"Grab a few jars and give me a hand. I've found some fragments here. Not sure what they are yet, but they're fascinating."

"Dr. Yates, I need to speak with you." Pete hooked his thumbs in the belt loops of his jeans.

"I'm listening."

"I need to take some time off," he said. "There's some stuff I need to work out . . . Personal stuff."

The professor continued pulling fragments from the soil. "I see." He dropped a couple of slivers delicately into the glass jar. "This wouldn't have anything to do with your brother's death, would it?"

The question caught him off guard. Pete didn't know what to

say. "What do you mean, sir? That was two years ago." He'd never mentioned Ricardo to Dr. Yates before. How did he know?

"The brother you think was murdered by the Redeemers?"

Pete nodded, ran a hand through his hair.

Yates stood and pushed his hat back from his forehead. His steely gaze bored into Pete. "So, has the infamous Miss Delgado worked her magic on you, too, Pedro Medina?"

The hair on the back of Pete's neck bristled. He'd never told the professor his given name, either. "How did you—?" Pete asked.

"Pedro Alonzo Mercucio Medina." Yates drew out each syllable. He screwed the cap back onto the glass jar and dropped it into the pocket of his shirt. He pulled a cigar from the same pocket and rolled it between his lips. "It's a fine name. Why'd you change it? Everyone knows you did. Why shouldn't I? I know more than you think, Pedro. Much more." He clipped the end of his cigar, then lit it. The slow and methodical ritual had a hypnotizing effect.

"How much more?" Pete asked, suddenly feeling threatened.

"Enough to know that you'll never forgive yourself if you continue with your investigating."

"Dr. Yates, this is something I *have* to do. I can't go on not knowing."

Yates puffed on his cigar. "You may not like what you find, Pete. I'm speaking from experience." Grief, or perhaps regret, seemed to pull at his mouth, making him look older.

"Maybe not, but I can't go on like this. I have to stop the questions, find the answers. You obviously understand such a need."

Yates raised a brow. "Is Miss Delgado in on this quest with you?"

"No." Pete *had* told Ruby some of it, but not all. Not the most important stuff. At this point, she didn't know enough to put it all together.

"She's trouble, Pete," Yates said, his voice tight.

"I know."

He also knew that in the short time she'd been in Las Montanas, Ruby had uncovered secrets and skeletons, literally and figuratively, that people assumed had been hidden away forever. She had a way of getting to the meat of things; he could use that ability.

Yates shook his head. "Damn it, Pete, I wish you wouldn't. I wish you'd just leave it alone."

"I can't."

Yates puffed on his cigar, unscrewed the lid to a new glass jar, and then pulled his hat down farther on his head. "You know I dismissed her . . ."

"Yes."

Yates returned to his work.

"I'll see you in a couple of weeks, Dr. Yates."

Yates said nothing more.

Pete had just cut the supports out from under himself. Now, all he had was Ruby.

❦

Ruby tried to open her eyes before she remembered the blindfold. She had to get it off, but her arms were taped behind her back. She lay still, thinking, trying to piece together the events that had brought her to this moment. Finding only jumbled answers and more questions, she moved to something more productive: escape.

She rubbed her head against the hard earth until the blindfold loosened and she broke free. A rush of blood swept into her head when she opened her eyes, making her feel faint. She quickly closed them until the wooziness passed. When she opened them again, a jackrabbit the size of a small dog was standing a few feet away from her. He rested his weight on powerful back haunches and held his small front legs close to his chest. His nose twitched rapidly, no doubt catching her scent.

Sitting up with a groan, she frightened the creature away. Next to her head lay the red bandana. Her abductor had used her own sacred relic to blindfold her. She winced at the irony.

The sun hadn't yet peeked over the horizon, but the glow made it possible to see. Damn, when would her head stop spinning?

She took a mental inventory. Part of her face, next to her right eye, felt dry and tight. The tape at her wrists cut into her skin, and she'd lost all feeling up to her shoulders. Her back ached from the way she'd slept, crumpled over on her side. And her mouth felt tight, too, immobilized, and she remembered the sound of duct tape being ripped from its roll.

Who'd done this to her? Dragged her out in the middle of the night and left her somewhere in the desert, tied, and gagged, and dressed only in her t-shirt and shorts? She tried to picture the man's face, but she hadn't seen him. She sensed he was large but she couldn't be sure, and he'd worn an astringent cologne. Plus, there'd been something familiar about his voice—a cadence or a rasp.

Her thoughts went back to how to free her hands. She struggled to her feet, then looked for a sharp rock to tear the tape. A large piece of oil-black obsidian nestled against some larger rocks. Crouching, she scooted closer and began to rub the tape against it. If she could manage a little tear, she'd be able to rip the rest apart.

After she sawed it against the rock a couple of times the tape gave, and she pulled and wiggled until she could separate her hands. Pain shot through her arms as the blood eagerly rushed back into them. Slowly, she eased the duct tape from her mouth.

Now that her limbs and mouth were free, survival mode gave way to anger. "That son of a bitch!"

"If you know what's good for you, you'll leave this village."

She rubbed her arms and stretched her legs and cramping feet as she looked to the horizon. *Where the hell am I?*

She started to walk. From the position of the sun she guessed it was around noon, maybe a bit earlier. Her bare feet gave her no mercy as she picked her way around rocks and prickly brush and weeds. Her throat felt parched, her tongue swollen, and her stomach ached from hunger.

Sometime later, numb from the hypnotic monotony of step after step after damned step, Ruby's head spun. Her tongue felt so thick, she feared she'd suffocate.

The sky whirled above her, and clouds dashed by. She stopped, resting for a moment—just a moment. *Pete.* She had to get to Pete. He'd help her.

Holding her hand over her eyes, she scanned the landscape. To her left, she saw the village in the distance. Shaking with relief, she moved forward. She just had to make it to Pete's house —Pete's cool, shadowed house.

She stumbled and fell to one knee as the horizon dipped and swayed in front of her.

She pushed herself upright, panting, crying. She took one step, then another.

If only she could get to Pete.

CHAPTER 17

"Ruby?" The voice was familiar. She blinked.

"Pete?"

"Thank God you're all right," he said, his voice rough with emotion.

"Where am—" She struggled to sit up and Pete helped her, propping pillows behind her back.

Pete's house. She'd made it to Pete's house. She lay on the Taos bed under an open window. "But how . . . ?"

"I found you at my gate," he explained. "What happened?"

"Oh, Pete." She started to cry. He wrapped his arms around her.

"You're okay, Ruby. I'm here now. But we need to get you back to the rectory. It'll be more comfortable for you there, and Rosita can take care of you."

She nodded, and closed her eyes, feeling safe in his arms. Nothing else mattered.

Not long later, they arrived at the rectory. Rosita immediately called Dr. Mendenhall, who came over to examine her.

"She'll be fine," he said to Rosita and Father Martinez, as if she weren't there. "She's dehydrated, has a few bruises, and her feet will be very sore for a while. Make sure she gets plenty of water, and I want her on bedrest for at least two days."

"*Sí, sí.*" Rosita nodded.

Father Martinez led the doctor out of the bedroom, and Rosita fussed over Ruby's bruises and raw feet. "Ah, what you must have been through," she said, clucking her tongue against her teeth. The housekeeper wrapped her plump, motherly arms around Ruby, and she welcomed the warmth. "But you must stop this, Ruby. You must go home." Rosita's voice was firm.

Ruby pulled back. "What do you mean?"

"It's too dangerous. You could have been killed. Please, go back to your *familia.*"

"Do you know what's been going on?" She grabbed Rosita's hands. "People are being murdered." She met the older woman's gaze. "I was kidnapped in my sleep, from this very bed."

Rosita freed her hands, stood, and turned her back to Ruby. The hand-wringing started again. "This is too dangerous for a young woman to be involved in. Please, do as I say," she begged.

"I can't," Ruby said flatly. "Especially now."

"Please, if you trust me, go home." She whirled to look at Ruby, her face tight, her eyes wide. "These people are not to be angered."

Ruby raised an eyebrow. *These people?*

"Who? Who are these people, Rosita? The Redeemers?"

"Just listen to the words of a wise old woman. It is best."

"What do you know?"

"Know?" Rosita's eyes lit with fear. "I know nothing. Only to mind my own business. You should do the same."

"What is it, Rosita?" Ruby asked, almost pleading. "Tell me."

Without looking back, the housekeeper walked out of the room, leaving Ruby alone and without answers.

Enrique Martinez stepped outside and walked down the main road of Las Montanas. Several people waved or nodded their greetings, but he didn't respond. His mind was too heavy with thoughts of Ruby and her current condition.

He hadn't meant for her to be harmed. She could have died in the desert, and then he'd have the blood of yet another person oozing its stain upon his soul. He'd only wanted to scare her, to make her leave Las Montanas. But the woman had no intention of leaving. Harming her only made her want to stay. He'd made a grievous error.

He'd only wanted to help the village. Five years ago, when he'd arrived in Las Montanas as a new priest, he'd come upon a community that had such abundant faith but no focus. No cohesion, no organization. The Brotherhood, though not sanctioned by the church, was floundering. As a priest, he could not condone their practice. But as he got to know its members, he realized that their teachings, their rituals, gave meaning to their faith.

The church of St. Mary Magdalene, too, had become lost without the guidance of the archdiocese. Father Alvarez had been ambivalent in his leadership. He had not kept contact with the bishop, and the bishop had other problems to deal with in Albuquerque and Santa Fe. Las Montanas had been forgotten.

It hadn't mattered. Father Martinez did not need the umbrella of doctrine and dogma of the Catholic Church. He could create his own church, and he had. Yet now, he felt he'd lost control of his followers. He'd lost control of himself.

The intensity with which the Brotherhood now practiced was beautiful and glorious, but some of the Brothers, like Gallegos, had started to take matters into their own hands. The passion that he, as parish priest, had encouraged in the faithful gained strength and power. But these days, that passion sometimes seemed like a dark, greedy giant. Like the impassioned scientist who'd created the atomic bomb, Martinez had created a demon that could not be stopped. For this, he was guilty. For this, he must be redeemed. If he repented with more dedication, perhaps he would be cleansed of his wrongdoing. Perhaps God would look on him with favor.

The Brotherhood had flourished under his guidance, but now it had turned into something else, something—dare he think—evil? Like beautiful vines smothering a once-serene garden. He could not blame anyone but himself. He hadn't cut and pruned where he should have. And now the Brotherhood was all he had left. All because of that Delgado woman.

He knelt to pray. Because of Ruby Delgado and her intrusion the archbishop had sent his people, his investigators, down to Las Montanas and they had uncovered his secret—that he had defied the Church and joined the Brotherhood. For this, he would be excommunicated. He could no longer live at the rectory. He would have to move. And soon. But nothing could make him leave the Brotherhood. His people needed him. He would make up a legitimate reason for his termination. The Church would not tell; they didn't like to admit their mistakes. And it *had* been their mistake. *They* had been negligent of the community of Las Montanas.

But he didn't need a title or official sanction to do his work. His work had made a name for itself. The people would not abandon him, would they? He looked at the scar of the cross he'd carved into his palm and remembered the pain. In that pain, he'd been redeemed. He'd paid the price for sins committed.

What would it take to absolve him of his blackest sin, of creating a demon out of the love of his faith?

⚜

"You look good . . . considering," Pete said as he placed a chair next to Ruby's bed and sat down. He leaned forward, his elbows on his thighs.

"Thanks, I guess." She took the glass of cold water he offered her and drank it down.

"Do you have any idea who did this to you?" he asked.

She shook her head. "Seems you might know, though."

His eyes fixed on hers, their mellow hue pulling her in despite her attempt to be unaffected. She needed more information from him and she wouldn't be pushed aside again, not even by his enticing eyes and tender care.

"What do you mean, I might know?" he asked.

"You keep doling out information to me in bite-sized pieces. If you had just come out and told me about the Redeemers and their burial place when I found those bodies, none of this would have happened."

Pete pulled his weight back so that he was sitting upright again, a cloud of confusion sweeping his features. "You're blaming me?"

"No," she clarified. "But I would have at least been able to watch my back, been on guard."

"I *told* you that you were in danger, that you knew too much. Did you think I was kidding? You got off lucky!"

"You think they would have killed me?"

He pursed his lips. "Didn't someone try to bury you alive out there in the sinkhole?"

Putting her hands to her face, she sighed. She didn't know if she had the strength to continue with this mess.

"Maybe you should just go home. This is too much," Pete said.

"No."

"But look at you. You don't need to be mixed up in any of this. You just happen to be the unfortunate person who landed on those bodies."

She sat up straighter and adjusted the pillows. "Pete, I've run from my problems for the past four years, and the running stops now. For some ungodly, bizarre, insane reason, I found those bodies. Now my life is in danger. If there is a God—and believe me, I have my doubts—He's put me here for a reason. Me, Ruby Delgado. Maybe this is my punishment, my penance; I don't know. But I am *not* running. I'm going to stay here and get to the bottom of this, and you're going to tell me everything. No more secrets."

He leaned forward again. "What about your scholarship?"

"I'm going to call UNM today and see what I can do. For now, I want you to tell me what the hell's going on."

"You're amazing." He smiled at her. "Beautiful, feisty, and the most bull-headed woman I've ever met."

Did he just say she was beautiful? She smiled back.

"All right, all right," he said, throwing his hands up in the air. "You win. I'll tell you everything."

"Thank you," she said, shifting to get more comfortable.

"I guess I'll just start from the first thing I remember . . ."

She nodded. He closed his eyes and took a deep breath. When he opened them again, there was a steely determination in his gaze.

"Ricardo joined the Brotherhood when he was sixteen," he began. "I begged him not to. At the time, I didn't know much about the Redeemers. I saw my father come home bloody and exhausted. I didn't want that happening to Ricardo. Besides, he would be spending all his free time at the morada and not with me."

"But he joined anyway," she said.

"Yes. It had been done in my family for generations. It was expected, really. My father was so proud that his favorite son would follow in the tradition. For years, Ricardo did his religious duty, and then one day they announced he would be Cristo."

"How did your father feel about that?"

"Honored. So did Ricardo."

"And you?" she asked, her voice gentle.

"Scared." Pete's eyes began to tear, but he blinked them away.

She nodded slowly. "You knew he might die."

He nodded. "In the past, Cristos rarely died from the crucifixion. The worst thing that would happen is that they would pass out from a lack of oxygen."

"Because they were tied to the cross with ropes?" Ruby asked.

"Right. But in the past five years, the Brotherhood decided to use spikes. That's when Cristos started dying. My brother was the third, two years ago."

"Who was the Cristo on the fourth year?" she asked.

"A guy by the name of Eddie Cordova. He also died."

"And this year it's Nicolas Baca," Ruby said. "Easter is only two weeks away . . ."

Pete nodded, leaning back to lift the chair's front legs off the floor. He teetered back and forth.

Ruby pushed the covers off and crossed her legs. "Painful as it is, nails, or spikes, wouldn't necessarily kill a man."

"Right," said Pete. "I raised such a stink, there was an autopsy done on Ricardo. The local press got wind of it, and that's how the investigation started."

"What happened with the investigation?" she asked.

"Nothing. They supposedly didn't find anything. Traces of some 'natural substance,'" he made quotation marks in the air with his fingers, "—were found in his system. No one looked into what that substance might be, though. It was probably the pulque."

"What's that?" Ruby asked.

"A drink the Redeemers make to see visions—you know, all that crap."

"A hallucinogen, then," Ruby said. "Could it be deadly? Poisonous?"

"I don't know. I suppose if you drank too much . . ."

"What's in it?"

"Peyote, other stuff." He shrugged. "Anyway, because of the lack of evidence from the autopsy the press lost interest. The case was closed indefinitely."

"But you didn't stop." Ruby frowned, realizing how alone Pete probably felt.

"No, I stopped," he said, his voice sad. "I'd disgraced my family enough."

"But didn't your family question Ricardo's death? And what about the other families?"

Pete set the chair back down on all fours, placing his hands on his thighs. "To die as a Cristo is a great honor. It assures a place for the family in Heaven, next to God. In the Brotherhood, a family's grief is outlived by their glory."

CHAPTER 18

The following day, Ruby felt well enough to get out of bed. After pulling on jeans and a T-shirt, she shuffled out to the living room to call her advisor at the university, Dr. Stone. She left a detailed message with his secretary in regard to her difficulties with Yates and his throwing her off the project. She hung up the phone, already anxious for Dr. Stone to call her back. If Yates had pulled rank, she didn't have a prayer. She'd have to head back to Los Caballos and the mundane life that came with running her parents' business, the Hop Stop Motel. The thought of returning to where she'd worked for more than half her life made her palms sweat.

She headed into the kitchen where Rosita stood at the sink, washing dishes. "Morning," Ruby greeted her.

Rosita nodded, not looking at her.

"Can I help you with that?"

Rosita turned to face Ruby with tear-stained cheeks and red, swollen eyes.

"What is it, Rosita?"

"He's gone," she said on a sob.

"Who? Who's gone?" Ruby asked.

"Padre. They made him go away."

Ruby tilted her head, confused. "Who made Father Martinez go away?"

Rosita turned to Ruby, betrayal in her eyes. "The archbishop and his people. They say Father Martinez is not a priest."

Ruby shook her head. "I don't understand." She did remember he'd been in street clothes the last time she'd seen him, though.

"They say that before he came to Las Montanas, he forged papers from the archbishop—his ordination papers."

Ruby went to the kitchen table and sat down, trying to process this information. "Where did he go?"

"He's going to live in the village," Rosita explained. "The people won't turn him away."

"He plans to stay in Las Montanas?"

The woman's brow furrowed. "Of course. This is his home. He is loved here. Why would he leave?"

Ruby shrugged. Wouldn't he want to run from his deception, just as she'd wanted to run from her failures? She didn't dare ask such a thing, though. Instead, she asked, "What's going to happen? With the church, I mean?"

"The old, retired priest, Father Alvarez, will take his place." Rosita stared out the kitchen window, her arms resting on the lip of the sink, her shoulders slumped.

"Is there anything I can do to help?" Ruby asked.

"No. No, you need your rest."

"Rosita, I'm feeling much better, really. Let me do something. Please," she nearly begged. "I feel as if I shouldn't even be here."

"You *shouldn't* be here in Las Montanas, but I know you are determined to stay." Rosita frowned. "Now that Father Martinez is gone I'd like the company, though. I'll give you work if it makes you feel better."

Ruby smiled. "It would."

Rosita wiped her tear-stained face with the dish towel, then turned to Ruby. "Father Alvarez needs help cleaning his place before he packs and moves in here. I told him I'd help him, but I want the rectory to look perfect when he arrives. If you wanted to help, you could clean his house."

Cleaning? Probably one of the things in life she did worst and liked even less. But she'd asked for it. "Sure. When do you want me to go?"

"Today. Now."

"Oh. Well then, point me in the right direction," she said with a smile, then was on her way.

When she arrived at Father Alvarez's house, he seemed more than pleased to see her. He grabbed her arm gently with a feeble hand and practically pulled her inside. She explained that she had been sent by Rosita to clean, but he shushed her and persuaded her to sit in a chair in the drawing room while he made tea.

He soon returned with two cups of steaming tea and a plate of biscochitos, delicious anise-and-cinnamon sugar cookies. He told her that *Señora* Garcia at the bookstore had made them for him.

"How are things going at the excavation site?" he asked.

"Well, uh . . . things didn't quite work out for me there," she admitted, her cheeks flaring with heat. "I'm staying at the rectory until I get instructions from the university. That's why I came to clean for you today: I'm helping Rosita in exchange for my board. And I really need to get started. I shouldn't be sitting here eating your cookies."

"Nonsense. You are my guest, and you will have tea with an old man if the old man pleases." He smiled widely at her, gaps showing at the back of his mouth where molars had once been.

Perhaps she should take this opportunity to learn more about Martinez and his dismissal by the Church.

"Father, this is very awkward, but—" She searched for the best words, wondering if she should even risk asking the question. "What do you think of this business with Fa— uh, Martinez?"

"Forging papers is a grave matter."

"But what will the Church tell the community?"

Father Alvarez ran his finger across one of his cookies. "Probably nothing. They will want to keep this quiet." He paused for a moment and sipped his tea. "Enrique Martinez has a strong faith. The people admire him as their spiritual leader."

"What do *you* think of him?" she asked.

"I've had my concerns."

"What do you mean?"

The priest offered Ruby another cookie and ate one himself. Ruby remained quiet, hoping he would answer her question.

"He's become obsessive about his faith and his followers. I know that sounds strange for a priest to say, but we are merely spiritual guides; not authorities to be revered and awed. We are servants. It's my opinion that Enrique Martinez lost sight of this. As I said, he is well-liked in the community. It's difficult to be aware of the power we hold, and yet not exercise that power." He looked directly into her eyes. "Why do you ask?"

Did she dare go further? Were the two men friends? Did they speak often? Would he tell Martinez of their conversation?

She tried to tamp down the questions in her mind and blurted out her biggest question. "Do you think he's involved with the Redeemers?"

Father Alvarez shook his head. "It's not impossible. Yet there has never been a priest associated with the secret society."

"But he's not a priest," Ruby reminded him.

"Yes, but still, the Brotherhood did not know this. I wouldn't have thought they would accept a priest."

"These Redeemers claim to do penance for the sake of others," she said. "And the last four Cristos in the last four years have died, Father Alvarez. They gave the ultimate penance."

He nodded. "*Sí.*"

"But can't you do something about it? Can you report this to the church?" she asked.

Father Alvarez shook his head. "It is for the authorities to handle. It is not a Church matter. These people have practiced this for centuries. It's not spoken of in the community, and it would do no good for you, or me, or anyone outside the Brotherhood to intervene. As a priest I must set the example, help people see God's love. I am but God's instrument to serve His people. I believe the Brotherhood will eventually stop their extreme practices. We must have faith. You must pray for them, Ruby, as I do. That's all we can do."

Ruby sighed, leaning back in the chair. She thought about the priest's words. Yates had tried to say the same thing, but in a completely different way. And Yates had an ulterior motive for getting her off the trail and out of Las Montanas: he didn't want her to dull his shine with her tiny bit of fame. Alvarez sounded sincere, and she believed he could help the community.

"Thank you, Father. Well, I'd better get to work."

The priest swatted the air. "Nonsense. I'll tell Rosita that you did a fine job."

She grinned. "Father, you would lie?"

"It is not a lie. You did a fine job of keeping me company. I've enjoyed our conversation and look forward to another one sometime."

"You'll be at the rectory soon?" she asked.

He chuckled. "I'm in no hurry to move, but yes, I will move to the rectory in the next few weeks."

"Well," Ruby slapped her thighs. "I'll be back to help you clean when you are ready. And, next time, you'd better let me do my job. I would hate to wear out my welcome at the rectory," she said.

"*Gracias*. And next time, I won't keep you from your duties."

Ruby stood, grateful he hadn't wanted her to clean. Her muscles and limbs still ached. She said goodbye and left him watching her from the doorway.

Ruby took the time on the short walk back to the rectory to sort out the jumble in her mind and loosen the knots in her muscles. She thought about the dead Cristos. Pete had said that Ricardo's body had been autopsied. She needed to find out more about the autopsy. And a coroner would be a good person to ask if pulque, the ceremonial drink, could cause death; maybe even give them insight into what else could've been the culprit.

Ruby had plenty to keep her occupied while she waited for Dr. Stone and the university to get back to her. It would drive her mad to idle away, waiting on the phone call that would inform her if she could pursue her dreams or if she had to go back to the mundane life of the Hop Stop Motel.

When she arrived at the rectory, she saw Pete's empty truck parked out front.

She walked inside to see Pete sitting on the sofa, eating biscochitos and drinking a Coke.

"Hey," he said, looking up. "Where have you been?"

"Father Alvarez's house. I asked Rosita how I could help her and she sent me to his house to clean for him."

The phone rang then, and Rosita walked into the room to answer it. Ruby motioned that she would do it and she hurried over, hoping Dr. Stone would be on the other end of the line. He was. After a brief conversation with him, she hung up the phone.

"What was that all about?" Pete shoved the last of the cookie into his mouth.

"I put a call in to the university to see if I could get my scholarship back."

"And?" he asked through his cookie-filled mouth.

Ruby shrugged. "Don't know yet. Dr. Stone said Yates doesn't have the authority to revoke my scholarship, so I may be able to resume my education in Albuquerque. He said he is working on it."

"That's good news." Pete's gazed flicked from hers to the can of Coke he held in his hand. Ruby couldn't tell if he seemed relieved or disappointed that she was going to stay, at least for a while.

"By the way," she continued, "I learned something interesting today." She peeked into the hallway to see if anyone was nearby. They were alone, but she didn't feel comfortable talking about

Martinez with the possibility of Rosita overhearing. "Let's go outside a minute." She walked past him to the front door.

He followed and closed the door behind them.

"Martinez isn't a priest," she whispered. "When the archbishop sent his people to investigate the Stigmata, they found out Martinez was an imposter. He had forged papers from the archbishop."

Pete looked stunned. "Where did he go? Did he leave town?"

"I don't think he plans to. According to Rosita, it doesn't matter to his followers whether he's a priest or not. Plus, Father Alvarez said something about the Church keeping quiet about it. Something about not wanting to admit they'd been mistaken about him, or negligent in checking him out. The archbishop and his people left without a word."

"They don't want to admit a scandal, I guess," Pete said, putting his hands in his pockets.

"Rosita said that Las Montanas had been forgotten—actually, *forsaken* was the word she used—by the Church. Perhaps they feel responsible."

"And as far as the Church goes, no harm done." Pete added.

"If they only knew . . ."

He sighed. "Unfortunately, nothing can be proven."

Ruby raised her eyebrows, challenging him. "Not yet."

"How do you think we're going to change that exactly?"

"I'm not completely sure, but I'm going to start by calling the coroner's office and see if I can get information on Ricardo's autopsy. Maybe ask a few additional questions, too," she said.

"I'm one step ahead of you. I tried calling a little while ago, but they won't give information over the phone. I have to drive to Los Campos, to the hospital. Wanna come?"

"Of course," Ruby said. "But what about Yates? Doesn't he expect you back at the site?"

Pete set his Coke down. "I asked for a little time off. If I know Yates, he'll have another crew out there within twenty-four hours. There's a whole slew of students who'd give their left arm to work under him. So I'm not concerned about the dig."

Ruby bit her lip. Students *would* give their left arm, and she'd blown her chances. Dr. Stone had told her that upsetting John Yates was basically giving her career a death sentence, but he'd see what he could do. Her mood threatened to sink, but then she felt Pete's fingertips on the underside of her chin.

"You okay?" His eyes met hers, and the depth of his sincerity sent a bolt of anxiety through her. She felt vulnerable, like a raw nerve. She couldn't let him see her weakness.

"Fine. When do you want to go?" she asked.

"Now."

"Great. Let me get my backpack."

CHAPTER 19

After eighty-five miles on the road with nothing to look at but clumps of native grass and an endless stretch of clear, blue sky, the growing number of billboards indicated their approach toward civilization. Buildings began to appear next, and Pete's truck pulled into the parking lot of the Los Campos Hospital. Ruby pointed to a sign directing them to the coroner's office. It was in the basement, probably the morgue.

They entered a dark, redwood-paneled room to find the reception desk empty. Diplomas hung on the walls, and a plush couch and leather armchair faced the desk. A swinging door stood to the left of the desk. Ruby walked through it, and Pete followed her down the long, sterile hallway with yellowed linoleum floors and glaring fluorescent lights. At the end of the hallway was a single door with a small sign that read "Coroner's Office, Authorized Personnel Only" hanging on it.

"Down there," she whispered. "Do you remember the man's name?"

"Dr. Perez, I think," he said.

They stepped through the door into a large, much colder room with the same austere linoleum and buzzing florescent lights. It smelled of disinfectant and formaldehyde. A petite woman in a lab coat with a blond beehive hairdo and cat-eye glasses sat at metal desk, her head bent over a pile of paperwork.

She looked up when she'd finished scrawling something on a pad of paper and tossed her pen down. "Yes?" she said, her voice sharp.

"We're looking for Dr. Perez," Ruby said.

The woman shot them a suspicious look. "Do you have authorization to be down here?"

"Is Dr. Perez here?" Pete repeated.

"Dr. Perez is deceased. I'm Dr. Madeline Jones. Now what is it that I can do for you?" Her eyes narrowed behind the upward sloping frame of her glasses.

"He's dead?" Ruby asked, surprised, but not as surprised as she probably should have been.

Dr. Jones nodded. "Yes."

"He did an autopsy on my brother," Pete said, stepping forward, "and we wanted to speak with him about it."

"Oh." Dr. Jones's voiced softened. "I'm sorry for your loss."

"Would you still have the report on file?" Ruby asked.

"We should if your brother died within the last five years," Dr. Jones explained.

Pete nodded. "He did."

She frowned. "Regardless, I'm afraid I can't show you the report unless the authorities request it. It's confidential information."

Ruby could feel Pete's disappointment reverberating off him in waves.

"Is there any way you could make an exception?" Ruby asked. "It's important."

"I'm sorry, no," Dr. Jones said.

Pete turned to walk away, but Ruby was not going to leave without pulling out all the stops. They hadn't driven ninety miles across the hot desert for nothing. "It's a matter of life and death," she said.

Dr. Jones held her gaze. "Have you discussed this with the police?"

"We can't," Ruby said with a shake of her head.

"Forget it, Ruby. Let's go," said Pete.

"Why can't you go to the police?" the doctor asked.

"It's a long story, but we can't go to the police—not yet. We think Pete's brother was murdered, but we don't have solid evidence. We thought the autopsy report might help."

Dr. Jones nodded. "If he was murdered, surely it would have shown up in the autopsy."

"That's what we were thinking, too," Ruby agreed, "but at the time they told Pete nothing in the report indicated murder. The police closed the case."

"Clearly, there wasn't enough evidence," Dr. Jones said. "How long ago was this?"

He swallowed loudly. "Two years."

"Hmm," she said. "It would take new evidence to reopen the case for investigation. You really ought to go to the authorities."

"Look, we said we can't." Pete's words came out clipped. "The police won't be cooperative. Believe me, I've tried. The Cristos will just keep dying if no one does anything about it."

Dr. Jones's eyes grew wide. "Did you say *the Cristos*?"

"Yes," Ruby said.

"You mean a Redeemer?" the doctor confirmed.

Pete nodded.

Dr. Jones tapped her pencil on the palm of her hand and looked from Pete to Ruby and then back to Pete. "What was it you said about the Cristos dying?"

"In Las Montanas, four have already died—one in each of the last four years. They've died very quickly, too, within minutes of being hung on the cross. My brother was the third to die."

Compassion filled the doctor's gaze. "Please, sit down." She indicated the chairs lined up against the walls.

"Look, we really don't have time," Pete said. "If you can't help us—"

"I don't know if I can, but if you tell me your story I'll see what I can do."

Amazed at her sudden change of heart Ruby grabbed one of the chairs that had been leaning against the wall, brought it over to the desk, and sat down. Pete remained standing.

"Why are you suddenly so interested?" Pete asked. "A few minutes ago, you looked ready to throw us out of here. What do you know about the Redeemers?"

"My college roommate was from Pueblo, Colorado. Her brother belonged to the Redeemers," she explained. "I'm more than interested."

"You mean, there are Redeemers elsewhere?" Ruby asked.

"They're all over the Southwest, mostly in remote areas."

"You say you're 'more than interested'," Pete repeated. "Interested enough to show us the report?"

The coroner tapped her fingers on the desk then crossed her arms, her body language making it clear that she knew she shouldn't continue this conversation, yet felt compelled to do so for some reason. "That I can't say for sure. Why don't you tell me what's going on and we'll see."

Pete looked over at Ruby and raised his eyebrows. She smiled at this small victory. He took a chair from the wall and sat next to her.

When he finished telling the story of Ricardo, the other Cristos, and the change in the ritual practices of the Redeemers in the past few years, Dr. Jones sat silent, taking it in.

"I can understand why you'd want to see the report," she said.

"And I can understand why you'd want to see it, too," Pete said with a smile. "Those men shouldn't have died so quickly, if at all."

"It doesn't make much sense," she agreed. "You say they started using spikes instead of ropes after the first Cristo died four years ago?"

Pete nodded.

"Dr. Jones, could they have bled to death?" Ruby asked.

She thought for a moment. "It's not impossible, but highly unlikely."

"What about tetanus? From the spikes, maybe?" Ruby tried again.

"Again, it's possible, but tetanus takes much longer to set in. Getting back to the spikes . . . If they used spikes, obviously the pain is severe. Do they use any sort of anesthetic? Something to ease the pain?"

"Pulque," Pete said.

"Never heard of it. What's in it?"

He shrugged. "I'm not sure. Peyote probably."

"Hmm." Dr. Jones adjusted her glasses. "Perhaps too much of the drug was administered and the Cristos overdosed?"

"Are you saying the deaths could have been accidental?" Ruby asked.

"Certainly. I'm assuming this pulque is some sort of home-made substance, and I'm sure most people wouldn't have much knowledge of chemistry or pharmaceuticals," Dr. Jones said. "I don't think it's wise to jump to the conclusion of murder until you examine all the possibilities."

Ruby had to agree with her, but they'd come for a specific reason.

"You're right, Dr. Jones. Perhaps we are jumping to conclu-sions, but will you show us Ricardo's autopsy report? We've driven nearly a hundred miles to be here."

The doctor tapped her pink fingernails on the desk and looked at her watch. The hesitation was a good sign.

"You really should speak with the police about this," the doctor tried again.

"We've explained to you why we can't do that. Not until we're sure," Pete said.

"Please, Dr. Jones," Ruby asked again.

Dr. Jones worried her lip. "I could lose my job."

Pete shook his head in frustration, stood, and walked toward the door. Ruby watched Dr. Jones's gaze follow him, then met hers. Ruby tried to keep her expression neutral.

"All right," Dr. Jones said with a sigh.

Pete turned to look at both the doctor and Ruby. "Are you sure?" he asked, leaving the coroner room to back out.

She nodded. "Just make sure no one's coming down the hall and then lock the door with the dead bolt."

That sounded like she was pretty sure to Ruby.

Pete did as the doctor directed and returned to the table. Ruby gave him a hopeful smile, but he didn't return it. His face had gone pale, his jaw flexing.

"I can't show you the report," Dr. Jones said, "but I can tell you what it says."

Pete sat down again. "Thank you," he said.

The doctor cleared her throat. "What was your brother's name, and when did he die?"

Pete gave her the particulars, and she disappeared through a doorway. He leaned back in the chair, hands folded in his lap, staring straight ahead—his face void of expression.

Ruby closed her eyes, hoping Dr. Jones would come back with some real evidence.

Seconds later, she returned. "I found it."

Pete looked over at Ruby, anticipation and fear in his eyes. She couldn't imagine what it felt like to relive Ricardo's death like this after so long. She thought of her son, of doing the same, and her stomach caved in on itself. She pushed the image away.

"There are two very interesting findings in the report. First of all, there were a number of natural substances in his bloodstream—traces of peyote and other desert vegetation known to be used in hallucinogenic mixtures. I'm assuming this is the pulque, but I can't be sure." Dr. Jones looked up at him. "Did your brother use drugs recreationally?"

He shook his head vehemently. "Never. He'd occasionally have a beer, but that was it."

The doctor frowned.

"What else?" Pete asked.

Dr. Jones met his gaze, hesitating. "Your brother showed signs of pneumonic plague. Do you recall if he was ill before the crucifixion?"

Ruby's thoughts were racing, piecing together the information, as Pete responded. "I didn't see Ricardo for two weeks before the crucifixion. They aren't allowed to see friends or family. They need to focus, pray, repent."

"I see," Dr. Jones said.

Then it hit Ruby. "What's *pneumonic* plague?" she asked, her voice cracking slightly.

"It's a disease that attacks the upper respiratory tract. The lungs fill with fluid."

Ruby clenched her jaw and looked at Pete. "Sound familiar?"

His eyes widened.

"What is it?" Dr. Jones asked.

"There's been a virus going around Las Montanas, but it's pretty new," Pete explained. "It wasn't around when Ricardo died. Although," he said, as if remembering something, "there were a few people who were sick around that time. Of course, no one knew why or what from. Many attributed the illness to evil spirits, possessions, or punishment for sin. My people are very superstitious."

"You seem fairly knowledgeable," said Dr. Jones.

Pete shrugged.

"What I'm saying, Pete," she continued, "is that even if Ricardo survived the crucifixion, he probably wouldn't have made it through the illness."

Shock swept over his face. "You mean, he would have died anyway?"

"I'm sorry, but yes," she confirmed.

Pete sank back into the chair, into the silence of the room.

"Chances are," Dr. Jones went on, "the strain from the crucifixion just added to the stress on his system, accelerating his death. He would have been in a severely weakened condition with pneumonic plague. There's no way he would have been able to withstand that kind of physical and emotional stress."

Pete sighed, running his hands through his hair. He and Ruby shared a look, his eyes searching hers, and then he excused himself and walked out of the room.

"He doesn't mean to be rude," Ruby said.

Dr. Jones gave her a sad smile. "I completely understand."

"Thanks for your help. For taking the risk."

"Certainly. If you can find out exactly what that pulque is made of, I might be able to get more information for you," the doctor added. "Maybe we can stop this from happening again."

Ruby nodded. "Thanks. I'll see what I can find out."

"Say goodbye to your friend for me," Dr. Jones said.

Ruby gave her a small wave, then headed after Pete. She caught up to him, and they walked out of the hospital toward the setting of the sun. They got in the car without a word, and Pete drove them to a nearby diner.

Neither one of them spoke after ordering their meals. The sounds of flatware clinking and people talking and laughing in the crowded restaurant highlighted the awkward silence. Pete just stared outside into the darkness of the parking lot, and Ruby fidgeted with her spoon.

"I'm sorry," she said eventually. "That must have been hard for you to hear."

Pete moved the food around on his plate. "He would have died anyway." He shook his head.

"The information might help us yet," Ruby said.

"I don't follow."

"It would be interesting to see if the other Cristos had some sort of illness before they died. Perhaps that's how they're chosen. They're already ill, so to the Brotherhood and to the villagers, it looks as if they died for the glory of God."

"Sounds pretty coincidental."

"Pneumonic plague sounds an awful lot like this virus that's been going around here lately," she said. "We need to look at all the options Dr. Jones laid out."

Pete blew out a soft whistle. The look in his eyes showed he was unconvinced.

She ignored it and continued. "We also need to work on the *who*, now that the *how* is in motion."

He shook his head. "What would be the point? Ricardo's dead either way."

Ruby leveled her gaze at him. "Nicolas Baca is the point. Everyone who might come after him is the point. We *need* to find out what's going on. If Ricardo had been treated, he might have made it. We have to give Nicolas the same opportunity. The way I see it, there are several things that need to be done." She absently tapped the handle of her knife against the table. "One: we need to discover what's in the pulque. Two: we need to find out if any other Cristo had a life-threatening disease or some kind of virus. Three: we also need to know more about the Redeemers." Her mind was going a thousand miles per hour now. "Have you told me everything you know?"

"Everything," he said with a wave of his hand.

"So how do we learn more?"

"It won't be easy. We'd probably have to get inside their operation, gain their trust and confidence."

"Do you think that maybe your fath—"

"Don't even think it, Ruby."

She sighed. Now it was her turn to push the food around on her plate. She couldn't stop thinking about Nicolas Baca and the fact that he could die as the next Cristo if they didn't find out what was going on, and fast. But she'd already caused such turmoil. She'd had no right to come in and turn everything upside down. She almost wished she had heeded Pete's advice and had not mentioned the bodies—or better yet, hadn't dug outside of her assigned grid in the first place and tumbled in on all those bodies. Because now even Pete was suffering. Possibly more than he had been already. His wounds had been reopened.

She was creating hell for so many people. But with the information she had, she had to keep going. To find the truth.

The ride back to the rectory was filled with more silence. When they finally arrived, Ruby asked Pete if he wanted to come in for coffee. He nodded, and they went inside.

Rosita greeted them with a plate of warm cookies. Just as they were about to eat, Rosita answered the phone and came to get Ruby. It was Dr. Stone from the university.

"I have good news, Ruby," he said, sounding cheerful. "I spoke with the scholarship committee today. They said you could come back to Albuquerque and start classes."

"Oh," she said, hoping he didn't hear the disappointment in her voice. "When?"

"Immediately. As soon as you can get here."

That meant she would have to leave Las Montanas, leave Nicolas and Pete.

"There's a catch, Ruby." Dr. Stone added, his voice now solemn.

"Yes?"

"We can't do anything to jeopardize our relationship with Dr. Yates. He's too important to the program, and he has stated that he will not work with you. I'm afraid we will have to ban you from doing fieldwork in the Southwest for the next four years."

His words felt like a punch in the stomach.

"I'm sorry," he went on, "but it's the best I can do."

"I understand, and I appreciate it." Her voice cracked with emotion. "I just need a little time to think, please. May I call you back in a few days with an answer?"

"Of course. I look forward to hearing from you."

"Thank you, Dr. Stone. I'll be in touch soon." She hung up the phone, feeling like a weight had settled on her heart.

"Everything all right?" Pete asked, brow furrowed.

"Yes," she said, mustering a smile. "Perfectly fine."

CHAPTER 20

Pete left the rectory and turned off the town's main street and onto the bumpy dirt road that led into the mountains. He thought about their visit with Dr. Jones and how she'd mentioned she could tell them more about Ricardo's death if she had a sample of the pulque.

When he came within a mile of the morada, he parked the truck and walked the rest of the way. He was fairly certain he'd find no one there, but he couldn't be too careful. Nothing good would come from being caught. He carefully stepped between clumps of grass, white boulders, Pinon trees, intermittent clusters of prickly pear cactus, and the long, spindly threads of cholla cactus. When he spotted the building, he squatted behind a large boulder and watched. No one entered or exited in the several minutes he waited.

He moved closer, hiding behind bushes and boulders. He picked up a few pebbles and threw them toward the building, aiming high for the windows. Nothing happened, reassuring him the place was temporarily vacated.

Once inside, he took off his sunglasses and hooked them on the collar of his T-shirt. Dense coolness enveloped him, and the smell of musty earth filled his nose. The air felt heavy with dampness trapped in the thick, adobe walls, and he shook off the growing feeling of claustrophobia. His eyes settled on a small wooden altar with doors to the left and right of it, then shifted to a large, looming crucifix, much like the one at St. Mary Magdalene's. His gaze traveled around the room to the twelve Stations of the Cross—images depicting the day of Jesus' crucifixion—framed in rustic wood.

Dust and flecks of uncooked rice covered the floor. He looked back at the doors by the altar. He headed for the one to the right and entered a small room. Shelves held hemp-tasseled whips, several bags of rice, rosaries, garden tools, coffee cans filled with nails, and other items one might find in a hardware store. He spotted a mayonnaise jar filled with a murky-brown liquid and reached for it, stopping when he heard footsteps.

Turning around, he found himself staring into the face of Sheriff Juan Gallegos as he stood in the doorway. Pete shoved the guilty hand into his pocket. He hoped the pounding of his heart was not visible through his T-shirt, and he fought to keep his other hand from swiping at the sweat trickling down his sideburns.

"Pedro, I'm surprised to see you here," Gallegos said, crossing his hammy arms over his chest.

Pete quickly tried to think of an excuse for being inside the morada.

"I, uh . . . I just wanted to . . ." He licked his lips, racking his brain. "What are you doing here?" he asked, trying to throw the sheriff off.

"I'm preparing for tonight's prayer service. I belong here— I'm an *Hermano*, remember? *Trespassers* pay for their crimes. I ask again, why are you here, Pedro?" Gallegos set a hand on his gun.

"I was just . . ." His mind raced. Why the hell would he be up here? Unless . . . "I've decided to join the Brotherhood," he blurted.

A faint smile parted the sheriff's lips. "So you've reconsidered," he said, drawing out the words. "Have you told your papa?"

"No," Pete said too quickly. "Not yet. It's not the right time."

"The time is now, Pedro. Why wait? You've made your decision, and it's a wise one." The creases near Gallegos' eyes deepened with his grin. "And about the gringa . . . I understand she was taken off the project—the excavation—no? It's amazing what happens when people get out of line, isn't it? I'm glad you've come to your senses."

Pete heard the threat in the sheriff's words but managed a smile. "I just don't want to tell my father yet. It will be such a shock to him that—"

"A *relief* for him, I assure you," Gallegos said.

Pete was pretty sure the sheriff didn't wholeheartedly believe him, that Gallegos was forcing Pete's hand to announce his intent to join the Brotherhood merely to better control him.

"You will come to the council meeting tomorrow morning, Pedro. Then you will tell your father, in the midst of the assembled Brotherhood, of your intentions."

"Fine." Pete felt like the life was being squeezed out of his heart.

Gallegos stood back from the door in a silent gesture for Pete to leave. "I didn't see your vehicle, Pedro. Can I give you a ride back to town?"

"I'd rather walk, thank you," he said.

"As you wish, Pedro. But be here tomorrow morning at nine," the sheriff ordered.

Pete nodded.

"And *don't* be late."

Pete watched the sheriff walk to his patrol car, expecting him to get in and drive off. But he didn't. Instead he leaned his backside against it and casually crossed his legs waiting for Pete to leave. He'd have to try to get the pulque another time.

Having no choice, Pete headed down the hill. Would Gallegos follow him? More than likely, he would just make sure

Pete didn't go back to the morada. Which is exactly what he wanted—and needed—to do. Though, joining the Brotherhood seemed like the only way to truly find out what had happened to Ricardo and all the others. It would put Pete in the thick of it all, seeing everything firsthand. He'd be able to learn how Martinez fit into the Brotherhood and monitor his movements, see what the other men did, see who all the other men *were*. He'd gain the knowledge they needed, but at what cost? The brutal initiation, the rituals, the giving up of the self, the giving *in* to their beliefs and practices . . . He shuddered. But the more he thought about his decision the more he realized it was the only way, even if Ruby didn't like it. Besides, if the Cristos *had* been murdered, it would be their word against the Brotherhood's. But if someone from the inside provided proof, then people might listen.

The truth would be known.

❦

Ruby sipped her iced tea in a corner booth of the café where she was supposed to meet Pete. Loud laughter from the other side of the room drew her attention, and she looked up at the entrance. Four men in black leather motorcycle attire, who looked as if they'd been riding for days, noisily walked in and seated themselves.

A middle-aged, pot-bellied man wearing a pearl-buttoned cowboy shirt and a formerly white apron came up to Ruby's table. "Are you ready to order?" he asked.

"I'm waiting for someone."

"Okay." He started to turn and then looked back at her. "I'm Xavier Piedras, the owner of this fine establishment. I haven't seen you around here before."

Ruby stuck out her hand and introduced herself.

"Just passing through?" he asked.

"No, not really. I'm working nearby. Well, I *was* working out at the site with Dr. Yates." She stirred some sugar in her tea and smiled.

"Ah, an archeologist."

"A student," she said.

The bikers loosed another uproarious burst of laughter. The café owner rolled his eyes. "Ay, those hoodlums," he said.

One of them, who had his blond hair slicked back in a duck-tail, gave Ruby the once-over, grinning. She quickly averted her eyes.

Xavier clearly saw the exchange. "You watch out for them, *señorita*. They're bad news."

"Don't worry," Ruby said just as Pete walked into the restaurant and over to the table.

Xavier shook his hand. "*You're* dining with this fine woman? She's much too good for the likes of you, no?"

"She is," Pete agreed, and Ruby felt her cheeks flush.

Xavier punched him playfully in the arm. "Your usual?"

"Yeah, thanks." Pete turned to her. "What about you, Ruby?"

"I'll have what he's having," she said, smiling at Xavier.

The man nodded, turned on his heel, and headed toward the kitchen.

"Have I got news for you," she said as soon as Pete sat down.

He pulled his flatware free of the napkin and napkin ring, but he wouldn't meet her eyes.

"What's wrong?" she asked.

"Nothing." He sounded defensive.

"Did you get the pulque?"

"No." He shook his head, still not looking at her.

"Why?"

"Don't ask."

She wanted to press him, but what she had to tell him couldn't wait. So she cleared her throat and continued. "I called the archbishop's office to inquire about Enrique Martinez. I said I was an old friend, but they wouldn't give me any information. However, Rosita told me that Martinez attended seminary in Colorado. So I called them. The guy I spoke to said they'd lost track of him, but they had a phone number for his former roommate. I gave him a call. He was all too eager to talk about old Enrique. Said they'd had a pretty big falling out."

"Over what?" Pete asked. Ruby was about to tell him when Xavier showed up with their order. He placed their plates in front of them.

"Can I get you anything else?" he asked.

"No, thank you," Ruby said.

"I'm good," said Pete.

After he'd walked away, Ruby continued. "He said Martinez was dismissed from the seminary for bizarre behavior." She paused for effect.

"And?" Pete prodded, lifting a forkful of pinto beans smothered in cheese to his mouth.

"Apparently, Martinez had come from an unstable background. Lots of trouble at home. But that's not all. This guy said he suffered from delusions."

"What kinds of delusions?"

Ruby leaned over her plate and lowered her voice. "He wasn't specific, but he said Martinez was obsessed with ridding the world of evil. To rid himself of evil, he would even cause harm and injury to his own body. He burned himself with cigarettes, cut himself. He tried to hide it, but when they aren't in prayer or in class these seminarians are pretty tightly knit. This guy said they all thought Martinez was weird. The head priest dismissed him."

"So how did Martinez get the necessary signed documents from the archbishop's office to become a priest?" Pete asked, his fork poised in the air.

"Well, if you think about it, Martinez must have had easy access to that kind of information, being in the seminary. It wouldn't be that hard to make up some fakes and forge the signature."

Pete nodded. "If what you say is true, Martinez believes that inflicting pain thwarts evil."

"Seems that way to me," Ruby agreed. "Sick, right?"

"But does that mean *he's* killing the Cristos? We still have no proof."

"Right you are," Ruby said. "The deaths could be accidental, as Dr. Jones suggested. Or the Brotherhood could be intentionally choosing Cristos with incurable illnesses, like Ricardo, to cause them pain and suffering, or because they figure they'll die anyway."

Pete shook his head. "That doesn't make sense. They couldn't guarantee anyone in the Brotherhood would have an incurable disease. And if Ricardo did have pneumonic plague, why didn't anyone else get it?"

"Maybe they did."

A plump waitress came out of the kitchen with another round of beer for the rowdy bikers, and they applauded her with lewd remarks. She narrowed her eyes at them and set their beers on the table with loud thumps. Ruby grinned at the woman's spunk, then turned her attention back to Pete. "What's wrong with you today?" she asked.

Pete twirled his fork in his fingers and then put it back down on his plate. He pressed his palms to his eyelids.

"Pete?" She thought he would be more enthused about the information she had revealed about Martinez.

"You're not going to believe what I did today," he said, taking his hands away and blinking hard.

Ruby waited, not sure she wanted to hear based upon his sulky behavior.

"I'm going inside."

"Inside?"

"I'm joining the Redeemers," he said.

"*What?!*" Her voice came out louder than she intended. The blond motorcycle guy grinned at her again. "What did you just say?"

He heaved a sigh. "It's the only way to get the information we need."

"Pete." He couldn't be serious. It went against everything she'd learned about him in the last few weeks.

He shook his head. "I've made up my mind."

"You're out of your mind! You can't do this."

"I *have* to do this."

"You're cutting me out," she said, crossing her arms in front of her chest.

He looked insulted. "What?"

"You're cutting me out of the loop."

"Ruby, there's a lot you can do. You can keep investigating from the outside, like you have been, while I work from the inside. It'll go much faster."

"Why are you doing this?" She couldn't believe what he was saying. Why would he subject himself to that kind of hell?

"It's the best way," he said.

"But what about—?"

"Please, Ruby. Try to understand. I still need your help. We just need to do it my way."

She hesitated, studying his eyes. She could see his resolve, his determination to finally end this investigation. "Okay," she said on a half-sigh. The fact that he was willing to risk his own safety, maybe his life, to get to the bottom of his brother's murder showed how much it meant to him. He deserved her support.

Pete slipped into silence and continued eating. Ruby did too, but kept sneaking glances at him. She sensed this decision he'd made weighed heavily on him. While she didn't entirely agree it was the best course of action, she was running out of ideas.

When they'd finished eating, Pete pulled out his billfold and set some money on the table. "I'll get this, but I gotta go. There are some things I need to take care of."

"Okay," she said. "Thank you. But will I see you before . . . before you go in?"

"I'm not sure. I have a lot to do."

Ruby reached out, setting her hand on top of his. She didn't want him to go. His eyes met hers. She didn't realize, until this moment, how much she had come to care for this tortured man. How their pain had somehow bonded them. How her heart, though fractured, showed promise of knitting itself back together again. He held her gaze a few moments longer and then slipped his hand out from under hers. "I'll be in touch."

Pete stood, shoved his billfold back into his pocket, and walked past the noisy motorcycle gang and out the door. Worry dug its claws into her chest as fear sank deep into her stomach. Pete might be up to the physical torture, but she didn't think he could handle the emotional toll this might take on him. In fact, she wasn't sure she could handle it either.

Xavier returned to the table then, with hot and delicious-smelling sopaipillas, traditional Mexican pastries served with honey, in hand. "Where's Pete?"

"He, uh, had some things to do," Ruby said.

The waitress joined them. "Xavier, we have to do something about those *malos*." She tilted her head toward the men. "They're going to tear up the café. I can see it coming."

"Ay, Josephina, relax." He gave the woman an affectionate smile. "This is Ruby." He turned to Ruby now. "This is Josephina, my wife."

The woman and Ruby exchanged greetings, and Josephina stared expectantly at her husband, one hand on her hip, one foot tapping against the floor.

"Don't worry," he said again. "They'll leave soon."

She walked away, flapping her arms and shaking her head.

"She worries too much," he said, glancing over at the disorderly bunch. "Today, maybe not. But usually, too much." He walked over to another table to clear it.

One of the bikers made a spectacle of chugging his beer in mere seconds. His pals laughed and hooted, making all the other patrons turn toward the gang. Ruby's attention, however, was focused on the man coming through the door. Every muscle in her body froze.

Dr. Yates.

He didn't seem to have seen her yet as he walked up to Xavier and shook his hand. He tipped his stained fedora to Josephina, who was now in the open kitchen. Walking toward a booth, he made eye contact with Ruby. She looked away, hoping he wouldn't say anything to her. She took a few more bites of her sopaipilla and then stood, careful to avoid looking at both Yates and the rowdy group. Unfortunately, both sat between her and the exit. Bowing her head, she stared directly at the floor and made a beeline for the door. She passed Yates without incident, but when she reached the motorcycle gang's table they stopped their drinking game. One of the men stuck his arm out, blocking her.

"Hey sweetheart, what's your name?" he asked.

"Don't talk to him, talk to me," Blond Guy blurted.

Ruby tried to step past the outstretched arm, ignoring them, but was jerked backward when the blond man caught her by the wrist.

"Where you goin', babe?" he asked. "I wanna talk to you."

Heart pounding, Ruby fought to remain relaxed and didn't pull away from him. "Let go of me," she said. She schooled her features and glared at him. Showing fear would just spur him on.

"But I don't want to, honey. I wanna talk."

"That's not all he wants," another man said much too loudly.

Ruby pulled her arm way and was about to tell them all where they could go, when she heard someone come up behind her.

"Leave her alone." Yates stepped up to the bikers' table.

"Just who the hell are you?" Blond Guy asked. "Mind your own business." He reached for Ruby again but she stepped back, accidentally knocking down a chair. Blond Guy stood up and started for her. Yates circled the table and stood in the biker's way.

"I told you to leave her alone." Yates' face took on the hard, stony expression she'd seen so many times.

The other three men got up, flinging their chairs behind them.

One of them scoffed. "Who does this old man think he is?"

Blond Guy lunged at Yates, grabbing him by the front of his collar. In seconds Yates had Blond Guy's arm cocked backward, and he sank to his knees. The hoodlum hurled obscenities. Yates made a swift jerk with the guy's arm and the sound of bones popping ripped through the air. Blond Guy screamed, writhing on the floor.

Yates released him, but before he could turn another biker jumped on his back while yet another lunged at him. Ruby jumped in front of the third man and he tried to push her aside. She clapped her hand on his, locked her thumbs over the top of it, and dug into his palm with her fingers. Then, dropping low, she shot under his arm and came back around, twisting it. Holding his hand palm up she jerked him down, falling to one knee, and then slammed his head into her other knee. The man wailed as blood spurted on her pants and onto the floor. Still holding his wrist angled in a direction that God had never intended she applied more pressure, making him squeal and curse.

She looked up to see Yates staring at her, wide-eyed. He had successfully subdued the other two men, and they squirmed on the floor in pain. Ruby couldn't help herself and gave him a satisfied smile. She turned her attention back to Third Guy and twisted his wrist a fraction more. He grunted in agony.

"Apologize," she said.

"Fuck you!" He spat, aiming for her shoe, but missed.

Ruby held the pressure on his cocked wrist. "You realize I could break your wrist at any moment, don't you?" she informed him. "Apologize."

He growled.

"I'm waiting."

"Fuck! I'm sorry, okay?"

She released him to the floor with a thud.

She pulled herself to standing, a little ashamed of herself for enjoying someone's pain so much. She gazed up at Yates, who smiled at her. By the twinkle in his eye, she knew she'd gained a little respect. Not much, but some. One of the patrons clapped, and then another joined in, and another, until applause filled the café.

Xavier Piedras approached the fallen thugs with a puffed-up chest. "Get out of my diner, you hoodlums."

The four men struggled to their feet, disheveled and bloody, and staggered out to the parking lot. In seconds, their motorcycles were revving and then began to fade into the evening.

Yates turned and headed back toward his table.

"Dr. Yates," Ruby said, stopping him. "Thank you."

"Looks like you didn't need much help after all," he said dryly before continuing to his booth.

Ruby followed him. "Why did you do it?" she asked.

"I thought you needed it."

"I did. Thanks again."

He waved her appreciation away and sipped at his beer. "I figured Pete would be with you. Where is he?"

Ruby's gaze fell to the floor, not sure if she could trust Yates with information regarding the Redeemers and Pete's plan. She didn't know *who* to trust anymore.

"Home, I guess."

Yates nodded. "Good evening, Miss Delgado."

Ruby sighed at his dismissive tone and left the booth. Waving to Xavier and Josephina, Ruby walked out of the restaurant. Suddenly fatigued from her exchange with Dr. Yates and the bikers, she headed for the rectory.

CHAPTER 21

Pete stood at the altar of the morada, stripped to the waist in front of the group of Redeemers. Men who, just like his father, had immersed themselves in something so deep they could no longer see right from wrong.

Enrique Martinez approached Pete, then placed both hands on his shoulders. "So, you wish to become one with the Brotherhood?" Martinez asked, his gaze probing.

Pete tried to keep his voice even. "Yes." Initially, he'd been surprised to find that Martinez belonged to the Brotherhood—priests had never been members. However, in thinking about it, the way things had changed with the Redeemers in the past few years nothing should surprise him. And Martinez was never a priest after all.

"Why do you seek to join us?" he asked.

Pete took a deep breath. "I have shamed my family and the Brotherhood in the past, but I've done my penance and am ready to carry out my family's legacy, if it would be permitted." He glanced at his father, who stood rigid and stoic. Pete knew Manuel would not be allowed to question him as an initiate; the bond of father and son was too close.

The room buzzed with muted conversation.

"Your family is surely proud," said Martinez. "Is this truly why you wish to join? To follow in the footsteps of one so great in the eyes of God; to follow in the footsteps of your brother, Ricardo?"

Pete avoided Martinez's direct gaze and nodded. "Yes."

Martinez smiled, his eyes twinkling. "Then it is time for you to give service to God."

One of the other men stepped forward. His face was stern, his moustache turned downward in a frown. "Why did you not wish to join the Brotherhood before, when Ricardo had?"

"I wished to go to school, to college. I put my own desires before those of God, and for that I am sorry."

"And did you complete school? Go to college?"

"No," Pete said, staring straight ahead like a soldier being addressed by a senior officer.

The man raised an eyebrow. "So you failed in your quest."

Pete clenched his jaw. He knew the interrogation was meant to shatter his esteem. "Yes," he said between tight lips.

"Are you now ready to put God and your family first?"

Pete forced himself not to hesitate. "Yes."

"So you're prepared to give thanks and praise to God, to serve Him through the Brotherhood of the Redeemers?"

Pete nodded.

The men backed away, leaving him alone at the altar.

"State your full name," Martinez ordered.

Once he did so, the others began to interrogate Pete about his faith and the teachings of the Catholic Church. They told him to cite his baptismal promises, say a rosary, and confess his sins.

After an hour, the questions ceased and Martinez approached him again. "You have answered well, Pedro Medina. Now is the time for initiation. If you pass, you will be accepted into the Brotherhood. However, because of your past violations against the Brotherhood, if you do not pass you will be required to take a vow of secrecy, telling no one you tried to join."

Pete nodded. His palms bloomed with sweat and his breathing quickened in anticipation of what would come next. He'd passed the first phase. They had bought his false sincerity and were willing to trust him based on his alleged penance. Now came the hard part.

What sort of torture did they have in mind for his initiation? He recited a quick prayer for strength and then made a promise to himself. Whether or not he passed this next phase, he *would* find out what had happened to Ricardo.

Martinez lifted a wooden cup to his lips, and Pete drank without a word. The stringent liquid burned his throat. This must be pulque, he thought with a wave of nausea. He flinched as it slipped down, but Martinez tilted the cup back up. "Drink it all."

Pete took a deep breath and gulped the rest of the pulque down his throat. Within minutes his vision blurred and the faces before him distorted, twisted, and stretched. He blinked hard.

Several men loosened his pants and pulled them off him. They fell to the floor with a whoosh. Then the men poured something on the ground and forced him to kneel. Pain lanced through his knees and up his thighs, making his skin tingle and sweat. Grains of rice against the hard brick floor stabbed at his knees, sending electric chills up his spine. At least the pulque dulled the pain.

Sights and sounds intensified. He must have been hallucinating. He heard laughter, lighthearted and silly, then it turned raspy and vicious. Something lashed against the back of his legs, sending a wave of burning pain through him. Instinctively he tried to move away, but someone held him still. The whip struck again and again. He could feel his skin tearing, warm blood trickling down his legs.

Finally, the blows ceased. The men who had held him in place helped him to his feet. One of them took Pete's face in his hand. He smiled and gently patted his cheek.

"Well done," the man said.

The men backed away and left Pete alone. His legs ached, but his kneecaps felt numb. Still, he couldn't move. Martinez ordered him to stay and pray, though the others filed out of the room.

As the biting pain started to subside, images clouded his mind and a waking dream distracted him from the burning ache. In the dream Pete sat on a tree stump near the water's edge, holding a fishing pole. Something tugged on his line. He turned the reel furiously as the object grew heavier. He fought with the weight until he finally pulled it to the surface. His hook had snared a human child, its body bloated and purple. Horrified, he threw down the pole.

Then the wailing began.

The mournful cry pierced the air and rang in his ears like a siren. She came toward him—the witch named La Llorona—the one who had drowned her babies and then walked the banks of the Rio Grande, crying for them in the night. Her eyes burned bright within the hood of her woolen cloak, and her moans vibrated against the water like the resonant dong of distant bells. Pete reached out to her, his fingers grazing the cloak. The hood fell back, and he gasped as he stared into the face of his own mother.

"Stop!" he yelled, forcing the vision away, but it was soon replaced by his father chopping wood.

Manuel swung the axe back, then over his head and down. The sound of splitting wood filled Pete's ears like a furious burst of thunder. Each time the axe made contact with the wood, it felt as if Pete's very soul was being split in two. He ran toward Manuel, begging him to stop, but he had no voice. He couldn't utter a sound. When he reached his father, the axe had turned into a hammer. The thunderous noise was replaced by a loud clinking sound as Manuel drove the stakes into the wrists and ankles of his eldest son, Ricardo. Pete tried to stop him, but his body wouldn't obey. Ricardo lay upon the cross, his body decayed and skeletal, the stakes ripping through his leathery flesh and springing fresh blood.

His own body and voice rendered useless, Pete could do nothing to stop the hallucination. The visions passed by like the pages of a photo album turning before him. Manuel and Ricardo faded away, and others appeared. He recognized none of them. The faces all stared at him and laughed, mocking not only his decision to be a Redeemer but his very soul.

Pete slumped to the floor, consciousness slipping away. He felt the rice dig into his flesh again, but he didn't care. He wanted to lose consciousness, to escape the visions. He moaned one last time, and then there was nothing.

CHAPTER 22

R uby spent most of the morning and early afternoon on the phone. She had to work around Rosita's cleaning so she could have some privacy. The housekeeper had again warned Ruby off any discussion of the Redeemers, and made it clear that she wanted nothing to do with the situation.

Ruby had called Dr. Stone and told him that, for personal reasons, she'd elected not to return to UNM right away. He'd been understanding, but had sounded confused at her declaration. It didn't matter. She'd made up her mind, and she would stick with her decision. She had to.

Then she called Dr. Jones for an update. The doctor had been studying Ricardo's file and had discovered that the bodies of two other Cristos had been autopsied at the request of the families. Both families resided on farms on the outskirts of Las Montanas, and she gave Ruby their names. Ruby planned to find those families today.

She asked Dr. Jones about Ricardo's symptoms of pneumonic plague, and she confirmed Ruby's theory of the spread of the disease—or lack thereof. But the other two Cristos had been in perfect health, so that blew Ruby's terminal-illness theory. It had been weak, anyway, but she was desperate.

"The only concerning similarity between Ricardo's and the two others' health was the fact they had all been smokers," Dr. Jones said, the tone of her voice altering. "Wait."

"What is it?"

"Only Ricardo suffered lung damage, obviously from the pneumonic plague and/or smoking, but not the other two."

"How do you know they were smokers, then?"

"Nicotine in the bloodstream. For all of them. There's something else I didn't mention," the doctor went on. "All three bodies had brown stains on their foreheads. I assume it was coagulated blood from the crown of thorns, but there's no mention of the cause of the stain in the reports."

Ruby wondered if the body that had fallen out of the coffin had the same stain. It had been too dark in the pit to tell at the time.

"What happened to the bodies after they were autopsied?" she asked.

"They were given back to the families for burial."

"More than likely, they were given back to the Redeemers," Ruby said, still thinking of the skeletal remains she'd found. Pete had said the burial place of the bodies was a secret, and until Ruby had literally stumbled over them no one had known where they were hidden—except the Brotherhood.

"Have you obtained a sample of the pulque yet?" Dr. Jones asked.

"No," Ruby said. "But we're working on it."

"Well, let me know when you do."

"Dr. Jones," Ruby said hesitantly, "may I ask . . . why are you doing this? Why are you taking so much time out of your busy schedule to help us?"

"Two reasons," Dr. Jones said. "I told you about my roommate's brother, but what I didn't tell you was that we were engaged to be married. I broke it off. I couldn't marry someone who had so many secrets. His life in the Redeemers was sacred to him, and he couldn't share it with me."

"And the other reason?" Ruby asked.

"I'm a sucker for a mystery."

Ruby laughed. "I really appreciate it."

"Sure," Dr. Jones said, a smile in her voice. "Let me know when you get that pulque."

"I will," Ruby promised. "Thank you, Doctor." She hung up and went to find Rosita.

When she asked the woman about the families of the other Cristos and where they lived, Rosita first scolded Ruby as if she were an impertinent child.

"I'm not going to tell you. You should go back to your college, *mija*. Stay out of this business."

"Please, Rosita. This is important. To both Pete and me."

At the mention of Pete's name, Rosita's face relaxed. Ruby knew she had a soft spot for him, liked to mother him.

"Eee, you are a stubborn woman, Ruby Delgado!" Rosita shook her finger at her.

Ruby smiled. "I know. I could say the same for you."

"*Dios Mio! Dame fuerza*," she said, invoking God for strength. With a sigh, she gave in to Ruby's pleading.

The Cordovas lived in a ramshackle plywood shack about five miles from the rectory. Their farm consisted of roughly four acres, some of which was used for alfalfa. The farm equipment that she could see was rusty and terribly outdated, and she wondered if it even worked. Several children played on a tire swing hanging from an oak tree outside the house. The rich beauty of the massive tree with its long, graceful branches covered with deep-green leaves contrasted with the broken-down hovel where the family lived.

In an open shed behind the house, an older man was bent over as he hammered something. The children, caught up in their play, took no notice of the stranger walking toward the back of their house.

At her approaching footsteps, however, the man turned to face her. "*Quien es?*"

"My name is Ruby Delgado. I'd like to ask you some questions."

The man's coal-dark eyes looked rheumy, void of any sparkle. The bitterness in his face and the sense of utter defeat in his posture told her that life had not been kind to him.

"Do you speak English?"

"Eh, *un poco*," he said, holding his thumb and index finger close together.

"I'd like to ask you about your son, Eddie. I understand he passed away some years ago. I'm so sorry for your loss."

The man frowned. "Eduardo. Yes."

"Um, I hope you don't mind my asking, but are you a member of the Redeemers?" She knew the Brotherhood liked to keep their membership a secret, but what did she have to lose?

He shook his head violently. "No. *Blasphemos!*" He used the Spanish word for blasphemers.

"Was Eduardo?"

"*Sí, sí*, he was . . . Now he's dead."

"I know, sir. I'm sorry," she said. "If you weren't a member, then why was your son?"

"*Mi hermano* was a Redeemer. But they tell me I can't join."

Ruby didn't want to make him uncomfortable. Pride was something none of these people lacked. She supposed it made sense that the Redeemers rejected some of the candidates who applied for membership. She'd just never considered the possibility before. "And your son was a Cristo?"

"*Sí.*" Tears pooled in his eyes but he blinked them back, his gaze turning hard. "They killed him."

"Who?" she asked. "Was it anyone in particular?"

"I don't know, but they killed him. He died too fast," he said in broken English. "He was healthy, strong." The man shook his head. "They took my boy away. He died, and then the *Hermanos* took him away. I can't even visit my son in his grave." His voice cracked. "I don't know where he is. They took *mi Corazon*, my heart, away from me."

Her own heart squeezed with compassion for the man. "Did you contact the police?"

"*Sí. Pero,* they have no time for me. They don't help. They went by the doctor's papers, said he died of no air. They don't care."

Ruby found it hard to believe that he'd reported it to the authorities, unless of course the authority had been Gallegos. As isolated as the family seemed to be, maybe the sheriff was the only authority he knew.

"I'm very sorry, Mr. Cordova," Ruby said. "Thank you for talking with me."

The man nodded, and returned to his work.

Ruby trudged back to her car. She couldn't help thinking the deaths were looking more and more like murders with every step she took in her investigation. She needed to find out how and who. This Cristo, Eduardo, died fairly early in the crucifixion. It seemed beyond coincidence that a healthy, strong young man like Eduardo and a sick one like Ricardo would both die in the same amount of time, within hours of being crucified.

She drove forty miles out to the other side of Las Montanas to contact the second family. But when she arrived at their little farm it was abandoned, the buildings ravaged by time and the elements.

With illness and bleeding to death ruled out, the only alternative at this point was the pulque. She hoped Pete would be able to obtain a sample soon.

Good Friday, and another crucifixion, would be there in only seven days.

When Pete woke, he couldn't open his eyes. Pain seeped through them deep into his head. He could feel the warmth of a bright light on his face as he struggled to pry open his eyelids. The effort made him dizzy and faint. Finally, the warmth faded away.

He could smell cool mountain air and hear crickets singing. From the damp breeze, he guessed it was early morning.

"Pedro? Pedro, open your eyes." He thought he recognized the voice. Martinez? He couldn't be sure.

Pete tried again. This time he managed to hold them open for a few seconds, but then pain forced them shut. Someone lifted his head and put something to his lips. Liquid. More putrid liquid. But this time it tasted different. It tasted like tea —*strong* tea.

Two hands gently placed his head back down. Within minutes, the pain began to subside and an energizing euphoria replaced it. Pete blinked open his eyes to find Enrique Martinez staring down at him.

"You have done well, Pedro," he said. "Drink. You need your strength."

Pete drank more and his head started to clear. He lay on a modest cot in a small room. Wooden shutters had been opened to let in the light, and the door to the outside stood ajar. Martinez sat next to him with a tray of food.

"Now you must eat."

Pete sat up slowly, swinging his feet around to the floor. His placed his hands to the side of his head in an attempt to stop the spinning, and the pain.

"Your head hurts?"

"Yes."

Martinez nodded. "Eat," he repeated, holding up a plate of beans and tortillas.

Pete's stomach growled as his senses took in the food. Martinez set the plate down on the floor at Pete's feet and then stood to leave.

"Wait, what happens next?" Pete asked.

Not answering, Martinez walked out of the room. Another man entered in his place—the frowning man from the interrogation.

"Hurry," was all the man said.

Pete shoveled the food in. When he finished, the frowning man motioned for him to stand. He did, but the pain in his legs pulled him down again. His body hurt so much that he'd forgotten about the whipping.

"Up," the man ordered.

Pete stood again, this time more slowly. When he felt stable enough, he twisted to examine the backs of his legs. The sight almost made him sick. The lashings were bad enough, but someone had dressed the wounds with a greasy, waxy substance.

The man gestured for Pete to go outside. He pushed open the door and ducked through the tiny doorframe. The sunlight assaulted his eyes, bringing back his forgotten headache. A group of Redeemers stood in a semicircle, waiting for him.

Still wearing only his boxer shorts Pete felt the cool, high desert breeze on his bare skin. A familiar young man emerged from the group. His face was almost recognizable, but Pete couldn't place him; not with any real certainty. He felt trapped in a dream he couldn't get out of.

The boy pulled a cart behind him—the death cart, with the skeleton El Muerte dressed as a witch, mangled hair sprouting from its skull. He wheeled it in front of Pete. The skeleton's bony fingers held a bow with an arrow nocked, waiting to fire.

Two men took Pete by the arms and harnessed him to the shafts of the cart. They pointed toward a hill and pushed him forward. He began to walk. Someone had put sandals on his feet, and he whispered a praise of thanks. He squinted in the sunlight that blanketed the area laden with boulders, small rocks, scrub brush, and pinons.

He turned around to see the skeleton, its hollow eye sockets glaring at him and its gaping mouth laughing.

Pete flinched at the crack of a whip. He faced forward again and began to pull the cart, walking as fast as he could with the ropes pulling strongly on his shoulders and chest. He saw his father in the distance, away from the other men, watching, standing still as a statue with his hands clasped in front of him.

What must he be thinking? Unless angry, he'd always been impossible to read.

Pete could hear the men heaving rocks into the cart behind him as he went. With each stone the cart became heavier, the ropes tighter. He searched for a distraction. He returned his gaze to his father. As they watched each other, Pete remembered one of the times he and Ricardo had felt the true wrath of their father. Once, when they were boys, Ricardo ten years old and Pete seven, they'd been late for Sunday Mass, preoccupied by a boyish game. They had only remembered their Sunday obligation when Mass was nearly over. Communion had begun, and they had sneaked into the church and scooted into the pew next to their mother, who had refused to look at them. Their father had leaned forward and glared at them, his eyes both hot and cold at the same time. Pete had known immediately that they were in trouble, and worried over the coming punishment.

That afternoon, their father had taken them to the shed and made them take off their shirts. He had beaten them with his belt until their knees buckled. "Do not ever, *ever*, turn your back on God again!" The expression in his father's eyes, like a living rage, had haunted Pete for years.

Now Pete no longer feared his father, but pitied him. Sometimes he even hated him.

A loud crack jarred Pete out of the memory. He forced himself to keep walking, beginning his journey up the hill, his aching legs bearing most of the burden. The rope cutting into his chest made him forget about the uneven, graveled ground beneath his sandaled feet. Rocks and clumps of prickly pear offered no refuge from his agony.

The whip cracked again, and Pete pressed on.

CHAPTER 23

Pete lay on the cot, unable to sleep. After the day's rituals, the Brothers had brought him inside and laid him down. He'd fallen asleep but woke a few hours later, trembling with pain. The muscles in his shoulders and legs ached with fatigue and overuse, and the skin on his chest and the back of his legs stung, the sores open and oozing.

He had spent the day toiling in the sun under the scrutiny of the Brothers. After struggling with the cart for what seemed like hours, he'd been allowed to rest for a few minutes. Then they prayed, the hot sun beating down on their bare skin. When he was allowed to put on his shirt again, even the soft cotton felt like burlap over the blisters and lash wounds.

Yet even in his exhausted condition, he couldn't quiet his mind. He studied the walls of the tiny room. The shutters had been closed again, letting in just a sliver of light. With Holy Week only six days away, many of the men stayed at the morada when they weren't participating in all-night vigils. Others went home to their families.

Pete thought about his own family. Weak from hunger and exhausted from the physical abuse, he longed for the comfort of his mother and his sisters. Occasionally, over the past two years, he'd seen them walking to the market or going into the café. Marguerite would be almost fifteen now and little Sophia, twelve. They had grown so much in the past two years. He missed their soft embraces, and their laughter echoed in his empty heart. And even as an adult, he wanted his mother. He wanted her to talk to him, tell him he was doing the right thing. He wanted her to hold his face in her hands and tell him how proud she was of him.

An image of his father forced its way into his mind, and he shut it out. They had not yet been permitted to speak directly, much to Pete's relief. He didn't feel ready, not yet. He would never be able to forgive his father for his passive acceptance of Ricardo's death, but he would have to pretend that he had.

How hypocritical of him, lying there bruised and battered of his own volition.

Oh yes, his father would be proud—but for the wrong reasons. If he only knew the blasphemy his remaining living son was committing by questioning the credibility of his beloved Brotherhood. If only he knew of Pete's determination to prove them murderers . . .

⚜

The next morning, one of the men served Pete the same scant fare as that of the previous day. After eating his beans and tortillas Pete had to drink more of the pulque, but thankfully the drink became easier to tolerate with each dose.

He met the Brotherhood outside the morada door when he was finished. They stood in a semicircle as they had before, waiting for him. Three of them supported a large wooden cross.

Martinez approached him. "Are you up to the task?"

Pete blinked slowly, drunk from the potion. "Yes, Brother. I'm fine."

Martinez smiled. "You are strong, Pedro. You were made to

serve the Lord in these ways. Today, you will take the cross to the top of the hill and then back down again. Do you understand?"

Pete nodded. He readied himself for the weight of the cross.

The men dragged it over and lowered it onto his shoulder. Pete's knees buckled. Splinters from the wood gouged his sunburned flesh. He gritted his teeth with the effort of holding it up.

"God be with you," Martinez said.

Pete offered another silent prayer for strength. A warm light consumed his mind, and he thought he heard a gentle whisper in his ear. Renewed energy flooded his body, and he began to walk.

Beneath the unbearable weight, Pete climbed the hill at a steady pace. The whisper urged him on. Halfway to the top, his knees gave way again and he struggled to keep the cross upright.

By some miracle he managed, but he needed to rest. Someone came to him with a damp rag and bathed his face with cool water. Grateful, he thanked the Brother, and for the first time he felt the sincerity of some of these men. They genuinely wanted him to succeed.

He got up again and continued uphill. The whispers intensified, yet he couldn't place whether they came from his own drunken mind or perhaps from his aching soul. They encouraged him to stay strong, keep going, and he obeyed. He *wanted* to obey.

Pete reached the top of the hill and fell to his knees again. Not out of fatigue, but out of gratitude. He began to understand. The Brothers believed in pushing a man to his limits in every way—physical, emotional, spiritual. They believed in the extreme. It was not to merely live one's life in comfort and ease, but to toil, to drive. To sacrifice for the Almighty in praise and thanks. To accomplish something great in the Name of God.

God, or perhaps it was his own soul, pushed him forward to achieve his goal. He stood again, rejuvenated. Carefully, he dragged the cross in a semicircle, turning around. The others joined him, and they prayed. Then he began his descent, the inspiring words of praise from the men who were following him ringing in his ears.

When the weight of the cross shifted to the front of his shoulders, he fell forward and almost tumbled down the hill. The tail of the cross pushed him from behind, and gravity pulled him to his knees. He hadn't imagined going down would be more difficult. He hadn't imagined *anything* could be more difficult than climbing that hill. He couldn't do it. He knelt on the hillside, chest heaving, sweat pouring from his temples and hairline. He didn't have the strength.

One of the Brothers approached. He grabbed Pete around the waist and lifted, bearing some of the weight with him. *For* him.

"It will be easier once you get used to it," he said. "It's just adjusting the distribution of weight. Pray for strength."

Pete turned his head and nearly collapsed when he saw the man's face. It was Nicolas.

"Thank you," Pete whispered.

Nicolas smiled in return. "Are you okay? I can help you for a while."

"Th-thanks. But I c-can do it," Pete stuttered in his exhaustion. He had to do this himself.

Nicolas nodded respectfully and backed away.

Gathering his strength, both physical and mental, Pete continued his descent.

Later that night, Pete and Nicolas knelt together in prayer on the dirt floor of the morada—Pete numb from the pain he'd endured and hungover from the pulque. He had no thoughts or prayers to petition. Exhaustion had consumed him.

He could hear Nicolas' steady breathing beside him. Pete flicked a glance at him. The young man knelt with perfectly rigid posture, his arms and hands poised in the prayer position, his fingertips lightly touching his lips, his eyes closed. Pete thought he had begun to understand this form of worship, this blind faith in the unknown. Religion provided hope for the hereafter.

The sound of the thick wooden door scraping against the adobe floor broke Pete's pseudo-concentration. Nicolas, immersed in his prayers, didn't react, but Pete turned to see his father enter the morada.

He walked up to Pete, his steps silent. "You've made me proud, Pedro," he said, his voice almost a whisper.

Pete didn't move, didn't acknowledge his presence.

His father continued. "Maybe now that you have seen the light, seen the purpose in your life, we can mend our differences."

The words snapped Pete out of his paralysis, but he didn't let it show. Mend their differences? If his father knew Pete's real motive for joining his beloved Brotherhood, their differences would never be mended. Part of him wanted to think that they could fix things, but his feelings for his father had changed. No longer did Pete admire him and adore him, as most sons did their fathers. No longer did he need to gain his father's approval. Pete couldn't forgive him—not now. Not until he knew the truth.

"Pedro?"

Pete stayed motionless. His actions needed to show forgiveness, even though his heart didn't have the strength to forgive.

His father sighed. "Very well. You need more time. At least you have begun the journey to God. For that, my heart rejoices. Soon, you will see the love I have for you and your brother. By joining the Redeemers, you have come back to life. I have my son again. For this, I am happy."

Pete squeezed his eyes shut even harder, shunning the words. He didn't want to hear the denial in his father's voice. His father lived in a denial so deep it would never be broken. Not until Pete found the truth.

"You pray, my son. Talk to the Lord, talk to Ricardo. They will show you the way." His father's hand gently caressed the top of Pete's head, as he'd done when Pete was a boy. The gesture broke down his guarded defense and emotion welled up inside him.

Fighting it, he again cleared his mind and returned to thoughtlessness.

CHAPTER 24

When Pete and Nicolas emerged from the morada at daybreak, the sun had just peeked over the horizon. Nicolas yawned and stretched while Pete picked up some small pebbles and zinged them at a large boulder. The activity felt good. His muscles were stiff and sore from the initiation ritual and then sitting all night. His head felt fuzzy, his thoughts muddled from lack of sleep and his knees aching from kneeling.

"It's a beautiful morning," Nicolas said.

"Yeah," Pete said, unable to pay attention to anything but his discomfort. He forced himself to concentrate on something besides the pain. He focused on the rose-colored glow that blanketed the land around them, the gentle colors and the fresh, cool air on his face.

"How do you feel, *amigo?*" Nicolas asked him.

"The truth?" Pete raised an eyebrow. "I feel like shit, Brother."

Nicolas laughed. "I'll never forget my initiation. It's amazing what the human body is capable of."

"Yep," Pete agreed. He studied Nicolas' face. Though he was six or seven years younger than Pete, Nicolas had a maturity about him, a wisdom that many older men didn't even possess.

Nicolas seemed to have an old soul, seemed to know much about life and living.

"Hey, Nicolas," Pete said.

"Yeah."

"Why did you help me?"

"I don't know." He shrugged. "I saw you struggling but I knew you'd be okay, even if I didn't help. I respect that. Praying with you last night, I could feel your passion."

You mean anger, Pete wanted to correct him. "I don't know if it's passion, but—"

"You're troubled, aren't you?"

"No, I don't thi—"

Nicolas' eyes stopped Pete's lie. An old soul, indeed.

"I'm working some things out," Pete said.

"That's where the passion comes from. I could see when you carried the cross—your determination, your strength. That's important."

Pete picked up another pebble, not sure what to say. He looked over at Nicolas, who had suddenly paled.

"Hey," Pete said, grabbing him by the arm. "You okay?"

Nicolas mopped the fresh beads of sweat from his brow. "Yeah, I'm just not one hundred percent yet. Only a week ago, I was lying in a hospital bed sick from snake venom."

Pete looked toward the glowing horizon.

"I was training for my role as Cristo. I had the cactus tied to my body and was walking toward the sunset. It started to rain, then it turned into a storm. Thunder. Lightning. I slipped and fell and couldn't get up," he explained. "After an hour or so, I started to struggle. I disturbed a rattler in the process, and it bit me on the hand. Next thing I know this beautiful woman, this angel of mercy, is standing over me in the rain, trying to help me. Somehow, she got me to the hospital. She saved my life." He shook his head, awed. "I don't know her name or where she's from, but she had the same kind of strength you do."

Pete nodded, not knowing what to say. It felt like a betrayal not letting on that he knew the entire story; that he was there, too. "How do you feel about being the Chosen One?" he asked instead.

"It is a great honor, but—" Nicolas lifted his face toward the rising sun "—I have no wish to die. I have a girl. Sylvia. We plan to get married in the fall if—"

"You'll make it," Pete said, knowing that it was very likely a lie if he and Ruby didn't find some answers soon.

"I have to. There's too much to see in life, too much to do. I want to do great things. Maybe leave Las Montanas, maybe even leave New Mexico. I want to see the world."

Pete patted him on the back. "I hope you get to do all those things. Let's get some breakfast."

"I need to ask you a favor, Pete."

"What's that?"

"Would you be my *Compañero* for Holy Week?"

Stunned, Pete didn't know what to say. He hadn't even finished his initiation yet. Plus, he barely knew Nicolas. Being *Compañero* meant taking the Cristo's place on the cross if he could not fulfill the obligation.

"Why me?" Pete asked. "There are many others better qualified."

"They don't possess your strength. With you behind me, I won't die. You'll pass your strength on to me when I need it most." He paused. "And there is one other reason."

"Which is . . . ?"

"Your name . . . You share the name of Jesus' best friend, his confidant."

Pete smiled. "He was also Jesus' betrayer."

Nicolas shrugged the comment off. "Jesus built his church upon the rock of Peter. *Peter* carried on where Christ left off. And you must do the same for me."

If he agreed, Pete would be thrown much deeper into the Brotherhood than he'd intended to go. He didn't know what to say, but the young man met his eyes with candor, with courage.

With need. He'd asked in sincerity and also out of respect. How could Pete say no?

He swallowed. "I'd be honored, Nicolas."

⊙⊱⊰⊙

Late in the afternoon, Ruby stopped at the Piedras' café for a bite to eat. When she came out of the café, she noticed Spike's motorcycle down the street at the cantina. It had been a while since she'd last seen him, and she hadn't gotten a chance to say goodbye. She hesitated, though, remembering the last time she'd gone there. She'd almost slipped. But Pete had stopped her.

Pete. Her thoughts of him had been constant, and to her surprise she actually missed him.

Leaving her car in front of the café, she walked toward the cantina. She noticed a black car parked at a wonky angle in the alleyway next to the bar. She sighed. The driver had probably driven drunk and then parked. A couple of children were playing on a rusted swing set in the yard of one of the houses on the street. She could hear their shrieks of laughter.

Her boy used to laugh like that. She closed her eyes and pushed the sounds out of her head.

She entered the cantina, allowing a minute for her eyes to adjust to the dark. Several men sat at the bar, and a few more were at the tables. She didn't see Spike. She walked a little farther into the cantina and heard the crash of billiard balls. In a little room off to the side of the main space she saw Spike, alone, shooting pool.

As he aimed for one of the corner pockets, he spotted her. "Ruby! What are you doin' here, girl?" He grinned and stepped around the pool table to greet her.

Lord, she'd missed that grin.

"I saw your bike outside," she said, giving him a hug.

"Have a seat." He pointed to a small round table with two chairs.

The top of it was sticky with spilled drinks, and the whole place smelled of stale beer. "Can I get you something to drink?" he asked, raking his fingers through his close- cropped hair.

"No, um, well, a Coke, I guess."

He walked into the other room and came back a few minutes later, a beer bottle in one hand and a Coke in the other. "Don't know how clean the glass is, but here you go."

She thanked him, and he sat down with her. Ruby didn't really know what to say to him. She wanted to tell him everything she'd learned, but she knew he wouldn't want to know.

"How's Dr. Yates?" she asked.

"Quiet. Moody. You know, the usual." Spike chuckled and then swigged his beer.

"Do you know about the Redeemers?" she blurted. She couldn't help herself.

He bobbed his head. "Everybody does."

"Did you know that Pete thinks his brother was murdered by the Redeemers?"

"Yep."

His answer surprised her. "Does Dr. Yates know he thinks they killed him?" she asked.

"Yep."

Ruby stared at him, dumbfounded, deciding whether or not to ask him another question—*the* question. She pitched her voice low. "Is Dr. Yates somehow involved in this whole business? Could he be covering for someone? Maybe getting funds for his project in exchange for his silence?"

Spike looked away from her, shaking his head. "I can't believe you would even suggest such a thing."

"I found out that Yates' funds from the private sector have been stopped due to something that happened in Peru—some problem with ethics. Yet the government has agreed to keep funding him, along with the university. I find that strange."

"Where'd you get this information?" he asked, his voice tinged with irritation.

"I, um, well . . . my source is reliable," she said, opting to avoid the truth. She didn't want to give Spike any reason not to trust her.

"All I'm gonna say is that John Yates is the most honest man I know. To a fault, even. I trust him with my life. What you say about the funding situation is true, but John would never allow himself to be bought. You have my solemn word on that."

She nodded slowly. "What happened in Peru, Spike?"

"You'll have to ask John about that."

"Do you think he'd talk to me?" she asked, trying to be hopeful but not counting on it.

"Don't know, little sister."

She frowned. If John Yates had such integrity, why would he refuse to acknowledge what was going on in this town?

"Thanks for the soda, Spike," she said, getting up.

"No problem. You take care, Ruby."

She said goodbye and walked out of the cantina, her head buzzing with more and more questions about Dr. John Yates.

☙❦❧

Twelve members of the Brotherhood sat at the long dining table. Among them was Nicolas, who sat in the center; Pete, seated to his right; and Martinez and Pete's father, who sat across from them. They ate in silence, their sparse meal consisting once again of pinto beans and flour tortillas. At least there was red wine this time.

When they had finished their meals, a portly, middle-aged man named Diego stood at the head of the table.

"We share this meal to salute our chosen Cristo, Brother Nicolas," he said, "and to wish him well as Holy Week is upon us."

All raised their glasses and turned to face Nicolas. Perspiration dotted Nicolas' stubbled upper lip. His face looked pale, and dark circles rimmed his deep-brown eyes.

"As is custom," Diego continued, "Nicolas, our Cristo, must choose a *Compañero* to help him fulfill his duties and to take his place, should he be unable to participate in the Blessed Event. So now I ask you, Nicolas, chosen Cristo of the Las Montanas Brotherhood, have you chosen your *Compañero*?"

With his hands pressed against the table, Nicolas stood. "I have chosen Pedro."

A hushed murmur filled the room. Pete glanced in his father's direction. He sat still, silent, not participating in the whispered comments, but his face beamed with pride.

Diego raised his hand to silence the men. "I'm sure you've chosen wisely, Nicolas, but Pedro has not yet completed his initiation."

"I know," said Nicolas. "But the determination and faith I saw in the rites he *has* completed convinced me that he is best for the role of *Compañero*. I request that his initiation be considered complete and his status elevated to Brother of Light."

Whispers filled the room again. Once more, Diego silenced them. "Tell us why you chose this man."

Nicolas showed no intimidation or reservation. Pete admired his strength in the face of the Brotherhood. "Because he is the one I want," Nicolas supplied. "And because he shares the same name as Jesus' own friend and confidant."

Diego sighed. "Brothers, the ultimate decision belongs to Nicolas."

Nicolas' wide smile split his face, but Pete couldn't share the same enthusiasm. Being so deeply involved would complicate his investigation. He would have to rely even more on Ruby to do the leg work.

He looked over at his father, who was staring at him, his eyes filled with joy. Pete felt a lump rise in his throat. Why couldn't his father be proud of him for just being who he was, not because of what he did? He turned away just in time to catch Nicolas, who slumped like a boneless carcass, pale and clammy, beside him.

"Hey Nicolas, what's wrong?" Pete asked, righting him in his seat.

Several of the men gathered around them to help.

"I'm fine, fine," Nicolas said weakly. "Must be the lack of sleep from the prayer vigil and all. I'll be okay. I just need rest."

"Let's get you home," Pete said.

One of the older men came to Nicolas' side. "I will take him, Pedro. I, too, must go early tonight; my wife is not well."

Pete let the old man take Nicolas by the arm and lead him from the room. Pete had just settled back into his chair when a black-robed, hooded man entered the room from another door. The men around him bowed their heads in silence at the grim figure's entrance. Pete did the same.

"*Jefe Mayor*," Diego said with great reverence. "It is our pleasure that you join us tonight."

The hooded man nodded.

"Nicolas has chosen his *Compañero*, sir," Diego said, holding his hand toward Pete and then beckoning him to rise and approach the *Jefe Mayor*.

Pete obeyed.

"This is Pedro Medina, our Brother Manuel's son," Diego introduced. "He is the one Nicolas has chosen."

The intimidating figure held out his hand and Pete took it, but suddenly felt the need to withdraw as the *Jefe Mayor* squeezed Pete's hand harder than necessary.

The *Jefe Mayor* then went around the room, shaking hands and speaking with the Brothers. Pete stood uncomfortably behind his chair, wishing he could get out of there and back to his little house in town. He needed to think.

When the *Jefe Mayor* finally left, the mood of the room lifted. Several of them gathered around Pete and introduced themselves, finally completely accepting him.

His father came up behind him and held his arms out for a hug. "My son, you do us a great honor. I am proud. Ricardo would be proud."

Pete bit his lip at the mention of his brother's name and stepped into his father's embrace.

"We will be a family again." His father released him, joy in his eyes.

Pete forced a smile and focused on the true reason he'd joined. "Father, I have a question."

"Yes, anything."

"Why does the *Jefe Mayor* wear a hood like that?"

"To hide his identity, of course," his father said. "The role of *Jefe Mayor* is a very powerful one. It is he who decides who will be Cristo each year. He also makes other important decisions about the rituals. If we knew his identity, it would be difficult for him to be a member of our community. People would look at him differently. It is for his protection, as well as ours."

Pete listened, trying to find flaws in his father's answer.

"Pedro, would you like to come home?" his father asked. "Tonight?"

Struck by the question he hesitated, not sure what to think or say.

"Just for tonight," Manuel clarified. "To visit with your mother and sisters for a few hours?"

Pete's resolve melted. He desperately wanted to see his sisters, his mother.

"Let us be father and son again." He extended his hand.

Pete studied the proffered hand, fighting the urge to lash out with the anger he'd held on to for so long. He had to play along, play the part of remorseful traitor. It was the only way to find out who murdered Ricardo. Hesitantly, he took his father's hand.

CHAPTER 25

When Ruby left Spike at the cantina, she had felt hopeful. His declaration that Yates would never get involved with the Redeemers gave her hope that, although he'd been an asshole to her, the man had principles. So what had happened in Peru? Perhaps Yates had been wrongly accused of something, and it had threatened his career?

And his marriage, she thought, remembering the picture of Yates and the two women.

Ruby headed down the street toward the café where she'd left her car. It was nearly dark, and a streetlamp flickered on over her head. She noticed the same black car from before now parked in front of the cantina. A shiver stole down her spine. Could someone be following her? She shuddered at the memory of her terrifying night in the desert. So much had been happening that she hadn't had time to even truly process the trauma she'd experienced. And she still didn't. Lives were at stake.

Ruby shook off the thought and continued to walk toward the rectory, her head down, even as the hum of an engine sounded behind her. The headlights shined brightly in her direction, casting her shadow, long and lean, in front of her. She heard the car accelerate, slowly at first, then gaining more and more speed. She quickened her pace, still concentrating on the sound. Just to be safe, she moved closer and closer to the buildings.

Suddenly, the engine roared. Headlights danced ahead of her, and she looked over her shoulder to see the car coming straight for her. She ran, staying close to the buildings, pushing her hand against them for balance. The car sped up, gaining on her. She reached the last of the buildings and slipped around the corner behind them. She slammed against something in the dark. Sharp pain seared through her body, and she felt the warmth of her own blood trickling along her skin in spots. She looked to see what she'd hit. A barbed-wire fence. The collision seemed to have loosened the wire from its wooden poles, and barbs sank into her hamstrings and the small of her back, the wire encircling her, trapping her.

The black car darted past her but then tried to stop, tires skidding on the dirt road. It turned around and came toward her again, its headlights blinding her. Ruby struggled in the barbed wire, the sharp prongs tearing at her skin. The car's engine roared, accelerating again. Ruby couldn't move for fear of shredding herself to ribbons. The smell of her own blood made her stomach churn and she covered her head, waiting to be hit by the car.

The sound of metal slamming against something shook her, and she braced herself for the impact. When nothing happened, she glanced up to see the car nose-down in a small irrigation ditch that ran along the back of the buildings, the glow of its headlights submerged in the water.

Carefully, she worked herself out of the tangle of barbed wire. No movement came from the car. Catching her breath, she winced against the pain of her lacerated skin. She limped toward the car, squinting to see inside. The figure behind the steering wheel moved, and Ruby froze. A groan came from inside the car, and then she saw the unmistakable glint of the barrel of a gun resting on the frame of the open car window. She dropped to the ground and scrambled around the building, pressing through all the pain. A shot fired, and she took off running for the cantina without looking back.

Someone didn't just want her to leave Las Montanas.

Someone wanted her dead.

෬ᢲᢙ

Pete and his father walked to the house, making small talk along the way. His father spoke of the farm, the disadvantages of getting older and, of course, the revered Brotherhood. Pete listened, but when his father mentioned Ricardo he tuned out his father's words to prevent his anger from surfacing. He must keep up the front.

When they reached the fence surrounding the Medinas' house, Pete's father told him to come through the gate but to wait outside. He had to prepare Pete's mother for his arrival.

From the outside the house hadn't changed in two years, and suddenly it seemed as if Ricardo had died just yesterday. In the yellow glow of the windows, he saw his mother's silhouette through the ruffled lace curtains she had sewn.

Sloppily rigged floodlights shined in the yard, illuminating the pristine garden. The beanstalks soared, and young yellow squash, zucchini, and gourds glowed in bright colors. That hadn't changed, either. He'd gained his love of gardening from his mother. She would let him dig little holes with a stick, then drop in the hard, tiny seeds and cover them up. With a sack made from a sheep's stomach, he would water the seedlings daily and wait for the sprouts to burst through the earth. His mother's garden, crowded with lush vegetation, reminded him of the neglect he'd shown his own yard. It was as dead as he'd felt.

His old, rusty bike was leaning against the adobe wall of the house. His youngest sister would be the perfect age for riding that bike; Marguerite was probably much too grown up for such play. He hoped Sophia enjoyed the bike as much as he and Ricardo had.

His father stood in the doorway and gestured for Pete to come inside. He took a deep breath and started for the door. His mother met him at the threshold.

"Pedro?" she said, her voice weak, disbelieving. "Pedro?"

Pete swallowed hard, forcing back the tears stinging behind his eyelids. "Hello, Mama."

"My son has returned!" she cried, and flung her arms around him.

Pete held her tightly. He hadn't realize how much he'd missed her.

She let go of him and stood back, taking in every inch of him. Her eyes drank him in as if she hadn't seen him for much longer than two years. Surely, she'd seen him in town. But in truth, he knew she'd obeyed her husband and considered him dead.

"You are thin," she noted. "I've made sopaipillas and biscochitos. Come eat." She took his hand and led him into the house.

Crammed with boxes and furniture, all neatly laid out, the house was just as he remembered. It smelled of tortillas and chili, and the hint of the cinnamon which garnished the sugar and anise seed cookies. A plethora of pictures, Santos, and retablos covered the walls.

"Where are the girls?" he asked.

"They are at Nanito's house, rehearsing," his mother said. "They will both play the part of Veronica this year during the Passion."

Pete frowned at the news. Another village custom. Chosen girls and young wives of the Brothers played the role of Veronica, the woman who had wiped sweat from Jesus' face as he'd toiled up the hill with the cross on his back. The bearers of the shroud.

Pete's insides twisted at the thought of his sisters participating in the Passion. They would watch another Cristo die. It incensed him that not only had his father been a participant in

Ricardo's death, but now his father would allow his daughters to be involved in another's death.

Pete's mother fixed a place for him at the small pine table and held a chair out for him. He sat, and she sat next to him. Her eyes had the sparkle he remembered, and her smile light-ened with each moment he stayed.

She pushed the basket of sweet sopaipillas in front of him and urged him to eat.

"You look well, Mama," he said.

She gave a small chuckle. "I'm an old woman, and I am tired," she said. "But you . . . look at you." She placed her weath-ered hand against his cheek. "You are still beautiful."

Just then the two girls burst through the back door, shouting excitedly at their parents. When they saw Pete they both stopped and stared, shock on their faces.

"It is all right, *mijitas*," Pete said. "I've come back to the family."

Sophia ran to him and wrapped her arms around his neck. She smelled of honey and fresh air. Pete held her close, fighting his tears once more. She had grown so much in the past two years, and he had missed it all.

"I missed you so much, Pedro," she said in her sweet voice.

He kissed her hair. "Me too, *mija*." He turned to Marguerite, who stood silent—suspicion in her eyes. "Don't be afraid, Marguerite. It's okay. I'm back."

At the sound of his voice, her bottom lip quivered and tears sprang to her eyes. Meekly she walked toward him, arms outstretched, and buried her head in the crook of his neck. Her gentle sobs pulled at his heart, and he hated his father for what he had done to these innocent children in depriving them of not one brother, but two.

Marguerite pulled back. "Are you here to stay?" she asked, wiping her tears away.

"No, just for a visit. I have my own home now, but we will

never be separated again," he said, conviction in his voice. "*That*, I promise you."

Both girls lunged at him and hugged him tightly again. He smiled and turned his attention to his parents. His mother wept, holding a soiled handkerchief to her face, and his father beamed. Pete took no joy in the pride in his father's expression. Guilt rose from his gut, filling him, darkening the joy of his homecoming. He would get his family back and find the truth, even if it meant betraying them again.

CHAPTER 26

Early the next morning, Pete sat in the comfort of his own bed after being awakened by his alarm clock. He hated to leave the soft mattress, still exhausted from the days of initiation at the morada. So much had happened. He'd been accepted by the Brotherhood, become *Compañero* of the Cristo, and had been reunited with his family—all in a matter of four days.

He longed to stay in his house for the entire day, just to sit and think about the events that had taken place, to figure out how to move forward with his plan. He also wanted to see Ruby, find out if she'd discovered any new information, but there simply wouldn't be time. He had to get back to the morada. If she found something, they had agreed that she would come to him.

It had been good to see his mother and sisters. The emptiness in his heart melted away at their smiles and hugs, and for the first time in two years he felt loved. But now, as he sat alone in his own house, the renewal of love was replaced with dread. He'd gone to them on false pretenses, pretending to be something he could never be: a true Brother of the Redeemers. Lying was the only way he could be with them again.

Interacting with his father had been more difficult. Anger

and pain still stabbed at his soul. Maybe someday he'd be able to forgive the old man, but not until he knew the truth about Ricardo.

Pete walked to the bathroom and studied his tired face in the mirror. A pale, weary man with lifeless eyes looked back at him. Turning his body he presented his back to the mirror and looked over his shoulder, wincing at the scabbing wounds he'd received from the lashing. His chest and shoulders also remained bruised and discolored.

Good Friday, the day of the crucifixion, was three days away. Who knew what else they had in store for him? One thing he did know, though, was that time was running out.

Later that morning, Pete and Nicolas sat at the top of the hill where Nicolas would be crucified. Nicolas had carried one of the large crosses to the top in preparation for Good Friday, and now his right shoulder was bloody and bruised and sweat seeped out of every pore. He still looked pale and weak, even though he carried the cross as if it weighed nothing. He'd made it to the top of the sand-covered hill without stopping a single time. At Pete's urging, he had finally set the cross down when they neared the top.

They sat in silence, looking out over the desert landscape. To the east, at the base of Manzanita Mountains, the earth spread down the sides of the jagged mountain crests and flooded into a sea of flat, brown land. To the west, the Las Montanas mountain range jutted high and majestic, its red earth glowing in the mid-morning sunlight. Rabbits scampered about, gathering food and then burrowing back into their holes.

Pete became aware of the sound of Nicolas' ragged breathing. He still had not caught his breath. "You okay?" Pete asked.

Nicolas held up a hand and nodded, unable to speak. After a few minutes his breathing finally slowed, but his complexion remained pale. His natural skin color was a dark brown, and the paleness made his face look blotchy, gray, and sickly. Pete hoped today's training hadn't harmed him.

"Can I ask you a question?" Nicolas asked.

"Sure."

"I see tension between you and Manuel. Why is that?"

Pete's stomach knotted. *Of all the questions . . .* He'd thought Nicolas was going to ask him for advice on women or something. He probably wouldn't be much help in that department either, though. "We haven't been together in a long time," he answered. "We've never really gotten along very well. I suppose things like that don't change."

"Why can't they?" Nicolas challenged.

"He's too old, too set in his ways. I see things differently than he does." He paused. "He was a difficult father . . . I guess we stopped talking a long time ago."

"That's too bad. I lost my father when I was seven. Sometimes I think about him, but not as much as I did when I was a kid. Still, I wonder what he was like. How we would have been together. You're lucky you still have your father."

Pete sighed. "Yeah, maybe."

"Is it true what they say?" Nicolas asked. "That your father was Cristo long ago?"

Pete only nodded.

"But he bears no scars."

"No. He didn't pass the final rite of his initiation," Pete explained.

"Oh," Nicolas said. "I'm sorry."

"I don't think he's ever recovered from the shame of it," Pete said. "But I'm not sorry he didn't make it."

"What do you mean?"

"I don't know if I could've handled watching him hang on the cross. I was little—only about four." A shudder swept through him. "Later, when Ricardo was Cristo, I couldn't watch, either. I refused."

"You love your father very much," Nicolas said.

"Yes." Pete frowned. To his surprise, the response had come automatically. So many thoughts of his father in the past few years had produced only anger and bitterness. But yes, he couldn't deny it. He did love his father.

"Your father must have been honored to have a son be Cristo, even though he himself could not be."

"He was. And now that Ricardo is dead, it gives us all honor." He hoped he sounded sincere, even as every muscle in his body wanted to let loose his anger and pain.

Nicolas looked at his hands and flexed his fingers, as if imagining the sensation of the large nails being driven into his wrists.

"You don't have to do this, you know," Pete said, watching him. "You're still not well. You're fatigued, weak—"

"I'm fine," Nicolas cut in.

"Well then, we'd better get back." Pete stood.

Nicolas rose to his feet and immediately faltered, falling back to the ground. He held his head. "Whoa, I feel kind of dizzy."

"Don't move. Just sit there." Pete watched the color drain from Nicolas' face. They shouldn't have come out here today. Nicolas hadn't completely recovered from the snake bite yet. Or was it the last of the flu-like virus that he'd suffered from? But he'd insisted.

"I feel better now." Nicolas stood again. Although he was still unsteady, he stayed on his feet this time. He took several deep breaths. "Must have stood up too fast the first time." He reached for the cross.

"Why don't we both carry it down?" Pete suggested. "I'll take the heavy end. You've had enough today."

To his surprise, Pete didn't get any resistance. They began down the hill.

"You should take it easy the rest of the day."

"Yeah, maybe you're right," Nicolas agreed.

As they made their way down, Pete wondered if Nicolas would be healthy enough to carry out his duties as Cristo. The way things had been going the past few days he seriously doubted it, which meant Pete would have to take his place. The idea made him break out into a sweat.

He had never intended for any of this to go so far. Either Nicolas needed to make a speedy recovery or Pete would have to come up with a plan to escape the crucifixion. The last thing he wanted to do was hang on a cross and die.

◈❦◈

At half past six in the evening, Ruby sat behind a large boulder amid the sage brush and a few pine trees, watching the morada. The sun hung lazily above the horizon in the west, refusing to rush its descent.

Chanting from inside floated on the breeze. Ruby envisioned the men kneeling in prayer, the choir of their melancholy voices filling the room.

How would she get Pete's attention when the vigil ended? *When* would it end, she wondered, thinking she could very well be out there until sunrise.

If only she knew someone who could get a message to him. But anyone she knew would either chide her for interfering in the Brotherhood or would have nothing to do with entering the sacred morada. She considered Xavier Piedras, but she wasn't sure of his relationship with the Brotherhood. Asking for his help would be too risky. There were so few people she could trust.

She hadn't a clue how to get Pete's attention. Absently she fingered the red bandana at her neck, and then it hit her. She placed the bandana, still knotted, on top of a large rock. Surely, Pete would know she was there.

The chanting stopped. Ruby listened, hearing only the chirp of crickets and the thump of jackrabbits stealing their way through clumps of wild grass. She peered over the boulder just in time to see the door of the morada swing open. The Redeemers spilled out into the dusky light of the evening. She watched them leave, straining to get a glimpse of Pete or Nicolas. Nicolas came out, accompanied by an older man. Then six or seven others filed out.

Pete finally appeared in the doorway. She stood up, and his gaze flitted in her direction. She sank down behind the boulder again, hoping he'd seen her or the bandana. She heard his soft, approaching footsteps in the sand. He sat down next to her and handed her the bandana. Ruby didn't say anything but studied his face. His eyes showed his fatigue as they locked on hers, but he still seemed glad to see her.

"I can't stay long," he said. "I've had to take a vow of silence for the next forty-eight hours. If anyone sees me talking to you, it's all over."

She nodded. "How are things going in there?"

"Hard to say. I haven't had the opportunity to find out much. They've kept me busy, and now we aren't allowed to speak. We have to stay the night, in prayer. We're just taking a break."

"Have you been able to talk to Nicolas?"

"Yeah. Great kid. But unfortunately, extremely devoted to the Brotherhood. He sees nothing amiss."

"Can you convince him of our suspicions?"

"I don't know."

Pete looked down at her arm and pointed at the rough scratches. "What happened to you?"

She shrugged. She had to stay calm, collected. "Someone tried to run me down in a car. I got caught in some barbed wire trying to get away."

"*What?!*" His eyes filled with alarm.

"Luckily, the car crashed into a ditch before it got to me. I was able to free myself from the wire and run away."

"Damn it," he said through clenched his teeth. "Who was it?"

She shook her head. "I couldn't see him clearly. I don't know."

"This is getting out of hand, Ruby." His eyes searched hers.

"I just need to be more careful," she tried to reason.

"I don't like you being out there alone. I wish I'd never done this, never joined the Brotherhood so I could—" He stopped, looking everywhere but at her. She was glad she didn't tell him the driver of the car had tried to shoot her, too.

"Protect me?" she asked with a slight grin.

"Yes."

"Thanks, but I can take care of myself." She smiled, flattered at his words.

"But someone is trying to *kill* you."

"I'll be all right. I'm worried about you, though." He took her hand and studied the scratches, ran his finger over each one.

"Wounds heal," she said quietly.

"Do they?"

His eyes met hers and held her gaze. Her skin tingled where he touched it, and she became aware of everything around her— the smell of the breeze, the feel of it on her face, the sounds of the crickets, and the stillness of the evening. Her heart pounded, overwhelmed by him, his tenderness, his fierce desire to protect her.

"What about your father?" she asked, breaking the tension.

Pete turned his eyes away. "My father has never been happier. And I was able to see the rest of my family—my sisters and my mother."

She gave a small smile. "I'm happy for you. How have you been treated—" she pointed, "—in there?"

"They're not very generous with meals or recreation. We spend most of our time praying, fasting, or partaking in the rituals."

"How's that been?" she asked, scrunching up her nose.

"You don't want to know."

"Oh." Ruby trailed her fingers in the sand at their feet. "Has Nicolas recovered?"

"Somewhat," Pete replied. "He *seems* frail, but his strength is incredible."

"Do you think he'll be able to perform as Cristo? Maybe if he can't, then he won't get hurt or killed."

Pete stared down at Ruby's hand, which was still in his, and he played with her fingers.

"What's the matter?" she asked, not understanding his sudden silence. Or his suddenly trembling hands.

"He chose me as his *Compañero*."

Her brow furrowed. "What does that mean?"

She could see in his eyes that she wasn't going to like it, even before he responded. "If he isn't well enough to hang on the cross, then I . . ."

Ruby's heart stuttered. "You?"

He nodded.

"No! Pete, you can't!" She shook her head almost violently. "You'll be . . . You can't!"

"Don't worry about that right now. We still have some time," he said, seeming much calmer than she would've expected. "We've got to find more information. *You've* got to find something. Just watch out for yourself while you try, okay?"

She swallowed, never expecting things to turn out like this. Now both of their lives were on the line, as well as Nicolas'.

"Who's out there?" a voice bellowed from the bushes.

Ruby and Pete stared at each other, wide-eyed. Pete pushed his fingers up against her lips. She held her breath.

"I have to go," he whispered.

"Wait. Have you got—"

Before she realized what had happened, Pete's mouth was covering hers. His kiss, warm and sensual, made her melt into his embrace. After what simultaneously seemed like seconds *and* hours, he pulled away. She stared at him with her mouth partially open, still reeling from the kiss.

"You had a question?" he asked.

"Oh, right." Her mind tried to focus. "Um, did you get a sample of the pulque?"

"I'll leave it on this rock tonight. You'll have to come back and get it."

She nodded.

He planted another gentle kiss on her forehead, then stood up. "Be careful, Ruby. I mean it."

CHAPTER 27

The Brothers ate a sparse meal of beans and rice in silence. Afterward they were allowed thirty minutes of free time before prayers, which couldn't work better for Pete. He snuck away and snagged a vial of pulque, hoping Ruby would see it on the same rock where she'd placed the bandana.

To his surprise, Ruby was still there. He didn't dare speak for fear someone might overhear. They communicated only with their eyes, and what Pete read in Ruby's suddenly slammed reality into him. He wanted her in his life. He hoped they'd both come out of this mess unscathed. Reluctantly, he walked away from her and returned to the morada.

Inside, Pete knelt next to Nicolas at the front of the room near the altar. Nicolas, deep in prayer, didn't move, didn't even twitch. But Pete fidgeted, his knees aching and his stomach still growling with hunger. He turned to see his father kneeling several rows behind him on the other side of the aisle, his head bent in prayer, his eyes closed.

In his glory.

When Pete turned back around, Martinez was approaching the altar. "I apologize for interrupting your prayers, but a serious matter has been brought to my attention and the Brotherhood needs to gather immediately. There has been a violation of the sacred vow of silence."

The men, careful not to speak, looked at one another, wide-eyed with curiosity. Sudden nausea hit Pete's stomach. He'd been caught.

"The vigil chain was broken earlier this evening when *that man*, the *Compañero*—" Martinez pointed at Pete, "—spoke secretly with a woman outside the morada."

All heads turned in his direction. Looking over his shoulder again, he met his father's glare. The old childhood guilt surfaced. He didn't understand how anyone could have seen him and Ruby. He'd been careful.

"Come to the altar, Pedro," Martinez ordered.

His face afire with shame Pete obeyed, knowing what would come next. How many times had his father lectured him and Ricardo on violating the sacred trust of God?

He walked to the altar, his back straight, and then turned to face the men. His eyes strayed again to his father's humiliated face. Pete swallowed hard.

Martinez pointed to two men, who walked toward Pete together and then split up when they reached the altar. They each took hold of ropes that snaked down on each side of the altar, suspended from the ceiling. The two men bound Pete's arms with the ropes and then hoisted his arms up so they were parallel with the ground. Panic gripped him, and he shot a pleading look at his father. But his father turned away.

"Don't do this," Pete said to Martinez, trying to steady his voice. "She's my girlfriend, and she's in trouble. I was only trying to help," he lied, desperate.

Martinez glared at Pete, the darkness in his eyes unforgiving, unemotional.

From the doorway the hooded *Jefe Mayor* entered, carrying his bullwhip. He handed it to Martinez.

"I will rid you of your sin," Martinez told Pete.

At the first crack, Pete nearly fell to his knees with the intensity of the sting. The world momentarily went black. The whip snapped again, tearing a new gash into his back. He howled at the impact, trying to use his anger to brace himself against the pain. The crack, again. Blackness, again. The crack four more times.

He hung from outstretched arms, his legs unable to bear his own weight any more. He fought the pain surging through his body. His mind went numb, his jaw dropped, and his eyelids hung lazily over glazed vision. The faces before him blurred. Crack.

Damn my father, he thought, barely able to keep his eyes open. *Damn them all.*

When Pete opened his eyes again, Nicolas' face hovered over him. Pete's arms had been freed and he lay on the ground, his head cradled in Nicolas' hands.

"Why did you do it?" Nicolas whispered.

"Didn't think I'd get caught," he answered honestly.

"Leave him now, Nicolas," Martinez said. "Finish your prayers. We will tend to him."

Silently, Nicolas helped Pete to his feet. Pete's head spun with the movement, and the pain blackened all his sensations. He allowed himself to slip again into the realm of soothing darkness.

⚜

The following morning, Ruby dressed and headed out to take the pulque sample to Dr. Jones in Los Campos. But first she'd pay a visit to Dr. Mendenhall. She wouldn't be any help to anyone if she didn't get her wounds treated. The areas that had been cut with the barbed wire were still red, swollen and tender to the touch.

She winced as she rolled the sleeves of her cotton blouse up to show the doctor the cuts on her forearm. He gave them a cursory look and then hustled around the room, grabbing supplies. He set everything down near Ruby and got to work cleaning the wound with peroxide. "It's infected all right," he said. The liquid bubbled furiously, and Ruby cringed against the sting. "You should have come in for a tetanus shot right away."

"I've been a little busy lately."

He gave her a look that said she should've known better. "How did this even happen?" he asked. She told him that she'd accidentally walked into the fence after dark—not a *complete* lie —and tried not to say anything more that could arouse his suspicion.

When he finished cleaning the wounds, he slathered them with antibacterial ointment and dressed them with gauze bandages. She watched him as he prepared the tetanus shot next.

"This is going to hurt," he warned, "and your arm will be sore for a few days."

"Thanks for being honest."

He raised a brow at her. "I've turned over a new leaf."

Ruby laughed, and he quickly gave her the injection. She clenched her teeth on the pain. He came at her with another injection.

"What's that?" she asked, pulling her arm away from him.

He chuckled. "Antibiotics."

"Oh." She cautiously showed him her arm again.

He gave her the shot. "That ought to do it. You must be the most accident-prone person I know, Ruby. You stay out of trouble, you hear?"

Right. She probably shouldn't tell him that someone was out to kill her. Sure, he'd been vindicated of wrongdoing by the media, but still.

"Anyone else come down with that virus?" she asked.

Dr. Mendenhall stood over the sink, washing his hands. "Yes, as a matter of fact—near the Four Corners area this time. It's quite an outbreak, and it's been going on for a few months now. But it doesn't seem to be transmitted from person to person."

"So you've found out more about the virus?" Ruby hopped down from the table.

"Yes. Turns out it's a zoonosis virus transmitted from animals to humans. In this case, it's coming from rodents—rats, rabbits, mice."

"Wow." She shook her head. "Do you think that the men in the cavern died of this zoo . . . zoonosis virus, then?"

"Doubtful. The bodies in the cavern had been deceased at least a year already."

"No government biological warfare testing?"

"I don't believe so."

She pressed her lips together, thinking. "But why are they all together in a pile like that?"

"The Redeemers have always buried their dead together," he said with a shrug.

Her jaw dropped slightly. "You know about the Redeemers?"

"I've lived and worked among these people for years, Ruby. There isn't much I don't know."

She could launch right in now. "What is your opinion on the deaths of the last few Cristos?"

"It's certainly odd," he said carefully.

"Damned right it is, Doctor."

"Don't do this." The warning in his voice alarmed her. "I know what you're thinking, but don't. Just leave it be. These people are almost medieval in their thinking, especially in their spirituality. They are insignificant to the rest of the world. Let them be."

"Dr. Mendenhall, four men have died. *For nothing.* You don't see anything wrong with that? You won't do anything about it?"

"I've interfered enough in these people's lives. It's not my place." He avoided making eye contact with her.

Ruby couldn't believe the immense power the Brotherhood wielded over the people of Las Montanas. Resigned to continuing the fight on her own, Ruby didn't press the doctor further. "How much do I owe you?"

"Nothing."

"But—"

"Stay healthy, Ruby. And please . . . please stay out of trouble." He turned his back on her and began to clean the examining room. Ruby sighed, and let herself out of the clinic.

⚜

When she arrived in Los Campos, Ruby told Dr. Jones what had transpired over the last few days. Then Dr. Jones analyzed the pulque, to disappointing findings. All the ingredients were natural. None of the substances were toxic, except maybe the nicotine, but it would have to be in highly concentrated form to cause death. She doubted the mixture would do anything except create vivid hallucinations and a nasty hangover.

Driving back to Las Montanas, Ruby felt defeated. Pete and Nicolas were still in danger, and they were no closer to figuring out what was going on. One idea kept coming to mind, though. She didn't like the option, but she knew she needed help. And there was one person left who would know how to help her. He wouldn't want to, though, so Ruby would have to persuade him.

During her drive to the dig site Ruby rehearsed over and over what she might say to Dr. Yates, but couldn't decide how best to say it. She pulled in next to Yates' truck and turned off the ignition.

Yates sat at the campfire, smoking a cigar, while two other men worked in the ruins. Ruby knew the professor had seen her drive up, but he didn't acknowledge her presence. Not surprised, she felt as welcome as a headache. She took a deep breath and got out of her car.

She walked to the campfire and sat in one of the chairs opposite Yates. His eyes trailed over her shoulder out to the desert. He rolled his cigar between his lips.

His eyes finally met hers across the dead campfire. "I thought you would've gone home by now."

"Well you thought wrong, Dr. Yates."

He pointed to her bandaged arms. "That looks unpleasant. What happened?"

"Someone tried to run me over with a car. Then they tried to shoot me," she said. "I guess they want me out of town."

"Or dead," he added.

She narrowed her eyes at him, wondering if he had been her assailant. Then she remembered Spike's vehement assertion that Yates was a good man, a moral man. *To a fault,* Spike had said. Ruby trusted Spike, so she'd take his word for it—for now.

"Is there something I can do for you?" he asked.

"I think I know why you don't want me to investigate the Redeemers."

He smiled and dipped his head, looking between his knees at the ground. She could see nothing of his face, blocked by his ever-present Panama fedora.

"I doubt that, Miss Delgado."

She crossed her arms. "You're involved."

He let out a deep, rolling, belly laugh. "That's ridiculous. Me? A Redeemer?"

"I didn't say you were a *member* of the Brotherhood."

His stony expression returned.

"I mean that you're involved in the cover-up," she clarified. "You know what's been happening out here and you won't do anything about it. Why is that, Dr. Yates? Someone paying you off? The government, perhaps?"

He gazed at her thoughtfully, twirling the cigar between his fingers. "I can assure you, Miss Delgado—Ruby—that I am not involved in any way. Nor do I know all that is going on with the Brotherhood of the Redeemers. I just know my business, and I try not to intrude upon other people's lives."

She scoffed. "You may as well be involved."

"Excuse me?" he growled.

"Did you hear about Enrique Martinez?"

"He took a leave of absence."

"He was never a priest, you know," she said. "He forged his papers from the archbishop. He's involved with the Redeemers, and could be directly involved with the murders."

Yates didn't say anything, seemingly unfazed by the information.

"Dr. Yates, I don't understand your apathy. The entire community is being taken advantage of, don't you see?"

Yates shook his head. "You are something else, Ruby Delgado. You've got tenacity I haven't seen since—"

"Since?" she urged.

"Nothing . . . Let's take a walk, Ruby."

CHAPTER 28

In his small room directly off the morada, Pete lay face-down on his cot. He couldn't move, paralyzed by heavy limbs and weak muscles. A quiet voice spoke to him from above. Foggy from pain he strained to hear, but couldn't comprehend the words.

His back felt as if it had been ripped open from shoulders to waist. Every fiber of him ached. Someone touched him, and he winced. Hands spread something smooth and cool on his back. He squeezed his eyes shut, fighting the pain. After several minutes the agony ceased and gave way to numbness. His head cleared, and he opened his eyes.

"There," the voice said. "That should make you feel better. You'll heal quickly with the salve."

Pete tried to turn his head to see the man to whom the voice belonged, but he couldn't manage it. He was too weak.

"I'll leave broth for you to sip, to gain back your strength," the voice said. "Right now, you must focus on rest and prayer. The Passion begins in two days, and as *Compañero* you will be needed."

The voice came closer, and Pete found himself staring into

two eye holes within a black hood. The eyes within were a deep, dark brown.

The *Jefe Mayor*.

"You've taken your punishment well," he said. "But I warn you, my friend, it will not be your last. You must stop this investigation, Pedro Medina. You will not defile the name of the Brotherhood of the Redeemers. You will serve God as you have promised in your initiation. And—" He paused, his voice lowering, "—you'll not see that woman again."

Pete glared into the dark, cold eyes. He was so weak that he couldn't do anything else.

"I will give you something to help you sleep," the hooded man said. "When you wake, you must drink the broth. Rest now, Brother."

Pete felt the sting of a needle in his arm. He fought for consciousness but quickly lost the battle.

❦

Before Ruby could get up from her spot around the campfire Yates was standing and walking at a brisk pace, moving past her and heading toward some nearby bluffs. She trotted to keep up with him. Neither of them spoke.

When they reached the ridge of one of the bluffs Yates stopped, scanning the landscape below. Ruby also admired the stunning view. The earth blushed pink and ran in rivulets to stacked mesas that bled crimson. The sharpness of the clear blue sky contrasted with brilliant, puffy white clouds. They shadowed the ground beneath them, making the jade-colored plants seem to glow.

Yates broke the silence. "You remind me of myself."

Her brow furrowed. "What? Me?"

He nodded. "Your passion, your determination, your sense of morality, your desire for justice."

Ruby bit her lip, listening, uncomfortable at him baring his soul to her.

"Your passion, though misdirected, runs your life; as my passion does mine," he went on. "I'm going to tell you something, Ruby. Listen well."

I'm all ears.

"When I was a younger man, about thirty, I was sent with a team from Cornell University to study a small indigenous tribe in Peru. Our mission was quite simple: to study the remains of the dead and learn more about their lifestyle, much as we're doing here with the Anasazi. But I became distracted."

He pulled another cigar from his breast pocket, clipped the end, twirled it in his mouth, and then lit it. "I had learned that the natives in higher jungles were killing any and all children born after a woman's first two. Population control. I couldn't wrap my mind around it. My wife and I had tried for a few years to conceive a child and were never successful. Our marriage eventually fell apart because of it, and these people who were so blessed with offspring were just killing them."

Ruby thought of the woman in the picture and the baby resting on her hip.

"My wife became distraught over this practice, as did I. We wanted a baby so much. As an anthropologist I knew some cultures still practiced human sacrifice for religious reasons, but this hit us hard. I contacted the Christian missionaries and told them what was going on. In a few weeks, they came out in an effort to 'educate' the natives."

Ruby cringed. That can't have been received very well . . .

"With time, we won our battle. The indigenous tribes agreed to stop killing their babies."

"You saved all those lives, all those children," Ruby said, feeling his victory.

"The entire village died from starvation." His voice was monotone and he shifted, putting space between them. Ruby couldn't see his eyes or read his expression. "It took several years, but the inevitable happened," he said. "Too many mouths to feed. Right or wrong, this form of population control had been a part of their culture. It had been so for centuries," he said, "and we . . . I . . . destroyed it."

He shifted again so that all Ruby could see was his bearded cheek and part of his chin.

"Because of my misdirected passion, I singlehandedly destroyed an entire culture. And my failure destroyed a part of me. I don't want to see you or anyone else do that. I won't permit it."

"Dr. Yates," she said gently, "this situation is different."

"How is it different?" He turned to her, his expression cold again.

"I think I know how the Cristos are dying," she lied. "I just can't prove it yet."

Yates stomped out his cigar on the ground and crossed his arms over his chest. "I'm listening."

Ruby told him about Ricardo and the coroner's report. She told him about Nicolas, and about Pete's entry into the Brotherhood. She also told him about her abduction and reminded him of her suspicions about Martinez. She told him about Dr. Jones, and how she was trying to help them. "Dr. Yates, someone is trying to stop me from investigating this. I can't quit now just because whoever is doing this has threatened my life, as well as Pete's."

Yates, still silent, stared out at the bluffs.

"When you helped me in the café I asked why you did it, why you risked your own safety for mine," she reminded him. "You said it was because I needed the help. Well, now it's Pete who needs you, and Nicolas Baca. You don't have to do anything for me again, but please, please help Pete. He needs you, Dr. Yates, and hopefully we can save Nicolas, too."

Yates pushed his hat back on his head and scratched at his temple. Without a word, he secured the hat on his forehead and started walking back toward the dig site.

"Dr. Yates?"

When they reached the camp, Ruby trotting behind him, Yates went directly to his trailer and shut the door.

I guess I've got my answer. So much for appealing to Yates' compassionate side; apparently, he didn't have one.

Flustered, Ruby got into her car and started the engine. She pressed her forehead to the steering wheel. Would she forever be unable to help those she cared about?

She'd just put the car in gear when Yates came out of the trailer and headed toward her. She waited, curious.

He leaned down and rested his arms on the frame of her open window. "I don't feel right about this, but I can't let Pete down. He's always been there for me."

Ruby smiled, relieved she'd gotten through to him. "Thank you so much. Really, you won't regret this. I promise."

"That's a pretty big promise." He straightened and slipped his hands into his pockets. "I think we should start back at square one: where you found the bodies."

Ruby let out her breath, relieved he wanted to move so quickly. "I'd like you to see the shrine down there, too."

"I'll get some gear together. Be right back."

She watched his lanky form stroll away from her. The sudden change of heart unsettled her a little. Did he really mean it?

Not long later, he came out of the trailer with a day pack. Ruby pulled her climbing gear from her car and together they walked to the sinkhole.

When they reached the opening, Ruby hooked them up with ropes and harnesses. She let Yates go in first, and then she followed. When she hit bottom she found him down on one knee where the bodies had been, hat in his hands, studying the ground. He smoothed his graying hair back, then centered the hat back on his head with the other.

Ruby's brows rose. She had never noticed his good looks before. Seeing him without his hat for that brief second was like seeing another man altogether.

"That brush over there?" He pointed to the thorny bush that blocked one of the entrances. "That plant does grow here, but it's rare. It's called *arbusto de chucillo*, bush of knives. The branches are used by the Redeemers to make the crown of thorns for the Passion."

She remembered the crowns on the tiny altar in the cavern.

"C'mon. There's something else you have to see."

They approached the hole in the wall that Ruby had made and crawled through to find the other cavern. Without warning, Yates grabbed her arm and covered her mouth with a rough hand. He pulled her up against the wall. Fear shot through her. What was he doing?

"Did you hear that?" he whispered, his breath warm on her ear, before he released her.

Her back against the wall, she caught her breath again and listened. It sounded like someone shuffling around. Yates leaned forward to see though the hole, and Ruby strained to see around him.

A man in a heavy coat and large hat sat on the ground near the altar. The upright coffins, having been returned to their proper places, framed the altar as a backdrop. The man wore heavy gloves and worked with thorny branches, fashioning them into perfect circles. He mumbled to himself—perhaps praying.

Ruby and Yates exchanged glances, then turned back to watch again.

The man took a small brush and dipped it into a wooden bowl. He lay the crown of thorns on the altar and bent over it, gently stroking the brush over the thorns. When he finished, he stood and admired his work. He then took the brush, placed it in a white paper bag, and set the bowl in a corner. He lay the spare branches on the altar. Then he lit the candles and knelt, bowing his head in prayer.

After a few minutes he rose, crossed himself, and blew out the candles. He backed toward the two of them, head still bowed in reverence, only turning when he neared the hole. With his hat pulled low, Ruby couldn't quite see his face. Fearing he would see them, however, they both eased into the shadows. Ruby held a hand over her own mouth, fearful she'd give them away. The man pushed himself through the hole then walked past them, completely unaware of their presence. They waited, not moving or speaking, until his footsteps faded and he was gone.

"That was close!" Ruby said, still whispering.

"Come on," Yates said, and climbed through the hole to see what was on the altar. Ruby followed him. He picked up the small wooden bowl.

"What is it?" Ruby asked.

"I don't know." He sniffed it. "Did you see he painted the crown of thorns with the stuff?"

She stared at the crown hanging on the altar, its thorns still wet from a translucent black substance. She picked up the brush, still in its white bag, and studied it.

"Could be some kind of varnish," Yates suggested. "For aesthetic purposes."

She slipped the bag off and turned the brush in her fingers. She held it to her nose. It smelled earthy, damp, with a sharp tang to it.

"Smell this." She handed the bowl to Yates. "Varnish has a toxic, *fumy* smell; this doesn't smell like that at all."

"Could be a drug," he said. "Maybe pulque."

"It doesn't smell like pulque," Ruby said. "But whatever it is could be the key to what's happening to the Cristos. Let's take a sample."

Yates pulled a tiny jar from his pants pocket. Careful not to touch the little puddle of liquid with his fingers, he lay the jar in the bowl. A few drops seeped into the jar, and he secured the lid. He wiped the wet jar on the dirt to dry it, then held it out to Ruby.

"Your coroner friend could probably tell us what this is," he said.

She nodded. "Probably. What do you think we should do now?"

"Let's see what Dr. Jones says first."

"Okay," Ruby agreed. "I'll go out to Los Campos. Do you want to come?"

Dr. Yates shook his head. "Just let me know what she says."

"Sounds good," Ruby said, but first she needed to see Pete.

⚜

Ruby watched the door to the morada from behind a clump of trees. She'd thrown on her grungiest clothes and bought an over-sized man's hat for a disguise. Pulling the hat down low on her head, she peered out from behind the trees. Two cars were parked near the entrance, but the morada remained quiet.

She took a deep breath and told herself she needed to inform Pete that Dr. Yates had agreed to help them. But really she missed him, she worried about him, and could no longer hide that she had developed feelings for him. Gathering her courage, she stepped out into the open. She hoped he was there. She'd checked his house in town first; when he wasn't there, she figured he'd be at the morada.

As soon as she came out from the cover of the trees two men stepped out of the morada, but they didn't look in her direction. She quietly slipped back to her hiding place. The two men walked to the two parked cars, got into them, and drove off. Relieved, she continued forward. When she reached the entrance she stepped inside, and strained to hear for voices or any sounds of movement. The place seemed to be empty, but she had to be sure. *Where could he be?*

The austerity of the room sent a chill down her spine when she recalled the sight of the twenty or so men kneeling on the very floor where she stood. Chanting as they flung the whips over their backs in self-flagellation.

She noticed a door behind the altar. Its only ornamentation

was a latch, which was closed but not locked. She flipped the latch open and pushed on the heavy door. It squeaked on its hinges, and when it had opened a few inches a ray of light hit the floor, illuminating the dark room. She stood a moment, letting her eyes adjust to the darkness, and then quietly stepped inside, partially closing the door behind her but leaving it open a crack for light.

The room smelled of earth and dust and something else. Something familiar. Something metallic.

Blood.

She looked around the room, noting the religious paraphernalia on the walls despite the dimness. She leaned close to see the items better and was startled by the distinct rhythm of someone breathing, as if in sleep. She blinked hard and whirled in the direction of the sound. Someone lay on his stomach on a dirty white cot, his head turned toward the wall, one arm dangling to the floor.

She walked toward him but stopped short when she saw his back. She gasped. The man had been brutally whipped, his skin purple and raw. A greasy salve coated the wounds, giving them a sickly sheen. She moved toward the man's head. One arm circled his face, making it impossible to identify him. She knelt in front of him, immediately recognizing the beautiful, silky brown waves of his hair.

Pete.

Tears stung her eyes, and she gently ran her fingers through his hair. At her touch, Pete stirred. He lifted his head and opened his eyes.

When he recognized her, his gaze filled with alarm. "W-what are you doing here?"

"What have they done to you?" she whispered.

Pete winced as he rolled to his side. "You have to get out of here. *Now.* Martinez knows something's up." He placed his palm on the cot for support, pain etched on his face. "Help me sit."

Ruby steadied his arms while he gritted his teeth and pushed himself up.

"I'm so sorry," Ruby said.

"Martinez saw us talking. I broke the silence of the prayer vigil. This was punishment."

She closed her eyes, but tears still escaped. "This is my fault."

"No," he said. "This is something *I* had to do. It's the only way." Pete raised his hand to her cheek. He caressed it, his fingers wiping away her tears. "This was just a warning. We won't be so lucky next time. You have to go. Now. You won't be able to come back, and I won't be able to leave." He gripped the cot, trying to hold himself upright. His knuckles whitened with the pressure.

"Maybe you should lie down," she said.

"Not yet. What have you found out? Anything else?"

"Lots. Two other Cristos were autopsied. Did you know that?"

He shook his head.

"Dr. Jones gave me the names. I spoke with the father of one of the Cristos, Eduardo Cordova. He thinks the Redeemers killed Eduardo, too. I couldn't find the other family. Mr. Cordova did tell me that Eduardo was in perfect health at the time of his death, no illnesses or anything. And Dr. Jones analyzed the pulque and said, in its present form, none of the ingredients could be fatal. And there's something else." She paused to press a gentle hand to his chest, over his heart. "Dr. Yates is helping us. He went with me to the shrine in the cavern, and we saw a man there painting multiple crowns of thorns with something."

"Who?" he asked.

"We never saw his face. But when he left, we got a sample of the liquid. I'm taking it to Dr. Jones. She'll be able to tell us what it is. We're almost there, Pete."

She didn't know if she was trying to give him hope or convince herself.

"Who's to say what's going to happen, Ruby?" He swallowed loudly. "You really should get out of here."

He sounded defeated, lost, as if all their efforts would gain them nothing. She wanted to stay and comfort him, to be there for him, but she would only get him in more trouble. She knew she had to leave.

"Just one more thing," she said. "Dr. Jones said all three Cristos had been smokers. Did Ricardo smoke?

"Smokers," he said, a flicker of new interest in his eyes.

"Yeah, the nicotine showed up in the autopsies."

"That was in my brother's autopsy, too?"

"Yes."

He shook his head. "Ricardo never smoked."

"Never? Did he chew tobacco?"

"Never."

Ruby leaned closer to him, her face next to his. She could feel his breath on her cheek. "I'm so sorry, Pete," she whispered, and kissed him softly on the lips.

A rattling came from the door, startling them both.

"Get down," Pete hissed. He flung his feet up onto the cot and spun around to lie on his stomach again. Ruby rushed to the corner of the room and sank to her haunches. The door opened wide and the room flooded with light.

"What the—?" A man wearing a black hood rushed toward her, grabbing her by the arms before she could react. When he pulled her to standing she lifted her knee, hard and fast, to make contact with his groin. He grunted and doubled over, his shoulder pinning her into the corner.

She punched at his ribs. Air rushed out of his lungs with each blow, but his grip remained steady. His shoulder pressed into her, squeezing harder and harder against her chest and ribs. She gasped for air, starting to feel lightheaded, as if on the edge of consciousness. Without air, she could no longer fight. She felt herself weaken. She struggled against him, pounding her fists on his back. "Let me go!"

She felt a sharp prick in her thigh, and within seconds everything was moving in slow motion. She tried to fight, to strike out, but her body wouldn't cooperate. Her head swam, and her arms and legs went limp. She felt herself falling, falling, falling.

And then, there was nothing.

CHAPTER 29

Ruby awoke in darkness. The air was hot, sticky, and suffocating, and her head was pounding. She tried to sit up, but nausea and dizziness overwhelmed her. She smelled the dank odor of earth. Was she underground?

A match flared to life, a familiar face lit by the glow. "Fa—Martinez," she gasped. She tried again to sit up, but the drug was still clearly in her system. She lay back down, defeated, and closed her eyes.

He lit a candle. "I tried to warn you. I thought I could get you to go away. It was bad enough you were asking so many questions, and then you reported your findings to the sheriff. You went too far."

Ruby finally pushed herself up to rest her upper body on her elbows. Pain seared the back of her eyeballs. "When the archbishop's people found out you were a fraud?" she snarked, her voice raspy.

"I *am* a minister of God. This village and its people have instilled this in me more than you could ever imagine. They've brought me back to faithfulness. They understand *true* sacrifice and worship, the way to genuinely love God."

"They're killing their sons and brothers," she snapped. "Their husbands." She fought the weakness that tried to draw her toward sleep.

"Nobody *killed* anyone." His voice was insistent. "Those Cristos have met God face-to-face. Don't you realize the honor bestowed upon them?"

Ruby couldn't speak anymore. Her arms buckled, dropping her back down. All she could do was lie there, wondering what he intended to do with her and how she could get out of it. If only she didn't feel as though she weighed three hundred pounds.

"He did it," Martinez murmured in a whisper. "He's the one, the voice in the dark. I've simply provided guidance. I showed them a deeper form of worship. I mean no one any harm, not even you, but you won't stop."

He sounded contrite, apologetic, but when Ruby pried open her eyes she saw in the flickering candlelight the madness in his gaze. What was he talking about? *Who* was he talking about?

"And because you won't stop, I have to do something," he went on. "I have to stop you. Don't be frightened. You'll be glorified, like the others, and it will give your family honor."

Ruby fought to keep her eyes open.

"We didn't kill the others. It was him, the voice. I couldn't stop it. I couldn't stop him."

"W-what voi . . . voice?" She struggled to form the words, but she slowly grew stronger. "A v-voice in . . . your head? Telling you t-to kill them?"

"No, no," he said weakly. "It's already been done."

"You won't g-get away with these murders. Too many people know about them now. There will be more questions, even . . . if you get rid of me."

He laughed. "You're wrong. No one questions the will of God."

Ruby's head began to clear. She sat up, forcing back the nausea that clutched at her gut. "So what are you going to do now?"

"I'm going to give you a gift." He smiled at her, a disturbing glint in his eyes. "The gift of eternal life."

Before she could blink he was on her, his fingers wrapped around her throat. Thinking fast she brought her arms around and down, hard, on top of his. He hissed in pain, his grip on her loosening. She slammed her arms into his again, this time breaking his hold. She rammed her left forearm under his chin, her right forearm swinging around the back of his neck. She squeezed her forearms together, her right hand grasping her left elbow, to lock his neck between them. He gasped and sputtered as his eyes began to roll back in his head. She kept the pressure constant, knowing it would neutralize him without killing him. And within moments, he lost consciousness and fell to the ground.

Ruby lifted her hands to her throbbing head. He would be unconscious just long enough for her to get away from him. She knew now they were underground. She didn't know how deep into the earth he'd taken her, but she took the lit candle and started through the only tunnel she could see. Minutes passed before light was visible in the distance. Ruby forced her heavy limbs to run, and in no time she was outside.

Nothing, however, looked familiar.

She spotted a black car at the foot of a cliff below her. The same car that had been used to try to run her down. Martinez's car. Following a narrow footpath she made her way down the steep slope, her equilibrium still off. Her head and the space behind her eyes ached, and her arms and legs tingled with fatigue. Finally, she reached the car. The doors weren't locked, but the keys weren't in the ignition either.

She looked around her, praying they had fallen in the dirt, only to find a coyote standing not six feet from her. It was the same one she'd seen in the sinkhole, the one with the scar above his eye. Their gazes met, and after a few seconds he moved away from the car and sat, his head cocked to the side as he watched her.

Martinez would be after her at any minute, and while she didn't want to startle the animal she had to get out of there. She ripped off the panel under the steering wheel and bent down to look at the wires. Waves of pain shot through her eyes, but she took a deep breath and blinked to steady her blurred vision. A primordial yell sounded behind her, and she looked to see Martinez sliding down the hill, heedless of the rocks and scrub brush. Focusing on the wires, she worked faster.

Martinez reached the car and slammed his hands against the trunk.

The coyote growled.

"Stop! Leave me alone!" Martinez hollered.

Ruby lifted her eyes from the wires. The coyote had Martinez's pantleg in his teeth, refusing to let go. Martinez swung at the animal, and the coyote released his pantleg but then sank his teeth into Martinez's arm. He hollered, trying to shake the animal off.

Returning to the wires Ruby managed to connect the right ones, the engine roaring to life. She put the car in gear and sped away in a flurry of dust. In the rearview mirror, she saw Martinez and the coyote continuing to struggle.

She focused on the landscape in front of her and saw the caves west of Truchas caverns. Now she could find her way. And with Martinez now out to kill her, she had to act fast.

※

Lifting his head Pete tried to get up, but he could hardly move. *Ruby*. What had happened to Ruby? What had they done to her?

The door opened then and Martinez entered the room, his forearm bandaged. "I see you're awake. Good."

"Where is she? Where is Ruby?"

"She won't be a problem any more, *Hermano*," he said.

Pete watched Martinez prepare a hypodermic needle; he was

about to be drugged again. Now, they just wanted him out of the way.

He intended to fight, but his bruised and beaten body wouldn't cooperate. He got in one strong swing, but Martinez only shushed him and jabbed him with the needle. The sting lasted only a few seconds, and Pete was again swept into unconsciousness.

❧

Ruby nearly jumped out of the car when she reached the dig site. "I was right about Martinez," Ruby said, running toward Yates and Spike. Breathless, she recounted the highlights of all that had just happened—finding the morada, Pete's condition, her being drugged, Martinez's lies, and his attempt on her life.

"We need to get the contents of that vial tested right away," Yates said.

"But shouldn't we get Pete and the Baca boy out of there?" Spike asked.

"They won't want them injured anymore until the Passion," said Yates. "They need both of them fit for the crucifixion. Spike, you stay here and keep an eye on things. I'm going with Ruby to see Dr. Jones."

Still feeling ill from the hangover of the drug, Ruby slumped in the leather seat of Yates' truck. Yates never took his eyes from the road, but the indignation on his face was clear. John Yates' sense of morality was showing itself, just as Spike had said it would. It was about time. Ruby knew she could probably get to Los Campos and Dr. Jones on her own, but it was nice to have help.

❧

Pete awoke with a start. His head pounded from the aftereffects of the drug. Mingled voices grew louder in the other room. It must be morning. And that meant the Holy Thursday ritual was about to begin.

He shook like a palsied man, and his legs wouldn't work properly as the Brothers took him outside. They guided him to a wooden chair where he would sit and watch the ritual.

Pete looked over at the cactus spines that lay neatly aligned on the ground at his feet, the ones that Nicolas would lie upon for several hours. A baby scorpion inched its way down the side of one of the spines. Fearing for Nicolas' safety, Pete tried to kick the menacing creature. But his leg felt too heavy. The scorpion seemed to understand, though, and decided to look for another feeding place. He sighed with relief as it crawled away.

Holy Thursday was the day before the crucifixion. Nicolas had to endure just one more day of ritual but, as they all knew, it didn't mean Nicolas would survive his role of Cristo.

Movement at the door of the morada caught Pete's eye. Nicolas stood in the frame, frail, pale, and painfully thin. The image of Christ swept through Pete's mind. Nicolas wore only white pants. His hair, slicked back as if just washed, glistened blue in its blackness when he stepped into the sunlight. Behind him stood the mysterious *Jefe Mayor*. Pete wished he knew who was under that hood . . .

The *Jefe Mayor* raised his hand, and two men immediately flanked Nicolas. He spread his arms, and each man took one and slowly led him to the cactus. Nicolas said something to one of them, and the Brother released his arm. The other did the same.

Nicolas clasped his hands together and fell to his knees in prayer. After a few moments he rose, and the men again took hold of his arms. Slowly, steadily, the men lowered Nicolas onto the cactus branches, chest down. Another man placed a rock under his forehead to prevent his face from meeting the ruthless spines.

Without speaking, the men who'd brought Pete outside helped him to his feet. Then all of them turned away, even Pete, leaving Nicolas alone with his suffering.

"So, you're the famous Dr. Yates." Madeline Jones' eyes sparkled with admiration when Ruby introduced her to the professor. "I've heard a lot about you over the years. It's a pleasure to finally meet you."

"Well, thank you," said Yates, obviously flattered.

"I'm afraid we don't have much time," Ruby said, handing Dr. Jones the glass vial of black liquid. "We saw someone painting the crown of thorns with this. We need to know what it is right away."

Dr. Jones nodded. "I'll give it a look," she said, walking toward the lab.

Ruby sank into a chair and shielded her eyes from the glaring fluorescent lights.

"Still feeling sick?" Yates asked her.

"A little. I'm feeling better, though," she said, trying to convince herself. "Are you all right?" Yates seemed distant, distracted.

"I've never lived in Las Montanas full time, but I've spent months at a stretch here and feel I've come to know the village and the people pretty well over the years." He paused, grazing his beard and neck with his hand. "It seemed like things *did* change after Martinez arrived."

Ruby tilted her head, listening. "How so?"

Before he could continue Dr. Jones returned, her glasses perched on the end of her nose. She still wore her surgical gloves. "Well, I'll be damned," she said.

"What is it?" Ruby asked.

"A highly concentrated form of nicotine," Dr. Jones told them. "It's typically extracted from tobacco leaves or perhaps leaf grindings. Absorption through the skin at such high concentrations is deadly."

Ruby's eyes widened. "That's why the nicotine showed up on the autopsy reports."

"And why the Cristos died so quickly. The moment the nicotine enters the bloodstream, it sends the heart into cardiac arrest," Dr. Jones finished.

Ruby jumped up from her chair, excitement making her forget her pain.

"We found it, Dr. Yates. We've really found it!"

Yates gave her a broad smile.

They had the murder weapon, and they had a suspect. Now they needed to stop the crime before another Cristo died.

◌⊱⊰◌

Pete came out of his drugged stupor to learn that Nicolas had fallen unconscious during the cactus ritual, and the Brothers had taken him to the hospital. Which meant Pete had been named Cristo in Nicolas' place.

The Brothers had prepared dinner and served Pete his meal. It was more food than he had been given in days. They wanted their new Cristo in top form to hang on the cross the next day. And while the thought made him too nauseated to want to eat, he knew he needed the strength.

After finishing his meal, Pete requested to be allowed to pray alone in his room. That's what he'd told them at least. What he really planned to do was figure a way out of this mess.

The shock of the news still had not worn off, even though part of him had known that Nicolas would be too sick to perform his role as Cristo. The effects of the drug they'd used to sedate him hadn't worn off yet, either, even after eating. He took a deep breath and rubbed his temples, trying to think.

Gradually, his mind cleared. He had to leave tonight, soon, if he was going to get out of this. He would have to leave his family forever. The disgrace his father would face would be unbearable. His mother's life would be a living hell—for a while, but then she'd recover. So would his sisters. He thought about Ricardo. His brother never would have backed away from this responsibility, even given the odds that Pete was facing. But if he didn't leave, he had no doubt he'd die on the cross tomorrow.

He tried to open the door, but it was locked. He slammed his fist against it. "Hey!" he shouted. "Let me out of here." He pounded on it a couple more times with no success. But he needed to get to Ruby. What had become of her? What if she was—

Dizziness took hold of him, and he made his way back to the cot and dropped down, gripping the sides tightly with both hands. A faint knock sounded at the door.

"Come in," he groaned. Pete looked up to see his father walk in, closing the door behind him. Torn between not wanting to look at him and wanting hug him, Pete chose to focus on the floor.

"So . . ." His father sat next to him. "You are Cristo." The words came out swollen with pride.

Pete drew his hands up over his face. He couldn't remember ever feeling so drained. "Yes, but I don't want to go through with it."

His father's eyes flashed with disbelief. "You would refuse the honor?"

"I don't want to die."

"You would defy the Brotherhood, defy your father and your family? Defy yourself?"

Pete shook his head. "Ricardo was *murdered*, Father. I'm certain of it."

His father jumped up, his dark eyes flashing. "What is this you speak of? You admitted your wrongdoing. You repented!"

Pete stood unsteadily and faced his father, feeling regret and remorse for the pitiful old man. Pete hadn't wanted to hurt him; he only had wanted to find out the truth of his brother's death, to save others from the same fate. His father had been brainwashed into believing that Ricardo died with honor.

"Father, listen to me." Pete took his father by the arms. "This whole thing—the rituals, the pulque, the Passion play, the crucifixion, the Brotherhood—if you want to worship like this, then fine, do so. But things have changed, don't you see? No one used to die during the Passion, but four Cristos have died in four years. Someone is *taking* these lives, and it's not God."

"You are a coward," his father spat.

Coward. His father would never understand. Coward or no, he *was* afraid to die.

"Maybe so," he said. "But I'm next to die, Father. Do you really want that?"

His father didn't answer, just walked toward the door. He looked back over his shoulder, his face lined with remorse. Pete couldn't decide if he wanted to please his father or curse him.

Wrestling with a thousand emotions, Pete slumped to the cot and tried to figure out his next move.

CHAPTER 30

"How are we going to deal with this when we return?" Ruby asked when she and Dr. Yates were back on the road. "I think we should go straight to the morada and stop this nonsense. *Before* tomorrow."

"I agree," Yates said. "We should get some of the Brothers together, tell them what's happening."

"You mean create a mutiny?"

He nodded. "Exactly. The less involvement we have with the public, the better. If the Redeemers can handle this themselves, that would be best."

Ruby thought about what he said. He wanted to handle the situation in the smoothest, most low-key manner possible, and she had to admit doing so might be best for everyone concerned. Ruby couldn't help but wonder if the idea stemmed from his experience in Peru.

"We'll drive up near the morada, stop several hundred feet away," Yates said. "I'll get to a few of the Brothers, talk to them."

"The place is probably guarded. How do you know we can trust them?"

"I don't know *who* we can trust right now, but no one at the morada knows I've teamed up with you."

She nodded. "That's true. But it still sounds risky."

"It's risky, yes," he agreed, "but I think it's the best shot we have."

"What happens if the conversation doesn't go the way we want it to? What if you get . . . I don't know . . . *detained?*"

"You'll have to go to Gallegos or, better yet, a higher authority. Go to the county supervisor. Do you know where his office is?"

"No," she said.

"The office is in Novio. It's a town about the size of Las Montanas on the other side of the mountains. It's about thirty miles east of here." He drummed a rhythm on the steering wheel. "He can call in county resources if we need them."

She worried her lower lip. She knew it might take her too long to drive thirty miles each way and still get back in time, but what other choice did they have?

⚜

Yates parked half a mile from the morada. He didn't want to draw attention to their arrival. Besides, Martinez would be on the lookout for Ruby, and he didn't want to endanger her in any way.

Dusk had fallen by the time they headed for the morada.

"What are you going to do?" Ruby asked.

"Talk."

"But they'll be suspicious."

"Perhaps, but they know I'm no threat to them. I can ask about the Passion, pretend I'm interested in the ritual."

"But what if—"

"I'll be fine." They stopped near a clump of pinons. "Just promise you won't move from here, unless you absolutely have to."

She nodded. "I promise," she said, her voice cracking.

"Good."

With that, Yates left her and walked out toward the morada, trying to act casual, as if out for an evening stroll. A few men milled about outside, talking and smoking cigarettes. They immediately noticed and moved toward him.

One of the men waved and smiled. "Dr. Yates."

Yates tipped his hat. "I need to speak with you about a delicate situation. It's important."

The men exchanged glances.

"Very important," Yates repeated.

Behind him, footsteps approached. He turned to see who was coming and was smacked squarely on the back of the head.

◈

Ruby clamped her hands over her mouth as Martinez walloped Yates on the back of the head with the butt of his gun. Yates fell to the ground. The other men standing around looked alarmed, and Ruby strained to hear their words.

"What are you doing?" one man asked, stepping forward. "He only came to talk."

"He was here to cause trouble," Martinez said, wiping blood from his gun with a handkerchief.

"You don't know that," another man said, pushing into Martinez's space.

Martinez raised his hands, stepping back. "We've received way too much attention lately. The Brotherhood is at risk," he reasoned. "The Delgado woman exposed us with the reporter, and if too many people know of our practices there will be trouble. You know this, *Hermanos*. It was bad enough the archbishop's people came. Please understand, I act only on behalf of the Brotherhood."

"But we never had these problems before," one of them said. "No one will bother us."

"They're trying to stop the Passion play," Father Martinez said. "Do you want that?"

The men discussed this amongst themselves, their confusion clear. "The Passion must go on," one of them said after a moment.

"Yes, it must," Martinez agreed. "Now get him out of here. Put him in the morada. We'll keep him quiet until the Passion is over."

The men carried Yates into the morada, Martinez watching. He turned, scanning the area. Ruby held her breath, hoping he wouldn't see her. But once they all entered the morada, Martinez included, Ruby ran for Yates' truck.

⚜

Ruby leaned her hands on the desk of the county supervisor. "But you've got to go out there and arrest him!" Her voice sounded shrill even to her own ears. "They've got Dr. Yates, and who knows what they'll do to him!"

The supervisor, Antonio Garza, smiled. Not a warm smile. A smarmy smile, on a smarmy face. He was enormously fat, the sides of his waist rolling out over the arms of his chair. He smelled of stale tequila.

"You have no proof of murder. What motive would Father Martinez possibly have?"

His voice, heavy with a Spanish accent and disdain, made her want to slap him.

"The man is crazy! He's not right in the head!" Ruby shouted. "Who knows his reasons? He talks about glorifying people and giving honor to their families by *killing people*. Tomorrow morning Nicolas Baca is going to hang on the cross, and I'm betting he won't live through it."

Garza laughed. "You have no understanding of these matters."

The man's pompousness raked through her like a pitchfork. "I have information that proves how the murders are committed. Nicotine is extracted—"

"La señorita es muy bonita para un pequena loca, eh?" Garza said to the uniformed guard standing next to his desk.

"I can understand you, you moron. I'm not crazy. Here, look." She pulled the small bottle from her pocket, set it on his desk. "This is highly concentrated nicotine. A small amount is placed on the crown of thorns so when it pierces the skin of the Cristo—"

"Very ingenious, eh, Beto?" Garza said to the guard. "Who would think a *señorita* could be so smart? Especially one so beautiful."

Ruby's rage bubbled up. The smug bastard. He wouldn't even listen!

Garza lifted his bulk out of the chair, moving around the desk to get closer to her. He put his hand out for the vial.

Ruby grabbed it off the desk. "Look, Mr. Garza, you have to listen to me. A man is going to die tomorrow, maybe sooner. Please. Please help me."

Garza moved closer to her, the smell of his breath turning her stomach. She didn't want to back away or back down.

"You see—Ruby, is it?"

Ruby could feel his hot, sour breath on her face.

"I've been expecting you. One of the Brothers said you might be coming." His smile widened, revealing coffee-stained teeth.

Ruby straightened her spine, holding her ground.

He chuckled a sinister chuckle. "What *you* don't know, is that I also belong to the sacred Brotherhood of the Redeemers."

Her stomach knotted, and tingling sweat broke out on her arms and legs. She'd run out of places to turn.

"It seems that someone as intelligent, as bright, as ingenious as you, *señorita*, would have heeded the advice to leave the Brotherhood alone," Garza said. "But unfortunately for everyone, you did not. Detain this woman," he ordered the guard.

"What? What the hell do you think you're doing?" Panic rose in her chest, her heart thumping a mad staccato.

"He's arresting you," Garza said.

"Arresting me?" She set her hands on her hips. "On what grounds?"

"Harassment."

The guard, burly and well over six feet tall, grabbed her by the arms and yanked them behind her back. She grimaced but refused to cry out, even though her arms felt as though they'd been ripped out of their sockets. The vial of liquid fell from her fingers to the floor. Garza picked it up.

"Someone's going to be murdered if you don't stop Enrique Martinez," Ruby said, fighting against the cuffs the guard put on her.

Garza placed the vial in his pocket. "You obviously don't understand."

"What are you doing with that? That's evidence!" she shouted.

"What evidence? I see no evidence." He held his hands out for her inspection. "Don't worry, you'll be released soon. *After* the ceremony."

With that the guard yanked Ruby, kicking and screaming, out of the room.

⚜

Yates came to, his head throbbing. In front of him, Pete sat upright on a cot, his face barely recognizable.

Pete didn't speak, just stared at him with vacant eyes. Yates struggled to sit up and managed to lean against the adobe wall. Coolness permeated his shirt and it felt good on his sweaty back.

"Pete, can you hear me? When do they crucify the Cristo?" Yates asked, hoping to snap him out of his daze. "What time?"

"Morning," Pete murmured. "Sunrise."

Yates stood, grimacing from the pain in his head. He moved over to his young friend and placed a hand on his bare, scabbed shoulder. "We've found what's killing the Cristos, Pete, and we think we know who the killer is, too. You've got to help us get out of here. We can put a stop to all of this right now."

Pete just sat and stared, not moving.

"This is what you wanted," Yates reminded Pete. "You were right. You don't have to live in confusion and shame any longer. I'm here to help you. Come on now, let's get out of here."

Pete lifted his head and looked at Dr. Yates. In Pete's eyes, Yates saw the same helplessness he'd seen in the eyes of the dying, of the hopeless, in Peru. He recognized little of his friend. From the look of him it was clear Pete had been beaten severely, more than once. And the dazed look was evidence that he'd been filled with pulque or some other mind-altering drug, as well.

"If I have to, I'll carry you out of here," Yates said. "It's over. Right now." He straightened, blood pounding in his ears. He moved to the door and tried to pull it open. It had been locked from the outside. The room had no windows, save for the narrow ones, covered with cloth, near the ceiling.

Someone pounded on the door and fiddled with the lock from the other side. The door burst open, and four men stood in the doorway. Three of them rushed at Yates, pulling his arms behind his back. He struggled as best he could, but they outnumbered him.

Enrique Martinez entered after them. "Dr. Yates, your friend Pedro has missed you." He pulled Pete, his eyes unfocused, to his feet. "Did he tell you he is the new Cristo? He gets the honor of hanging on the cross. If you behave, we'll even let you watch."

Yates' jaw dropped. "You?" He struggled against the men's hold as Martinez led Pete out of the room.

One of the men uncoiled a rope and secured Yates' arms behind his back. *"Lo siento,"* he whispered in Yates' ear, apologizing, then forced him to sit so he could tie his feet together.

"You don't have to do this," Yates said to the man. He sensed he could reason with this one. "We can stop this right now. Together. You know what they're doing is wrong."

The man looked at Yates with sorrow-filled eyes. He turned away and left with the others in silence.

Yates slumped against the wall. He only hoped that Ruby had gotten to the county supervisor in time and that help would soon arrive.

❦

Pete stood alone in the dark, swaying, the pulque still in full effect. He thought he remembered speaking with Dr. Yates, but he couldn't be sure. He also wasn't sure of the time of day. Several of the men had brought him to the desert to pray and told him he'd be there until dawn.

The ground swam in the moonlight, and his knees threatened to buckle. They'd filled him with pulque, and a fever from his infected wounds made his body burn and his mind feel like mush. He couldn't muster any emotion. No regret, no anger, not even pain. He felt nothing, and was beginning to enjoy the sensation. Simple existence had become enough.

The moon made a lazy semicircle in the dark sky. Young women in colorful skirts danced, twirling in the glow of the moon. His sisters. Then he saw his father, the white moustache prominent on his face, his sombrero shading him from the light. His mother stood at his father's side. His two sisters leaped in and out of the halo of the moon, their dark hair plaited and falling in neat rows to their waists. They danced around a seated figure. Pete squinted to see better—Ricardo.

Pete's heart soared. Ricardo was alive!

Ricardo rushed over to him and threw his arms around him, but Pete felt nothing. He blinked. His arms were empty. He blinked again and everyone had disappeared, all except the moon. His heart broke, and he fell to the ground.

CHAPTER 31

Yates' hands and feet had gone numb. He sat against the wall, cursing Martinez. If only he'd realized the gravity of the situation sooner. His resentment toward Ruby had clouded everything, but she'd been right all along. Yates had known about Pete's trouble with his family, but since Pete had never mentioned it Yates thought it best to leave the matter alone. It would never have gone this far if he'd just listened to Ruby from the beginning. He could have stopped this. Could stop it still if he could free himself of these ropes and get out of this room.

If only he could get to the pocketknife he always carried. For now, he'd have to improvise, at least until his hands were freed. He searched for something sharp to cut his ties. His eyes landed on the cot and the butterfly bolts that stuck out from the screws near the hinges. If he could rub the rope on the grooves of the screws, he could probably tear his way through the ropes. It might take time, but he could do it. And then he'd use his freed hands to release his legs with the pocketknife.

Pulling himself by his heels, he scooted toward the other side of the room. The movement strained his thighs and abdominal muscles as he made his way, inch by inch, across the dirt floor.

When he finally neared the cot, he turned around and leaned

his back against one of the butterfly bolts. Raising his tied hands as high as he could, he strained to reach the screw. He leaned forward, giving his arms more mobility, but still the effort tugged at his pectoral and shoulder muscles, causing sharp pain to radiate down his arms. He pushed through it and rubbed the rope against the screw for a while, then lowered his arms to rest.

He repeated the same steps again and again. Sweat poured from his face, chest, and arms, and his neck ached from being thrust into such uncomfortable positions. Finally—*finally*—he felt something give. The ropes loosened. Encouraged, he rubbed the rope against the screw harder and faster. Another pop. Soon, he'd be free. He pressed on, sweating and cursing, and imagined each fiber ripping loose and unraveling.

At last, his wrists fell away from each other. He wriggled his hands out of their binds. He pulled his arms forward, stretching them, and had started to reach into his pocket for his knife when the door opened.

Martinez stepped into the room, and Yates thrust his hand into his pocket and pulled out the knife. He opened it and held it out for Martinez to see. "Stand back," he said.

"Put your weapon away," said Martinez. "You don't want to kill me."

"Maybe not. But I could certainly hurt you."

"A peace-loving man like you?" He scoffed. "I don't think so."

"I've dealt with plenty of nasty creatures. I have no qualms about taking down scum like you."

Martinez stood over him, but Yates held the knife higher. In an instant Martinez's boot came down on Yates' shins, sending excruciating pain up his legs. He thrust the knife toward Martinez, hoping to cut him, but Martinez caught his arm mid-thrust and dug his fingers into Yates' triceps. Yates pried the fingers from his arm with his free hand and twisted Martinez's arm so that the elbow faced upward. Then he slammed his free elbow into the fake priest's, the snap of the break audible.

Martinez howled in pain, and the noise brought more of the

Brothers into the room. They converged on Yates and detained him once again. Martinez lay on the floor, clutching his broken arm and cursing Yates.

"He's trying to sabotage the Passion, Brothers. Tie him up again. Get the pulque." Martinez leveled a stare at Yates. "You'll pay for this." He stood, his arm dangling at an unnatural angle until he secured his other arm under it.

"You won't get away with it this time, Martinez. Tell me, are you the killer or are you just his puppet?"

One of the men kicked Yates in the face with the heel of his boot. Stars spread out before his eyes. He tasted blood going down his throat and he coughed, choking.

Another of the men held him down and held his bloody mouth open. They poured hot liquid into his mouth and he choked and sputtered, trying not to swallow. They held him tightly, so tightly he needed to swallow in order to breathe. The fluid burned as it went down.

After several minutes, his energy was gone and his head was fuzzy. The men released him and he slumped to the floor, watching blurred visions moving in front of his eyes.

"That ought to take care of him for a while," Martinez said, still clutching his arm. "In a few hours, give him some more. It'll keep him quiet and out of the way. When this is over, I'll take care of him."

Yates heard the door shut. He lifted his head to see his ex-wife, Melissa, standing next to him, her blond hair streaming behind her in the breeze. He relaxed into the image, enjoying the sight of her sheer cotton dress clinging to her body—her expression serene, peaceful. She turned from him, but when she turned back her face had changed. The skin and eyes were now dark like chocolate, and she held a baby on her hip. It was the woman his wife had befriended. Melissa had fallen in love with her baby boy. The dark woman held out her arms to him, her face pleading. Her skin clung to her bones and the baby started to shrink, his skin sinking into his bones. Starving.

Dying. The woman fell to her knees, her free arm outstretched. The baby cried from hunger, his wails echoing in Yates' ears.

Mother and son fell to the ground, and though he tried by sheer will to quiet the cry of the baby it only grew louder. He put his hands to his ears to block out the sound, but it wouldn't stop.

❧❧❧

Ruby paced the five-by-seven-foot cell, her fists clenched. "Damn it!" she yelled through the bars. "Let me out of here, you jerk!"

She knew no one could hear her, and if they could they probably wouldn't care. She was stuck here until tomorrow, or maybe longer, and by then the Passion would be over and Nicolas would be dead. She had to get out before it was too late.

The guard came through a metal door and walked toward her cell. She rubbed her arms at the shoulders, remembering how he'd manhandled her to get her into the cuffs. He pulled a folding chair over to the cell and sat down, guarding her.

Maybe she could appeal to his compassionate side. If he had one.

"It's cold in here," she said. "May I have a blanket please?"

No answer.

"What's your name?" She tried smiling.

He smiled back but didn't say anything. He stood, circled his hands around the bars, and leaned his elbows against them.

"Looks like it's just you and me tonight," he said. "Everyone's gone home."

Ruby's legs went weak with fear, but she managed to smile up into his face again. "How about that blanket? What was your name, again?"

"Armando."

"Ah, Armando. Nice name."

He pulled a flask from his pocket and chugged from it. He

wiped his mouth with the back of his hand and passed the flask to Ruby. "Want some?"

"Sure. Why don't you come on in here and we'll share?" Ruby unscrewed the top, held the flask to her lips, then lowered it again. She backed away from the cell door. "Or maybe we won't. Guess you'll have to come get it, if you want it."

Armando's face spread into a grin. He fidgeted with the keys on his belt and unhooked them. He searched for the right one and unlatched the door.

Ruby's heart pumped hard and fast, her mind searching for a strategy. The guard, who looked like he spent hours each day lifting weights, stepped inside the cell and clanged the door shut. He hooked his keys back onto his belt and moved toward her.

He grabbed her by the arm, his grip strong, and jerked her toward him. Her head snapped backward as he pressed his body up against hers. "If you cooperate, you won't get hurt." His breath was hot in her ear. "Who knows, you might even like it."

"Oh, I'll like it," she whispered. She closed her eyes, her body trembling, her mind paralyzed, but she had to play along to get away. He let him wrap his arms around her, and then she slammed her knee up into his groin. He howled, bending over but still holding her arm.

Ruby grabbed the fleshy part of his palm with her fingers and wrenched his arm backward like a linked chain that could be twisted no farther. He cursed at her, unable to move. With her other hand she reached for his pistol, but she missed. Ruby lost her grip, and with a powerful blow he knocked her to the ground. Still doubled over in pain, he tried to hold Ruby down. Taking advantage of his weakened state, she kicked him squarely in the face. She scrambled to standing, and while he writhed on the ground holding his bloodied nose and aching crotch, she grabbed his keys and unhooked them from his belt. She also grabbed his gun and stuffed it into the waist of her jeans. Heading for the door, she fumbled for the keys.

The guard groaned and shouted obscenities at her as she

tried several keys in the lock. She worked fast, flicking occasional looks over at him as she did so. He pulled himself along the floor toward her, and before she knew it he was on his hands and knees.

Click.

She pulled open the door just as the guard's hands encircled her ankles. He yanked on her legs, pulling her to the ground. She lay half-in and half-out of the cell, trying to claw herself free from his grip. He pulled her closer, and she kicked at his face. His hold loosened and he attempted to grab her knee, but her foot swiftly made contact with his already-broken nose. He bellowed and cursed some more, holding his hand over his bloody face.

Ruby scrambled to her feet and over the threshold, then pulled the door shut. Locking the guard inside the cell, she then threw the keys into the farthest corner of the jail. The guard lay in the cell, still shouting obscenities at her. She couldn't help but smile as she opened the door to the building and raced out into the night.

CHAPTER 32

Someone shook him. "Cristo," the voice said. "Wake up. They're here for you."

Pete opened his eyes and flinched at the brilliant light of morning. A man pulled him to his feet. "We must go."

Pete leaned heavily on him and then noticed there were others. Among them was the hooded *Jefe Mayor*. Two Brothers flanked Pete and began to lead him back to the morada. When Pete lifted his head, he saw a large male coyote sitting on a rock in the distance. His yellow eyes followed Pete as the men took him away.

When they neared the morada, several people came into focus. The entire village had turned up, surrounding the building and waiting for him. All of them wore black. The women had covered their faces with sheer black veils and the little children carried spring wildflowers.

Three men lowered a large wooden cross from the side of the building and dragged it over to Pete. They propped it up while several of the village girls, portraying the role of Veronica, washed his bare chest and face with soft cloths. He didn't see his sisters and said a prayer of thanks. At least his father had had the decency to protect them from this. The rags the girls used bore crude penciled drawings of Jesus' face, and Pete shuddered.

His father walked up to him and took Pete's hands in his. Tears flowed freely down his cheeks and into his mustache. Pete's chest tightened, and he wished he could say so many things to the father he both loved and hated. He wanted to make him understand the true purpose for his joining the Brotherhood, the reason he'd come this far—to prove his brother had been murdered. But even if he could tell him, his father had always been deaf to the truth. He wouldn't listen.

"Son, you don't realize the honor that is bestowed upon you and our family. You have redeemed yourself to our family, to our faith and, most importantly, to God. I am proud to have you back. You are alive within my heart and always will be. God bless you."

He put his hand behind Pete's neck and pulled him close so that their foreheads touched. Pete closed his eyes, feeling the warmth and love radiating from his father's embrace. Why couldn't things have been different? Why hadn't he been able to earn his father's acceptance and love before he was so near death?

Pete saw his mother emerge from the crowd.

"Mama," he whispered.

She buried her face in her handkerchief. He wanted to touch her face, wipe her tears away, but he couldn't move his arms. His eyes met hers. "After today, we'll be together again. I'm sorry I left the family. I didn't realize how sorry until the other night. Be brave, Mama." He scanned the crowd. "Are my sisters here?"

She shook her head. "No. They didn't want to watch you—"

"I won't die, Mother. For you, for them—I won't leave you." He felt his resolve grow. "I promise."

She yelped when someone abruptly pulled her away. Anger returned to his numbed mind. Gaining his strength back he thrust his shoulder forward, pushing the men next to him and knocking three of them down. He tried to turn and run, but several Brothers were on him instantly.

The *Jefe Mayor* stepped forward. "Sometimes a man cannot control his fear. For his sake, we must restrain him and help him do his duty as Cristo. Do not fear, Brothers. This is the way for him."

Reassured by the *Jefe Mayor's* words, two of the Brothers held him while several others hoisted the cross onto his shoulder. The weight of it sent him to the ground. While on his knees, they tied the cross to him with ropes and then unbound his hands. The sound of a whip snapping pierced the air. Fearing its contact on what was left of his skin, Pete struggled to his feet and began to move. The hooded *Jefe Mayor* pointed up the hill behind the morada, directing Pete where to go.

His journey had begun.

⚅⚅⚅

Ruby found her way to Yates' truck in the parking lot. Just as she put it into gear and spun it around she saw the guard run out the door, arms flailing, face bloody. He must have had another key. She knew he'd be on her in a matter of minutes. She slammed the truck into gear, pressed hard on the accelerator, and spun out of the parking lot in flurry of dust.

She guessed the time to be between 5:00 and 5:30 a.m. on Good Friday, the morning of the Passion. Sunrise would be in an hour. She hoped she wouldn't be too late to stop the crucifixion.

After forty minutes of driving as fast as the truck would go, Ruby reached Las Montanas. She sped through town and up the winding road to the morada. She parked the car some distance away and continued on foot, running.

Using bushes and rocks for cover, Ruby made her way toward the morada. When she reached the double doors at the entrance, she peeked in to find it empty. She slipped through the doors and into the main room. Hearing a loud, rhythmic thumping, her eyes rested on the door behind the altar, which was secured with a padlock. She could hear something behind the door moving. She pressed her ear to the door, pulling the gun out of her waistband.

"Pete?"

She heard more muffled sounds.

"Ruby?" It didn't sound like Pete. "Ruby, break the lock."

"Dr. Yates! Give me a sec."

She searched the room and found wrought-iron candlesticks with melted wax stubs on the altar. After taking the remains of the candlewax out, she hit the lock with the candlestick. She hit it again and again. Four heavy blows did nothing but numb her hands. She tossed the candlestick aside.

Shooting the lock open with the gun would make too much noise, so she couldn't risk that. She studied the metal door hinges and then began going through her pockets.

"Dr. Yates," she said through the crack, "do you have any change? A dime, maybe?"

"Um, yes," he said, confusion in his voice.

His fingertips peeked out from under the door, and he shoved a dime at her feet. She snatched it up and went to work on the hinges. Within minutes, she'd unfastened the screws that held the hinges in the wood.

She shoved the heavy door to the left until it tilted open, held by the padlock.

Yates sat on the floor, ropes strewn loose around him, his nose and cheeks caked with blood.

"Dr. Yates, my God, are you okay?" She rushed over to him. "What happened?"

He moved his mouth to speak, but winced and grabbed at his jaw. "Martinez."

She looked around the room. "Where's Pete? Where's everybody else? The morada is empty."

"They must have started the Passion," he said. "What time is it?"

"I don't know. Oh, God. We have to go. We have to save Nicolas."

"Not Nicolas," Yates said, trying to stand.

Ruby helped him. "What do you mean?"

"Nicolas won't be on the cross."

Adrenaline raced through Ruby, making her head spin. "It's Pete, isn't it? Pete is the Cristo? Come on, Dr. Yates, let's go."

Yates didn't move. It seemed as though he couldn't. Ruby lifted his arm around her shoulder and pulled him forward. "Come on. We're the only ones who can stop this."

⚜

Pete walked halfway up the hill and then fell to his knees. Rocks and gritty sand pierced his kneecaps through the thin fabric of his pants. Two brown hands holding a tin cup appeared before his eyes. Thinking it was more of the hallucinogenic pulque, he turned his face away.

"It's water," whispered a woman's voice.

He let her hold the cup to his mouth, and he drank all of it. The water refreshed and strengthened him. He heard the whip crack behind him and he instinctively wanted to stand, but he fought it. Whip or no, he would rest, if only for a few moments.

"God, give me strength," he said.

He stood, staggering under the weight of the cross. He raised his head and looked to the top of the hill. Reaching the peak would rid him of the heavy burden of the cross, but reaching the peak also meant he would be crucified on that very cross. He wouldn't let it happen. Somehow, he would fight.

"Tell me what to do." He raised his eyes Heavenward.

At the top of the hill, in the dawning sunlight, the image of Ricardo beckoned Pete onward again. Why did his brother urge him toward death? Did he want him to die? To join him in God's kingdom?

Pete moved onward, anticipating the moment when he

would again meet his brother face-to-face. When he finally reached the top of the steep hill, he collapsed to the ground. His shoulders and torso hung from the ropes that bound him to the cross. Immediately, several of the men hurried over to him and cut the binding ties. They pulled him from beneath the cross and let him rest on his back.

He stared up into the sky. It glowed pink and yellow and expanded into white. Then a beautiful face appeared in front of him. It was the girl who'd given him the water. She again held the cup to his lips. He drank, marveling at her beauty. Her eyes were large and brown, her lips as pink as a blooming rose in spring.

He motioned for more water and drank eagerly from the third cup. He'd swallowed a mouthful before he realized it was pulque.

"For the pain," she said.

He tried to spit it into the dirt, but there was nothing left in his mouth. The delirium hit swiftly, taking him from reality.

He heard the men setting the cross on the ground and then the clanking of the stakes as they prepared them. The men lifted him and lay him on top of the cross. Knowing what would happen next he tried to struggle, but he was rendered helpless against the power of the drug. His limbs wouldn't obey.

Soon he heard the sharp sound of metal on metal as the hammer hit the stake. His wrist burned as the metal sank into his flesh, the impact of the blows cracking his bones. He screamed. He felt himself slipping into unconsciousness and tried to fight it, but he couldn't.

When he came to, faces swam before him. His sisters, his mother, and Ruby.

Ruby.

Her image had been with him the whole time—her warm, dark eyes and soft pink skin. He regretted he'd never been able to come to terms with his feelings for her, but he knew now. He loved her.

He felt himself being lifted. He drew in a deep breath.

The men raised the cross at an angle and then let it slip into the hole in the ground.

Pete groaned.

The men stood the cross upright.

Pete's bones snapped as gravity pulled his body down. His flesh tore. His chest burned, heavy and tight, and he struggled to breathe. Gravity would win this battle.

Something hard knocked against the cross. On his left someone drew close, climbing the cross. No, climbing a ladder.

It was the *Jefe Mayor*. He placed his hooded face only inches from Pete's.

Pete looked into the eyes through the crudely cut holes. They were familiar, but . . .

"Now receive your rightful crown," he said, holding the crown of thorns over Pete's head, one hand covered with a heavy black glove, the other resting in a sling.

"Wait."

The *Jefe Mayor* paused, the shadowed eyes questioning. "You have a request?"

"Take off your hood," Pete croaked.

The *Jefe Mayor* froze.

"If I die, I want to remember your face when I'm in Heaven. I want to be able to forgive you," Pete said.

The eyes stared at him, hard and cold. Slowly, the *Jefe Mayor* lifted his left hand and grasped the point of the hood. He pulled it up, revealing his face only to Pete, and then pulled it back down.

"Gallegos," Pete whispered.

The sheriff raised the thorns above Pete's head. "Now for the crowning . . ."

CHAPTER 33

R uby and Yates ran toward the hill where the Passion play was taking place. Ruby's heart was thumping in her ears as she saw Pete's body hanging limp on the cross and the hooded man preparing to set the crown of thorns on his head. She ran faster, planning to knock the ladder over, sending the *Jefe Mayor* to the ground before she shot him dead.

"It's Gallegos," Yates exclaimed.

"Don't do it, Gallegos." Ruby reached the base of the cross and pointed the gun at him. He froze. Several of the men moved toward her but Yates stepped in front of them, protecting her.

"You don't understand," Yates said in a loud voice, drawing the crowd's attention. "If that crown of thorns is placed on his head, he *will* die. You've all been deceived."

The men looked at one another, confusion on their faces. "We must continue with the Passion," one of them said.

"If you continue this man will die, just as the past four Cristos have died."

"If he dies, he will be with God. He is chosen," another one said.

"No. If he dies he will have killed by the hand of man, not chosen by the hand of God," said Yates.

"The crown of thorns is laced with poison," Ruby said. "That's how the last four Cristos died; right, Gallegos?" She shoved the gun closer to him.

"Poison?" one of the men asked. "But why?"

"Ask your *Jefe Mayor*," she said calmly, the butt of the gun heating up with her desire to pull the trigger.

"No!" A shrill cry came from the crowd. A man ran toward them, waving his arms, white mustache bold against dark skin. Manuel Medina. "He must die!" he yelled, and lunged for Martinez. One of the Brothers caught hold of him. "Father, the Cristo must die!"

Ruby stared in shock, horrified to see Pete's father demanding his death.

"The thorns. He must die by the thorns! His death will assure us a place in Heaven. He will redeem me." Manuel's eyes were aflame with passionate madness. With a sudden lunge, he broke free from Martinez's grip, reached up the ladder, and grabbed the crown from Gallegos' gloved hand. He held it in front of him like a weapon. "Don't come near me."

Ruby gasped as blood dripped from Manuel's hands as his skin came in contact with the thorns.

"You were to be our savior, my son. The perfect sacrifice." Manuel looked up at Pete. "Sacrifice of my blood. It would have been perfect, beautiful, but they ruined it!" He whirled toward the crowd, staggering, the nicotine taking effect. "I will not let it be so." He raised the crown above his head and thrust it down onto his own forehead. Blood oozed from under the thorns and crawled down his face. "Forgive them, Father," he said, and fell to the ground.

A woman screamed, but the Brothers and other villagers circled him in silence. Ruby looked over at Pete, still limp on the cross,

"Madre de Dios!" a woman shrieked, pointing at the fallen man.

Blood oozed from Manuel's wrists, rolling down the sides of

his arms. At his ankles his shoes and pant legs seeped crimson, and his shirt became stained as a puddle of blood settled underneath him, below his ribcage.

Ruby's mouth fell open. The Stigmata.

Several of the people surrounding Manuel's body fell to their knees, crossed themselves, and began murmuring in prayer. Ruby stared, dumbfounded.

"We have to get him down from there." Dr. Yates' voice snapped her out of her daze.

"Pete!" Ruby cried. "You." She motioned to several of the men. "Help him. Now."

She held the gun steady, trained on Juan Gallegos as he stepped down from the ladder. Afraid to take her eyes off him Ruby motioned for him to stand away from the cross, away from the crowd. She could hear Martinez ministering to the fallen Manuel, giving him his last rites. When he was finished, several of the Brothers apprehended him.

"I've heard this man's confession for years," said Martinez. "His was the voice in the dark."

"You allowed this to happen," one of the men said. "You were in collusion with him, with the sheriff, too. You've betrayed us!"

"I didn't mean to!" Martinez pleaded. "I thought it was what you wanted."

The two men assisting Dr. Yates had used bolt cutters to cut the spikes holding Pete to the cross. When Pete was released from the cross Ruby rushed to him, forgetting about Juan Gallegos, forgetting everything else.

Barely conscious, Pete shivered uncontrollably. Dr. Yates ripped off his shirt and lay it over Pete. "The bleeding at his wrists and ankles is beginning to clot. A good sign," he said.

"Pete? Pete, it's Ruby," she said, tears streaming down her cheeks. "You're going to be okay. I promise."

"Ruby?" he groaned. "Ruby."

She smiled as she lay her hands on his chest, so grateful he hadn't been taken from her. "Yes, yes, I'm here."

"We need to get him to the hospital," Yates said, standing above them.

Ruby nodded, then stood up and scooted out of the way so the men could lift Pete. Without warning someone grabbed her, pinned her arms to her sides, and wrenched the gun from her hand. Then he shoved her aside.

Juan Gallegos pointed the gun at the crowd. "No one moves, or I'll shoot." He backed away, waving the gun.

The pop of a rifle rang out, and all eyes turned to a man in the distance who lowered his rifle, aiming it at Gallegos' head.

"Put it down, Sheriff!" Nicolas Baca's voice echoed in the stillness. He moved toward the sheriff. His eyes were sunken but resolute. His face bore a sternness that Ruby hadn't thought possible.

Gallegos turned the gun on Ruby. "I'll kill her. Get that rifle off me."

"Why did you do this to us?" Nicolas asked. "We believed in you. We believed in Father Martinez. You made us believe that we and ours were Chosen. You lied. Men died, and you made us believe God took them. You were willing to see me die."

"We didn't know that Manuel was killing them!" Gallegos shouted. "I swear."

Nicolas shook his head. "You are the law. You stood by and let this happen."

"I didn't know. I didn't realize what was happening. I thought God had taken them, too."

Nicolas twisted his mouth, clearly wrestling with his emotions, the rifle still aimed at Gallegos' head. "You've made a mockery of our beliefs. You used it for yourself, for power over other men. You destroyed all that we believed in," he said.

Ruby saw Nicolas' trigger finger move. She dove at him, knocking the rifle out of his hands. He moved like lightning to reach it again, but Ruby grabbed it and held it above her head, Gallegos still aiming the other gun at her. Ruby pointed the rifle at him. "Don't do it. I just stopped him from shooting you, but I have less to lose. Hasn't there been enough killing here?"

Gallegos gritted his teeth, moving closer to her. "*You*. You ruined everything," he whispered, his jaw tight.

Ruby rested her finger on the trigger. "This madness started well before I arrived. Those young men died, and you let it happen. You didn't stop it. Nicolas is right. *You* had the responsibility to protect and serve these people, but instead you deceived them. You let them be led astray. And for what? To feel important?" She glared at him. "It's over now, Sheriff. The truth is out, and it's all over."

"You stole all of this from us," he said. She heard the click of his trigger, and she pulled hers. The gun flew out of Gallegos' hand and landed on the ground. He howled in pain and bent over, holding his bleeding hand between his knees. Two men descended on him and shoved him face-first to the ground. They pulled his arms behind his back. One of them took off his tie and secured the sheriff's hands.

Ruby lowered the rifle, her whole body shaking, her mouth dry. Nicolas rushed toward the pistol and picked it up. He opened the chamber and let the bullets fall to the ground. He walked toward Ruby and held it out for her in exchange for the rifle. She handed it to him and took the pistol in her trembling hand. Nicolas rested his rifle on his shoulder.

"Thank you, Ruby. Thank you for everything." His eyes brimmed with moisture.

"You're welcome, Nicolas," she said, smiling at him.

"See that he is safe." Nicolas pointed to Pete, lying on the ground.

"I will," she promised. "Always."

He nodded to her, turned, and walked away from the crowd.

"It's over, folks," Yates said to everyone. "Go home. We've got to get this man to the hospital."

"What should we do with the sheriff?" one of the men asked. Ruby wanted to say *Whatever you want*, but she refrained.

"Take him to the state police," Yates said. Two of the men hoisted Gallegos to his feet and led him away.

Mothers clutched their children and men gathered their families, hugging them, reassuring them.

The smell of sage blew in the breeze as Ruby watched them go. She turned in a wide, slow circle, suddenly aware of the peace on the hillside. It was a gorgeous day. Puffy white clouds floated across an azure sky. The distant mountain range, purple with the rising of the sun, stretched far into the distance. And closer, just above on the hillside, Ruby saw a coyote sitting on a large boulder, erect and proud, his nose sniffing the breeze.

"Ruby?" Yates called out. "Are you all right?"

"Yes," she said. "Let's go."

Ruby followed several feet behind the men carrying Pete. She didn't want to forget this moment, this day, this hour. She had saved a life. Two lives, really.

She thought about her son, Matthew, and wondered if saving Pete and Nicolas Baca would allow her to forgive herself.

Only time would tell.

On the way down the hill Ruby saw Father Alvarez standing some distance from the crucifixion mount, his hands clasped behind his back. He raised one hand above his head and made the sign of the cross in a slow, exaggerated gesture. When Ruby passed she held her hand out to him, and he grasped it. He placed his other hand on her forehead and whispered another blessing.

Ruby looked into his eyes and knew he recognized her pain, her loss. He wiped away a tear that ran down her cheek. "Go in peace, Ruby Delgado."

DID YOU ENJOY THIS BOOK?

I hope this book has brought you some entertainment and enjoyment! I am so grateful and honored that you have chosen to spend some time with me.

If you are so inclined, I would appreciate your spending just one more moment and writing a review. It doesn't need to be long, just a few honest words about your reading experience.

I'd also love to connect with with you on a more personal level. Sign up for my mailing list via my website to participate in special giveaways, receive news and information about my events and upcoming releases at https://www.KariBovee.com.

ABOUT THE AUTHOR

Empowered women in history, horses, unconventional characters, and real-life historical events fill the pages of award-winning author Kari Bovée's articles and historical mystery musings and manuscripts.

She and her husband, Kevin, spend their time between their horse property in the beautiful Land of Enchantment, New Mexico, and their condo on the sunny shores of Kailua-Kona, Hawaii.

Kari would love to connect with with you on a more personal level. Subscribe to her mailing list to participate in special giveaways, and to receive news and information about events and upcoming releases at https://www.KariBovee.com.

ALSO BY KARI BOVÉE

ACKNOWLEDGMENTS

Bones of the Redeemed has been a labor of love for too many years to divulge. It is the book I cut my teeth on. Many authors and industry experts will say that the first couple of books you write should often go under the bed or on the shelf indefinitely—and I heeded their advice. Those first two books shall never see the light of day.

Bones is the third novel I wrote under a different title many years ago. While it may have deserved a place under the bed as well, I simply could not give up on it. And thank goodness, there are others who didn't give up on it either.

I'd like to thank my first ever agent, Anthony Schneider. We have lost touch over the years, but Anthony, if you are out there somewhere, thank you for your many, many helpful comments, suggestions, and words of wisdom. Also for all the pep talks and making me feel like I had some talent as a writer and would one day realize my dream of being published.

I'd like to thank David Corbett for his help and guidance. When I retitled the book, I wanted to do another strong developmental edit. I handed the book to Mr. Corbett after I had made attempts to better it myself, and admittedly, it was a bit of a mess. Thank you for your diligence in straightening it out!

I would also like to thank my current editor, Danielle Poise of DoubleVision Editorial for putting the final touches on it, and making the piece shine.

Lastly, I'd like to thank my late father, Jim Cramer, for the inspiration for this book. He and I shared a love of the South-west, particularly New Mexico, and its rich and fascinating history.

CPSIA information can be obtained
at www.ICGtesting.com
Printed in the USA
FSHW011535111120

9 781947 905108